A war for life and liberty . . .

Tom Dobb and his son Ned came to New York in the summer of 1776, as the violent clamor for independence reached a fever pitch. Caught up in the emotion and drama of the time, Tom and Ned both joined Washington's army to drive the British out of New York. But a humiliating defeat quickly soured their dreams. Only the passionate commitment of young Daisy McConnahay, to Tom Dobb and to the newly born nation, saved them from despair and rallied them through the bitter days at Valley Forge. From there they would test their bravery on the field of honor and find their destiny in the crucible of

REVOLUTION

PACINO
REVOLUTION

AL PACINO

REVOLUTION

Starring DONALD SUTHERLAND

NASTASSJA KINSKI

WARNER BROS., GOLDCREST and VIKING

present
an IRWIN WINKLER PRODUCTION

A film by
HUGH HUDSON

Music by
JOHN CORIGLIANO

Executive Producer
CHRIS BURT

Written by
ROBERT DILLON

Produced by
IRWIN WINKLER

Directed by
HUGH HUDSON

DISTRIBUTED BY **WARNER BROS.**
A WARNER COMMUNICATIONS COMPANY

REVOLUTION

A Novel by
Richard Francis

From the Screenplay by
Robert Dillon

BANTAM BOOKS

TORONTO · NEW YORK · LONDON · SYDNEY · AUCKLAND

REVOLUTION

A Bantam Book / January 1986

ISBN 0-553-25760-9

Published simultaneously in the United States and Canada

PRINTED IN THE UNITED STATES OF AMERICA

H   0 9 8 7 6 5 4 3 2 1

REVOLUTION

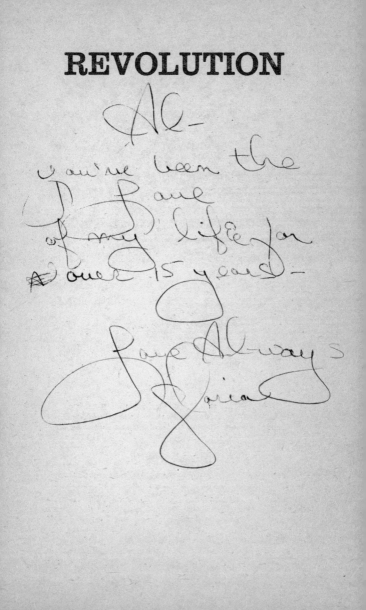

Al—
you've been the
love
of my life for
over 15 years—

Love Always
Lorian

1

Hands, stumbling over themselves in their hurry, slipped a noose around the king's neck and pulled it taut. The rain was teeming down, and rivulets ran over the pudgy monarch's face, streaming like tears down his cheeks, dripping from nose and chin. The hands, finishing their business, withdrew, and a seedy-looking man in a drenched blue jacket and a cocked hat resembling a waterlogged boat, clambered down the flimsy ladder and rejoined the crowd which jeered, cheered, and shouted.

The square was jammed with people. It was the biggest and most popular open area in New York, the Bowling Green near the old Battery. All around it were merchants' houses, built in stone or brick, their windows firmly shuttered against the scenes outside. The mob didn't come from houses like these. Many of them didn't come from New York at all. They were soldiers, militia men from all over the colonies; mechanics and farmers, clerks and storekeepers, often young boys away from their families for the first time—the "long faces," as George Washington called them. Fat Henry Knox, Boston bookseller turned gunner-in-chief, said that the army was a "receptacle for ragamuffins." Certainly, in ill-fitting uniforms or none at all, poorly armed, ill-disciplined, homesick, and now soaked by the rain, they were a force more calculated to put fear into law-abiding citizens—like the merchants peering at the square through the cracks in their shutters—than to intimidate a professional army like the British.

The faces of the American soldiers were not long at the moment. They had just come from a parade at which a document had been read to them, a rousing document full of long words and promises—the Declaration of Independence, signed only five days before, on July 4th 1776, at a meeting of the Continental Congress in Philadelphia.

> We hold these truths to be self-evident, that all men are created equal, that they are endowed by their Creator with certain unalienable rights, that among these are Life, Liberty, and the pursuit of happiness.

Not all these points, barked out at them on a parade ground in the pouring rain, had struck home, but they'd gotten the general drift—toward happiness.

Nothing much had happened since the outbreak of hostilities a year ago, at Lexington Green and Concord Bridge in Massachesetts. But now the situation was becoming more ominous, and day after day, week after week, the American troops had gone down to the Battery or the docks to watch the biggest fleet Britain had ever put to sea arrive in New York waters. Over a hundred vessels were here already; many more were on their way. Big wallowing ships had moved in slowly one at a time, to be greeted by the sudden dull boom of cannons from those who had arrived already. For the last week the commander of the British forces, Sir William Howe, had been engaged in landing troops on Staten Island. Soon a total of thirty thousand would be stationed there, an army far larger than anything the Americans could bring together. Some of the Hessian mercenaries that the British government had hired were so well-disciplined that they stood at attention on the landing craft that took them over to the island.

Clearly the next move on the part of the British would be to transfer part of their force across the Narrows to Long Island, so that New York City itself could be held in a pincer.

The American soldiers were confused and scared. Like any amateur troops, they thought of the people, places, responsibilities they'd left behind—girls, parents, friends; trades neglected, apprenticeships abandoned, farms left to be coped with by wives and children. And here they were in New York, many miles, for some of them, from their own colony. Meanwhile, day by day, the British were sailing in. Day by day the spring was being tightened, the trap set. Day by day the prospect of a large-scale battle with a trained European army got a little nearer. In these circumstances it was a comfort to the soldiers to listen to the Declaration of Independence, and find out what they were fighting for: Life, Liberty, the pursuit of Happiness.

After the reading, the soldiers merged with the street mobs of the city. They were ready for action; at least, they were ready to make a gesture. They livened up the rain with catcalls and fist-waving, convincing themselves for the moment that they were in charge of their own destinies and that of the city. For the time being they could forget or disparage the huge fleet bobbing silently in the waters of New York harbor, forget the soldiers drilling on Staten Island and the distant crackle and whine of the British troops carrying out their musket practice. They called out obscenities, made jokes, gave themselves up to the headiness of the moment, shouted themselves out of trouble.

But as the rope was pulled taut, the crowd fell silent. The king, still mounted, hung poised above his former subjects for a long second. Rain gleamed on his metallic features. And then the enormous statue leaned on its plinth and slowly fell in a large arc toward the pavement below.

For a moment after it struck, it held the memory of its shape. The bronze king rested on his side. Then collapsed into a number of pieces.

The crunch of impact triggered the mob again. They whooped and hollered like huntsmen or Indians, and surged toward the metal corpse, arms and hands groping for fragments in blurred unison. Near the front were some bullet-headed youths dressed in rags, weaving their way through the throng more expertly than most. They were wiry street urchins who could now pursue their activities as local toughs and petty thieves in the name of revolution. They called themselves the Mohawks, in honor of the Boston gang they'd heard of, which had dressed up as Indians, raided some cargo ships in the harbor, and dumped their loads of tea overboard. The Boston Tea Party. Everybody had talked about it. That was the kind of war this New York gang understood. They were Indians of the street, and *Tory* was the name they gave to their victims, knowing every nook and cranny of their territory, breaking Tory windows, picking Tory pockets, ambushing Tory passersby.

Like most of the rest of the mob, the Mohawks were poor, unemployed, resentful. Now, like the others, they wanted scalps, and they scrabbled on the ground for pieces of the king.

The mob was made up of hundreds of individuals, each with his own reasons for being there, his own story to tell. But every now and again the bodies were jammed close enough together for its individuals to have feeling and emotion in common, for the mob to develop a mind of its own. Now such a moment came, and an idea flowed through the mob as the wind blows over a field of wheat. The idea was: run.

The people had heard officers, politicians, street orators, telling them about the glorious cause: independence from Britain, freedom from the tyranny of George III. But now they had deposed the king for themselves. And suddenly their instinct was to run with his pieces. Not to flee, but to run together purposefully. To run down to the harbor where the king's armada was arriving, and to take what they had of the king with them.

So the mob ran. Only those in front had had the time to pick up fragments anyway, and most of the king and his horse was left behind, a broken giant slumped across the center of the Bowling Green. Later the remains would be melted down and molded into forty thousand musket balls. As Ebenezer Hazard put it, "The bloody-backs"—alias the lobsters, the redcoats, the British soldiers—"will have melted majesty fired into them."

The mob ran along narrow, twisting streets. Passersby who had ventured out unaware of the activity on the Bowling Green flattened themselves against walls and found themselves even flatter when the mob had passed. Windows were smashed and shops emptied of their goods almost magically as the crowds swarmed past. The funneling effect of the streets increased the mob's momentum and intensified its sense of having its own identity, making its own laws, acting on its own motives. For its members this provided a welcome relief from coping with the poverty and distress of their daily lives. A number of blacks ran with the rest. Not slaves. Slavery in New York was a condition these people could actually envy. The slaves did the household chores in rich houses; cleaned, mended, drove; were dressed up in ribbons, sashes, satin jackets, knee breeches, gold braiding, even powdered wigs, to act as dandified footmen or doll-like coachboys. They would have beds to sleep in, food to eat. Their merchant masters would grumble about hard times, but there was still enough to go around in their city houses and country mansions.

Hard times had come quicker, and harder, to the docks. The blacks who worked here were free, paid by the day. In recent years the workdays had become fewer as trade restrictions had increased. Now, with the British blockade, they had ceased to exist altogether. The dockers lived in lean-tos, huts, canvas shelters, in the recesses beneath the planking of the ropewalks and wharves, behind warehouses and customs sheds. At the best of times they were poor; now they were starving. Theft and looting was a last recourse, and the unrest in the streets made those desperate acts much safer, almost legitimate. So the blacks ran, shouting with the rest while keeping an eye open to opportunity. They didn't, of course, know that a fellow Negro, Crispus Attucks, had been shot in the Boston Massacre of 1773, and had therefore qualified as the first martyr of the revolution. They had no more knowledge than Attucks himself of the issues at stake, and for good reason, since those issues had nothing to do with them. But for the moment they had a place in the mob, albeit a moving one, and in the rain. A place to run. And there was satisfaction in seeing the statue brought down and buildings smashed up. And somewhere, in all the chaos, there might be a chance of seizing food, or rum.

The mob rounded a corner, and up ahead were bigger buildings, warehouses, commercial offices, chandleries, rigging sheds. The roadway broadened out into yards and unloading areas. Beyond were the wharves and the spiky masts of ships, and beyond them the gray sea, its swell puckered and flattened by rain. Farther out, in a line across the harbor mouth, clustered near Staten Island, the British fleet rocked at anchor.

From another direction altogether a closed carriage galloped along the cobbled streets toward the docks. It was varnished, well-sprung, elegant. The horses, even in this downpour, clopped friskily. A black coachman, his livery glazed with water, tickled them from time to time with his whip and held the traces impassively, unsubdued by the weather. Inside, behind the steamy windows, sat the McConnahay ladies: Martha, wife of Joseph McConnahay, the biggest sugar and molasses trader in the city—indeed, in the whole colony of New York—and her three daughters, Daisy, Betsy, and Amy.

The girls were in their teens, all pretty, in summer gowns decked with ribbons and straw bonnets, dressed for the sunshiny morning that had greeted them when they awoke, before gray squalls blew in from the northeast. Their mother was handsome but more sedately dressed, as befit her age; more luxuriously also, which befit her seniority, in satin and lace.

The McConnahay women were returning from a morning expedition, both commercial and social, which had been successful on each count, and there was an atmosphere of contentment and celebration in the carriage, at least on the part of three of its passengers.

Martha had led the excursion. She knew her way around New York as well as any member of the Mohawk gang; except that hers was a different New York. A few days before, at a social gathering at the Burnells', she had heard rumours of the arrival, somewhere uptown, of a quantity of yellow muslin, deposited there heaven knows how, smuggled by some trader or got from the British garrison by fair means or foul. It was said British officers had brought a quantity of such stuff with them, perhaps to bestow as favors on pretty girls they met; perhaps, some claimed, in exchange for services rendered. There was much outrage, and curiosity, about this matter amongst the female members of New York society. They had seen their husbands and fathers struggling to maintain their businesses as this foolish squabble between the colonies and the British government dragged on and on. Trade became difficult, circumstances confined, lives drab. There was less money for purchases and fewer items to buy. And then along came the British to settle matters once and for all, and these roguish officers had apparently loaded their trunks and kitbags with gewgaws and rarities to use as presents, and perhaps as bribes. It showed effrontery and cynicism. Surely it broke all the accepted rules of warfare. The ladies agreed to stand firm, and resist bravely until the end.

But the yellow muslin was different. It had been spotted by an acquaintance of Martha McConnahay's, who acted as a sort of advance guard or scout for supplies and fashion at the house of a cloth trader. It might have been stolen, she'd said, and surely that would make it acceptable to purchase. Or perhaps it had been given, after all, and then sold. Best for all concerned not to enquire too closely. To Martha's fury, her source would reveal no more. She lapsed into secrecy, and coyness, and knowing looks. Martha knew what she required: pleadings, beseechings, offers of favors in return, flattery. In her own way, the source was as unscrupulous as those rascally officers, Martha thought, and would have none of it, having too much pride and independence of spirit. So this morning she and her girls had taken the carriage and gone to reconnoiter.

She had been fairly sure that the material would not have found its way to the cloth dealers and dressmakers in the main streets of the city. Others, besides her own spy, would have spotted it in that case. Nor in the dockyard area. She herself patrolled that territory pretty thoroughly, since Joe had interests there. She believed it was deposited in one of those streets in the upper part of town where buildings gave way to woods and fields. It was just the sort of region where a girl who didn't want to be recognized by her friends might go, or a smuggler who was keeping shy of the authorities. So Martha had explored those parts, and after barely an hour had caught up with her prey and devoured it whole.

She was put in mind of such bloodthirsty imagery because of the nature of the place—not a proper cloth dealer's at all, but a trader in hides. There were heaps of skins and pelts everywhere, and the most dreadful stench of animals. What a person of that sort was doing with a bit of good cloth, heaven only knew. Ask no questions and be told no lies was the maxim Martha had decided to adopt. She purchased the whole bolt on the spot and asked for it to be wrapped and transported to Joseph McConnahay's Sugar House on the wharves, where she would collect it later that morning. Then she and the girls had decided to take advantage of being at the edge of the town, and ordered the coach to proceed on into the country, where they'd visited their friends the Rennslers on their estate and crowed to them about their triumph.

Now they were on their way to the McConnahay Sugar House to pick up the trophy.

"Fanny Rennsler has not yet read Tom Paine," Daisy, the oldest daughter, was telling her mother. She had long brown hair, dark eyes, a pale sensitive face.

"Then Fanny has some common sense," Martha replied.

There was a short pause, and then Betsy squealed with

amusement at the allusion. Amy regarded her in puzzlement, and shook her head at yet another example of the mental deficiency of others. Daisy raised her eyes to the roof of the carriage in exasperation. Tom Paine's great words came back into her mind. She had read and reread the tract since it was first published in January, and knew it almost by heart:

> Everything that is right or reasonable pleads for separation. The blood of the slain, the weeping voice of nature cries, "Tis time to Part."

It was like an anguished poem. The rhythm of the phrases, the terrible images, then the sadness and restraint of "Tis time to Part." The words haunted Daisy, and she would find herself reciting them to herself at moments through the day, as a Catholic might recite her rosary. There was a romance and passion in Tom Paine's phrasing that moved her feelings and imagination more than anything in the pile of novels and journals that her sisters accumulated.

Betsy turned and glared at the provoking Amy. "*Common Sense* by Tom Paine," she said stoutly. Then, to her mother, as though by way of apology, "I haven't read it any more than Fanny. It looks drier than Papa's *Gentleman's Magazine*."

Martha nodded approval. Confident of her ground, Betsy continued: "But I can play the harpsichord better than her. She is so slow, I thought I would quite fall asleep during the 'Prince and Maiden.'"

Martha was giving Daisy a hard, appraising stare. The girl was sitting with eyes half closed, murmuring to herself. She'd been given to these strange fits in the last few months, ever since the troubles had set in. One could think she'd become half crazed with the anxiety of it all. There was another explanation, which Martha didn't want to think about. Daisy was a serious young lady, a great book reader, who seemed to feel that she was a cut above the pastimes of ordinary girls— the water coloring, singing, talking of young men, following the fashions—all the simple pleasures girls of her age habitually indulged themselves in and which signaled a healthy development towards the sphere of wife-and-mother. It was that sphere, if all went well—or rather, Martha thought, if all went according to plan—in which her girls would find their allotted place.

Daisy had a taste for large, dense volumes, and for matters

of politics and philosophy; she was an enthusiast by nature, with her head in the clouds and her mind preoccupied by great, insoluble questions. Sometimes Martha feared she would become one of these bluestocking ladies, who had more taste for print than for husbands, and who produced pamphlets and articles when they ought to be bearing children.

"It is a more befitting pastime for a young lady than reading seditious tracts," Martha said, leaving it unclear whether she was referring to Fanny's harpsichord or Betsy's sleep.

Daisy took the bait. "Mama!" she said earnestly. 'With Father hard at work at the commissary, surely we must all try to understand the principles of our revolution.'

New York was full of what was grandly called the Continental Army of the United Colonies, or States, as the rebels had taken to calling them. In point of fact, as Martha had seen with her own eyes, they were nothing but a bunch of hireling soldiers, country boys for the most part, who couldn't whip a dog let alone the might of King George's army. Nevertheless, even asses need hay, her husband had said, and these gollumpus troops required provender. So a commissary was set up, where the scanty supplies available in New York after all the difficulties of recent times could be auctioned off to militia leaders, quartermasters, and the like. Naturally, Joe took charge, and the other big merchants formed a cartel to assist. It was reasonable and prudent to sell where the customers were, even if the customers were loutish and unmanly in the extreme. No doubt better terms might be arranged, and more civilised negotiations transacted, with certain dashing infantry officers over at Long Island. But as Joe pointed out, such arrangements could be misunderstood in the present delicate state of affairs, and given the unruly nature of the common people these days, might lead to broken windows, daubing on the walls, or something even worse. A perfectly respectable attorney of their acquaintance, Joshua Slaney, had had his house broken into by a bunch of scallawags, and the poor man was dragged out and placed upon a cart, merely for stating in public his loyalty to the king. They had pulled him off to the street corner, where a barrel of pitch was heating, and proceeded to tar and feather the poor wretch. Mrs. Stuke, who saw the whole proceeding from her window, said it really was a most comical sight, even though her heart bled for the victim. He stood upon his cart like a monstrous fluffy chicken, singing

"God Save the King" in his quavering furious voice while the mob roared all around him.

Joe McConnahay had too much sense than to run the risk of any inconvenience of that kind. But Daisy, zealot that she was, insisted on viewing his work at the commissary as evidence of a belief in the glorious cause, and to hold him up to all and sundry as a model patriot and example to wealthy Loyalists everywhere: a sort of rebel merchant who would put the new republic on to a sound economic footing.

"I do not need to be taught principles by some immigrant corsetmaker," Martha told Daisy in her most crushing tones. She had been informed quite recently that this Tom Paine, whose name had been for some months past so tiresomely on everyone's lips, had been a practitioner of that humble trade before leaving England to come to America and stirring up trouble.

"I imagined," Daisy replied, borrowing her mother's sarcasm, "that you were interested in all matters concerning dress."

But Martha was not to be outmaneuvered. She ignored Daisy's barb, choosing to interpret her remark as a legitimate and tactful change of subject. "This has been an extremely successful expedition," she said with utmost satisfaction. "You will have a gown apiece that will turn the head of every young buck in the British army." She gave Daisy a gimlet look of triumph.

At this moment the carriage entered the small paved area in front of the Sugar House, and was drawn up sideways by the great doors so that the bolt could be loaded on more conveniently and the horses could then head directly homeward. As this was done, however, the McConnahay ladies suddenly became aware of other sounds outside, beyond the drumming of the rain on the roof and windows. There were cries, screams, screeches, squawks, a human hurdy-gurdy of raucous noise. The mob was careering around the corner of the Sugar House and approaching the carriage.

"Oh, heavens," said Martha McConnahay, as she realized what was going on. "This will give me the headache, which is exactly what I do not need today."

She unstrapped her window, poked her head out, and called up "Drive on!" But it was already too late. With the rioters approaching headlong, there was nowhere to drive on to, and the horses were already rearing and backing between their shafts.

Crowds swarmed about the McConnahay carriage. An arm came through the window Martha was still struggling to close. It was bare, hairy, and it made strangely independent motions while in the delicately scented world of the carriage, as if nobody owned it. Betsy and Amy watched it with a kind of horrified pleasure. No naked male arm had ever been quite so close before. They wondered what it would do next. Daisy, meanwhile, reached across to it.

"Daisy!" Martha snapped.

"Daisy!" Betsy said, with something close to admiration in her voice.

Daisy grasped the hand. The fingers uncurled, and she took from them a rolled-up paper. The arm immediately withdrew. Instantly Martha pulled the window up. Then she took the leaflet from Daisy. "A Declaration of Independence," she read, "Scum," she added. She screwed it into a twist and passed it to Daisy. "Good for the fire," she concluded.

Betsy and Amy giggled. Daisy ignored them, and her mother. She turned to the window. The crowd was blurred behind the steamy glass, frothing about the carriage and Sugar House like a fast-flowing jangled river. She wiped the pane with her hand and gazed out at the smeared figures running past. There were women, girls of her own age or even younger, running with the men. Some waved as they went past. She didn't know whether they were taunting her as street women sometimes did, gesturing and making signs, or whether it was done out of kindred feeling, sister to sister. Surely there were too many women on this street for them all to be street women, she thought, poor though most of them obviously were.

Daisy had already seen the Declaration. She had obtained it hot off the press from patriot friends the night before, and read it and reread it, as she did Tom Paine, with passion and intensity. All men are created equal. She thought of the contrast between these four women, sitting in the McConnahay carriage, outside the McConnahay Sugar House, and the desperate river of people sweeping past. Who was it, she wondered, who had to do the declaring? Was it simply a matter of the representative of each colony putting his signature to the written document? Or should every man make the declaration for himself? And every women?

On impulse she pulled the catch on her door and pushed it open a little. She needed to refresh herself from the oppressive atmosphere of the carriage and come a little nearer to the energy and vitality of the people rushing past outside.

As soon as she'd done so, she realized she'd made a mistake. It was a sheer impossibility to hold a door slightly ajar in the face of an oncoming charge of rioters. The door swung violently open, she lurched forward with it, and women's arms grasped upward at her, whether to assist her down or pull her out, she never knew.

She caught a glimpse of a forehead with a pair of crossed swords drawn upon it, long swirling hair cascading down; then an impression of the carriage, her mother's eyes blazing with fury, Betsy's popping slightly with envy and alarm, Amy's looking coolly speculative.

Daisy continued to feel that she was acting without any will of her own. She didn't know whether she was running with the mob or being dragged along by it. Certainly, however, she found herself turning the corner of her father's Sugar House and heading toward the wharf.

As the mob had begun its run towards the Sugar House wharf from the Bowling Green, and the McConnahay ladies had jingled toward it along the cobbled dockside road from the north of the town, Tom Dobb and his son Ned, aboard their battered, square-rigged longboat loaded with furs, were approaching it from a third direction: the river. As luck would have it, all three groups arrived at the same place at more or less the same moment.

2

___

Tom Dobb had been upriver for two weeks, collecting furs from a trader's. He'd dropped some off at a merchant's just to the north of the city and was bringing the rest around to sell at a warehouse by the docks. Tom was a weatherbeaten thirty-five-year-old who had traded up and down the Hudson since about fourteen, the age of his son Ned. He sat in the stern, collar up, head hunched against the rain that had soaked him anyway. Water pooled along the bottom of the boat and saturated the pelts. It was a comfort to sniff the sausage Ned was cooking on a little charcoal stove.

As they rounded the point, the British fleet came into view, even larger than the last time they'd been here, arranged in a line across the sea road and in a tangle of spars and bowsprits alongside Staten Island. Everything else appeared the same. Tom recalled that at the dealer's that morning there had even been a fine lady making purchases of raw pelts, for some reason. And there had been several young ladies in the carriage, peering out at the fur strippers and boatmen, grinning behind their gloved hands. He knew they wouldn't have been out of doors if anything bad had been happening.

It was no use asking people what was going on, Tom thought. They told you every story you could think of, about what the British were up to, and what the colonists were going to do about it. People talked scared or boasted, according to their nature. But no one had anything bad to say about battles or any kind of real fighting, not since it had gotten hot for a while last year up around Boston.

But Tom had seen militia on the march a couple of times. A scarecrow bunch they looked too, not so much marching as sauntering along, talking and laughing with each other while officers yelled at them to lift their feet up and get in step with each other. And this British fleet hadn't sailed over here for nothing. When two sides began preparing for each other in this fashion, something was going to come of it. It was like what you saw in the trading camps upriver. A couple of lads would be drinking together, have a few angry words; the others, for lack of something better to do, would whip them up a bit more, and then you could see them moving toward it, knowing they were going to beat hell out of each other. They would look at one another, eyes screwed up as if they were calculating how to get the advantage. But Tom guessed they were wondering how they got there, why couldn't they just lay back down on the floor, drink a little more, and talk about old times, like they did before. But there was no way of avoiding the fighting once the initial moves were made.

Tom kept out of anything like that. He would sit in a corner, say nothing, keep watchful, and look after Ned. Then, when things got hot, he'd move off with the boy. If there was a free for all, they wouldn't make allowances for a child; anyone within range was fair game.

It was the same with this business with the British. Maybe there were good reasons for it all, maybe not. Tom hadn't enquired and he had a suspicion that nobody in the fur trade along the river would give him a good answer if he did. But one thing he was sure of—once these things were set in motion, they were hard to stop. It didn't make a lot of sense when you thought about British fighting Americans. You could understand it when it was British against French, or Indians—when opponents spoke a different language and carried on their business in different ways. But this would be kin against kin. Nevertheless, as with the lads in the trading camps, there'd be broken heads before it was finished, because when you got to a certain point you couldn't go back. Tom wasn't going to hang around and see what happened though, any more than he did in the fur villages and camps. He was going to dispose of this batch of pelts and go upriver, carry on his business way up there as best he might, and keep Ned out of trouble. There was no way he'd come back to New York again till the trouble blew over.

He planned to moor on the wharf between the ropewalk

and the Sugar House. He swung the boat around with the long steering oar, and moved in toward the docks. As he got closer, he heard a noise spread out in the air like the sound of the rain, only deeper and getting louder by the second. It was a roaring noise, and then you could hear particular screeches and cries in it. It was like nothing Tom had ever heard before. He'd already gotten his sail partway down, and the boat was swinging into the wharf. Ned's sausage was just beginning to pop.

The mob rounded the corner of the Sugar House and ran toward the wharf. There was a wooden cart there, obviously waiting for some cargo to arrive and be unloaded. The mob surged around it, and several of the girls climbed up on it to get a better view of the harbor, the girl with the crossed swords on her forehead among them. Daisy found herself standing nearby. The girl was young, about her own age, and she had long loose hair that streamed down to her waist. Her fierceness made Daisy think of a witch, except she wasn't an old crone, but youthful and striking, with flashing eyes, white teeth, and a wide, expressive, angry mouth. She was wearing patched skirts and an old blue bodice held together with string. She could be a market stall girl or a fishwoman. But she had a liberty sash like the other girls, and her shirt was open at the neck to show *Liberty or Death* written on the upper part of her chest. She was chanting words, inciting the mob, almost a leader. The Liberty Woman, Daisy thought. She felt glad that the rain was beating down on her own frills and ribbons and soaking her bonnet. It seemed an equalizing rain, making her more like the rest of the people there.

As the mob reached the edge of the wharf, they threw their pieces of the statue over the side while hurling abuse at the British ships. Again Daisy thought of magic, as though scattering the king upon the waters would bring a curse on his ships and send them back over the ocean from where they had came. Her heart swelled as she understood more fully what it meant. They were deposing their king for themselves. It was not to be left to the politicians in Philadelphia, or even the generals in the field of battle. The question she'd been asking herself in the carriage a few minutes ago was surely being answered. Each man was making his own declaration of independence. She looked up at the girls in the cart, and saw that each woman was making her declaration too.

The mob was leaning over the side of the dock, calling out, waving fists, throwing things. Tom ducked and dodged as chunks of metal clattered on his boat and peppered the water all around him. All he could think of was, Why me? What have they got against me? Ned crouched over his sausage, his arms protecting his head.

Tom peered up as best he could. Some of the mob was rough, but that didn't explain why they were hurling things at him. And there were women among them, some of them high up, standing on something, shouting. And soldiers, a lot of soldiers, most of them just boys, in jackets too big for them. Perhaps they think we're the British, Tom thought. The boat clunked against the wharf. He couldn't tie her up, not with all these people milling about.

The metal stopped flying; now it was just the rain. Tom looked up again. Maybe he didn't want to moor anyway, with this crowd here. They were looking for action, and could get it into their heads to loot his boat, steal his pelts. Tom wasn't used to seeing so many people together at once. His life was on the river, with just Ned for company, sailing past small townships and villages, scattered farms, fields and forests. All these faces together blended into each other, like the faces in a pack of animals, eyes glaring, mouths wide and shouting. "Libert-y. Libert-y." What were the women? Fishwives? Fishwives could shout, as a rule, and hold their own on the docks, but you always expected them to be old, not young girls like these, with all their teeth and more. Nor whores. They weren't like whores. One standing nearby was a proper lady, all dressed up, her finery beaten down like a sugar cake left out in the rain. It was a mystery to him where they'd come from. He'd never seen the likes of them before.

Jane Hankin, standing on the cart by the Liberty Woman, hardly knew where she'd come from either. Or rather, she knew where she came from but didn't know how she'd gotten there. Jane was an eighteen-year-old farm girl from Staten Island. Here she was now, on the cart, her dress torn and pinned together, her moon of a face, pink with all the running, opening and closing on "Libert-y, libert-y."

A week ago she'd been living with her sick father, keeping the farm going, working hard, worrying about when she'd find herself a sweetheart. Nobody had ever asked her whether she was a Loyalist or a rebel. She'd never asked herself. She had other things on her mind. The British fleet had piled up near the harbor, and the longboats began rowing ashore, day after day. Their farm was on a low hill, and she could see them coming quite clearly. She would stop her work and watch them. Some of the soldiers stood upright as they came, stiff as statues in the wobbly boats.

One British officer, Lord Rawdon, described the welcome British troops received from the inhabitants of Staten Island after long weeks at sea. They'd had their first taste of fresh meat and it had the unfortunate side effect, Rawdon pointed out, of making them "riotous as satyrs."

One evening at dusk Jane carried a pail of milk across her yard to the churn shed at the bottom. It was dusk. The windowless shed was dark. As she entered, hands seized her, dragged her inside, shut the door behind her. She was attacked, writhing on the milky floor under the weight of each man in turn, squawking like one of her own hens in the next shed.

Jane saw nothing at all until the ravishers began to leave. Then she could make out their shapes against the paler dark outside, and saw that each one had to duck his head to get through the doorway. After they'd gone, she lay on the floor for more than an hour, telling herself that because she'd seen nothing, nothing had really happened; acts of darkness, not necessary to remember. When she was able to walk again, she'd walk away from it.

It took her a long time to realize she might have a baby. As soon as the thought came to her, she noticed the milk that had saturated her dress and lay pooled around her on the floor. The sweet smell made her retch.

Later that night she threw pebbles at the window of a friend on a nearby farm. They talked in the fields. Alice said there was less disgrace in being raped than in letting yourself become pregnant willingly.

"Do you know the fellows?" she asked.

"No," Jane replied, shocked.

"I mean, their regiment."

"I saw nothing," Jane said. "Save as they went, that they were tall men."

"Grenadiers," Alice said. "They are the tallest."

Jane could not guess how she knew so much of regiments, but repeated what Alice had told her when she came before Lord Haworth at a Committee of Inquiry.

"And how, young lady, did you know these men were grenadiers?" the earl asked.

"Oh, God," she replied, suddenly weeping. "They were so big."

His lordship raised his heavily wigged head and looked at her for a long time. His chins began to tremble, then he roared with laughter. They all did. Jane was waved out, through a storm of mirth.

As Lord Rawdon commented: "A girl cannot step into the bushes to pluck a rose without running the imminent risk of being ravished, and they are so little accustomed to these vigorous methods that they don't bear them with the proper resignation."

Jane didn't know, of course, whether or not she was with child. But everyone on Staten Island, including her sick father, knew she'd been with the soldiers. So now she was on Manhattan Island, with no home to go to, chanting "Libert-y, libert-y." She chanted it with her eyes almost shut and nothing in her mind save the one word: Libert-y. It was as though, for the moment, the word was enough to live in. Of the Liberty Woman beside her, she knew nothing at all. Nobody did, not even the other girls who came from these parts. She seemed to come out of nowhere.

"Libert-y!" gave way to "The boat! The boat!" Tom's bewilderment increased. Yes, a boat. Of course, a boat. This is a harbor. In one direction, the river; in the other, the ocean. But he said nothing. This mob was concerned with his boat. They'd thrown things at it. Meanwhile the boat was still rattling about the wharf pilings, loose on the water. Tom had hopes it would catch an eddy and begin to drift out. He didn't dare do anything to help it on its way, though. Instead he turned his back on the faces and began to stow his sail.

Then a gravelly voice called down at him: "You there! Are you American of the United States?"

Tom turned back and looked up once again. It was an

American officer, much older than the boy-soldiers. He was grizzled, a real soldier who'd perhaps fought French and Indians. The crowd quieted.

Tom swallowed. The question was a trick, Tom was sure of that. The officer was gazing down at him, smiling, good-humored, looking as if he just wanted to satisfy his curiosity. Tom felt his heart pounding. He remained silent for a moment more, wondering what to reply. He could smell the meaty smoke of Ned's sausage.

"I'm a New Yorker," he said at last. It was as true as any reply could be. He and Ned lived on the longboat, wherever it might be moored. Now he wished it was somewhere other than this place.

The Liberty Woman called out something to him, and Tom switched his gaze to her. She was high above the captain and the other people lining the wharf, standing on something so she looked like a statue. Her face was ashy white, but with the swords drawn on her forehead, her blazing eyes, and the long hair hanging straight down, she suddenly looked the part of some savage, with scalping on her mind.

"I didn't hear you," Tom said.

"That's the United States."

"What?"

"New York. It's the United States."

"It wasn't last week."

"Well, it is now," the captain shouted. "We're independent now."

Tom felt a chill in his heart. Independent. He knew what that meant. War. Proper war. Not some trouble around Boston, or the troops coming to New York, but war everywhere.

The Liberty Woman repeated the captain's words, as if he might not have understood. "We're independent! We're declared!"

Tom understood. Independent, declared—he understood those words. There were all sorts of ways of saying it. American against Briton. Briton against Briton. Rebel against Tory. However you said it, it meant suffering and killing. Neighbor against neighbor. Father against son. Ned was all the family he had left.

"The army of the United States needs your boat to drive the British away from New York," the Liberty Woman said.

Before she spoke, Tom knew what she was going to say. The crowd had been chanting "The boat, The boat," before.

He still couldn't see what use they could have for it. He turned and looked at the massive British warships moored across the entrance to the harbor, then along the wharf at all the boats tied up. There was a large barque alongside the Sugar House, but otherwise it was all fishing dinghies, barges, rafts, canoes.

Toy boats, toy soldiers. These people must be mad, he thought.

"Not my boat," Tom said softly. He turned to Ned. "Back water, Ned. Head for Greenwich Cove."

Ned had been watching the wharf with flat curiosity, like a child. His last few years on the boat with his taciturn father had left him young for his age in some ways, old in others. He was small for fourteen, though solidly built, with close-cropped hair and a broad strong-looking face. He was still crouching over his sausage as he watched, turning it from time to time on the charcoal cinders. Now he left it and grabbed an oar.

"You're a citizen, Mr. New Yorker," the Liberty Woman said. She said *citizen* as if it meant enemy. "You should give it to them."

"Not my boat," said Tom, just as if he had something else to give. He had nothing else to give. That was why he couldn't give his boat.

Suddenly another voice spoke up. "Take the boat," it said. A woman's voice, high and clear.

It was the lady. The young lady in the rain. Her clothes were trim and expensive, sodden. Her bonnet limp with dampness. It was straw and ribbons, not made for bad weather. Tom glanced at the people around her. Beauty was a luxury the mob couldn't afford. What was a lady like this doing here? Why should a girl who was so rich want to take from him the one thing he owned?

"No," he said. "Ya won't."

"Take the boat! Take the boat!" the crowd chanted.

"Take the boat," the captain said briskly.

Suddenly soldiers were swarming aboard from the wharf, across from the moored boats. They grabbed the pelts. The boat swayed. Tom flailed out, and soldiers grabbed each arm. Ned fought. He spat and hit like a cat, but they held him too. The pelts and furs disappeared from the longboat, then other things: Tom's razor, his chest of fish hooks, his wool blanket; Hands coming from all angles, like fish.

"Not my personals, ya bastards!" Tom shouted. He tried to throw himself forward, but they had him fast. Then hands were shoving, lifting, and he felt himself rising out of the boat, and suddenly the rich girl was grabbing hold of him from the wharf and he was standing there with the crowd all around him, the Liberty Woman still above, on a cart with some others.

"Give the patriot a cheer," the Liberty Woman said.

"Patriot," Tom said, almost whispering. "Take my boat and my skins, I'm a patriot?"

Ned arrived on the wharf beside him, in a tangle of clothes from the struggle. Tom looked back down at his boat. The scavengers had stripped it clean.

"Captain Lacey," the Liberty Woman said, "give this man a note."

The captain scratched on a piece of paper, and passed it to Tom. "Take this to Wall Street," he said. "Show it to the Provisional Commissary."

"Who the hell's that?"

Lacey pointed his thumb up toward the Sugar House. "Joe McConnahay," he said.

"Him? The Sugar King?"

"We don't have kings now," Lacey said. "You want the cash, you see him. He's at the old auction house."

The crowd was moving on. Tom made out the Liberty Woman shouting about victory. He looked down at the chit Lacey had given him. There were some words scrawled on it. They could say what words they liked, or write them, but what it all meant was that in a few moments they'd stolen his home, his living, his goods, his personals. Everything.

No, not everything. He still had Ned.

He put his arm around the boy's shoulders and they went off in search of the Provisional Commissary.

Tom and Ned made their way through the teeming, intricate streets of New York, squishing through horse dung, slops, picked over litter. Pigs ran loose and wagons staggered over the cobbles. Soldiers were calling at stores and warehouses, requisitioning supplies, and people hurried from shop to shop in their wake, in search of what had been overlooked. A small mob beat on someone's door. Boys were fighting in the street. There were signs everywhere. Ned picked some of

the words out. PISS ON BRITISH. DAMN TORIES. There was a big
banner outside a row of brothels, hanging from a rickety
balcony. GOD SAVE something, Ned read.

Tom pulled Ned under a balcony, out of the rain, and gave
him the paper. Ned ran his finger under the words and
spelled them out.

"Boat and pro-vi-dents. Seventy dollars."

Tom grabbed the paper from him and peered at it closely,
as though, even lacking the ability to read, he ought to be
able to make out better news than that.

"We been robbed," he said at last.

"We got no money, Pa?" Ned asked.

"No."

"Where we gonna sleep?"

Tom grasped his shoulder and they hurried on through the
rain, turning into Wall Street. It was wider than the others,
but too narrow for its traffic, wedged with carts and wagons
and thronged with men, most of whom were hurrying toward
a big sooty building a few hundred yards farther down. There
was a sign nailed to it, with three words: OF in the middle;
the first began COM. Ned made it Commissary of Provisions.
New York was full of new signs. The city was rewriting itself.

Just as they were about to go in, Tom stopped. He looked
down at Ned. They'd taken his boat already. Best to keep
Ned away from these declarers and independents as much as
he could.

"You wait here, Ned," he said, and before the boy could
argue, hurried into the commissary yard.

Ned watched him go in surprise, then shrugged his shoulders. He put his hands into his breeches' pockets and toed
the sidewalk. Men hurrying toward the yard pushed and
jostled him as they went past. He moved out of their way,
into the middle of the muddy street. There was music coming
toward him. He watched it come, a fife and drum band. He
stared fascinated as the smart young bandsmen marched past.

Inside the commissary yard supplies and provisions were
piled high—casks of salted food, barrels of rum, coils of rope,
heaps of pelts. Tom wondered if his had found their way
here yet. Soldiers were guarding the commodities; brokers,
quartermasters, and dealers scurried about pricing them and
bartering. Men with chits in their hands were hurrying past

into the auction room doors at the side of the building. Tom went in with them.

People were crowded into a huge room. At intervals were desks, where clerks scratched away. Men milled about with their papers. Every sort was here, all of New York: English, Germans, French, Walloons, Spanish, Portuguese. All the trades: boatmen, dockers, farmers, craftsmen. As they got to the desks, they called out what had been taken from them, inventories of what they no longer had: hogs, sheep, boats, cord, hay, wine. Just words, Tom thought again. The *things* were outside, in the rain; the *words* were in here. This United States seemed to be a place for turning your possessions into scraps of paper. And at the desks the clerks were busy turning the scraps into more scraps. These they gave to the men, who complained and argued.

Tom asked someone what was going on. Everyone here seemed to know where to go, what to do, what to moan about, except himself. He had discovered this before. You went to a new place, new things happen, and the other people there seemed to know what was going on, and you didn't. They seemed to be able to grab information out of the air, even if they couldn't read any more than he could.

The man explained. The paper Lacey had given him was a requisition chit. All the other men here had them too. It was a receipt for the goods taken. The clerks took it away and gave you a promissory note. This was a promise of payment in the future.

"Ain't they gonna pay us now?" Tom asked in horror. Two minutes ago he'd felt poor with seventy dollars; now he was going to get nothing but a promise.

The other men in the room felt the same way. A chant began: "We want cash. We want cash." Tom thought of those women chanting Libert-y, libert-y. This was a chant he understood.

After a few minutes two men appeared on a small rostrum at the end of the hall. The men moved forward to listen. One of the two began speaking. He was a fussy-looking man in smart black jacket and breeches, with a lace cravat around his neck. He had a plump face and a sharp pointed nose. "Mr. Corty," the man standing next to Tom told him. "The other one's Joe McConnahay." McConnahay was thickset, middle-aged, of plainer appearance than Mr. Corty, and he stood just behind him, looking watchfully about the room. The Sugar

King. "He runs this place," the man went on bitterly. "He owns it, if you ask me. He owns us. He owns our stuff. He owns the whole goddamned war."

Joe McConnahay whispered in Mr. Corty's ear, and then Mr. Corty began to speak. He had a strong Irish brogue, and an oily manner.

"There is no cash," he began. The men groaned and called out. "It's gone to war," Corty continued. He smiled, and showed his teeth. "But these notes are issued by the Treasury of the United States, God bless our Congress, and they'll be redeemed in gold."

"When?" men called. "When do we get it? How we gonna live?"

More whispers from the Sugar King. Corty nodded sagely. It was like watching a dog with its master, or a doll in a puppet show. Mr. Corty gave the Sugar King's answer.

"Two weeks."

The complaints diminished into murmurs. Two weeks. It wasn't good, and it wasn't bad.

Corty followed up his advantage. "When the war's won and the British thrown back into the sea." More whispers. "Two weeks and you'll be paid with interest. That's the word of Mr. McConnahay, a man you all know and trust."

He turned, touched his master on the shoulder, and smiled at him. McConnahay whispered back. Corty announced: "He says, the notes in your hand are worth more than gold. They're the future of your country."

The men stirred restlessly. McConnahay suddenly smiled. He'd been looking grim up till now. His smile made him look younger. A rogue's smile. It seemed to say, I'm a rogue, but you like rogues, so you'll go along with me.

Sure enough, the noise began to die down.

Then Tom called out, "You can starve in two weeks," and the smile faded away. Other men took up the cry, and Corty and McConnahay left the room. Tom thought to himself, If men like them say two weeks, you can wager your life it'll be four. He felt shaky at having called out. He thought of how the Sugar King's smile disappeared and those cold eyes flicked to him. It was always his plan to lie low when he came across people like McConnahay. The enemy. The enemy were everywhere. The Liberty Woman. The wealthy bitch. Captain Lacey. The Sugar King and his puppet. The British across the harbor. They were all the same. They all wanted what little he had. Well, they had it now, so that was the end of the matter. Tom shuffled into a line and waited.

At last he was given his promissory note, and could leave the commissary. Promissory. Commissary. Liberty. He spat as he walked across the yard. The rain had stopped, and it was warm and humid. He had to push against the men coming in with their scraps of paper. For the first time he thought of Ned, waiting for him on the street all this while, and he pushed harder, began to run, pushed and forced his way out through the yard gates, suddenly panicky at the thought of all that time passing without Ned coming into his mind even once. He was all he'd had to think about, and he'd not thought. Worrying about Lacey's piece of paper when he'd known it was just paper all along. A boat, it's there, you can touch it. Paper, he couldn't even read. Your son, you can touch him too—he's something to hold on to. He's everything. The only thing.

He rushed out into the street, but he knew.

He knew because it had to happen, after what else had happened today. Still he looked up and down, ran across the street and looked from the other side, pushed people out of the way, ran up the steps to a door to get a better view. But no.

Ned was gone.

3

Ned followed the band till it halted at a big square. There was a pedestal in the middle with nothing on top. The recruits squatted, talking to each other or to their girls, who'd tagged along. The sergeant paraded the band. Ned stood near a young drummer, who was about his own age and had a long, comical face. Ned asked him his name, and the drummer whispered back, "Merle Smith." The band began to play again, and Merle beat his snare until it sang. Ned stood very still, listening.

The rain fell, but Ned was oblivious to it and the recruits who sat on their haunches. He was wrapped up in the roll of the drum, the skittering beat, the sudden sweeps and plunges. Whistles tootled in and out of the drum roll. Somewhere beyond, the sergeant was saying, "These brave young men! Some from farms. Some from the city! Some indentured! Now they're free. Every man Jack's a hero, come to the aid of his country."

The drum roll rose and gusted. In his mind's eye Ned saw trees in a windy forest, feet flying at dream speed, and he heard, "The United States wants you-you-you."

Merle's sticks beat faster than hands could move. They became indistinct and fuzzy, blurred into the drumskin. But the sound remained clear, and the sergeant's voice wound itself into the rhythm. "Sixty dollars a year. A hundred and fifty acres to every discharged veteran."

Suddenly coins were jumping with the vibrating skin, clinking on the sticks. "And five shillings bounty on the drumhead now."

The sergeant's face loomed toward Ned's. "What about you?" he asked.

Ned was shaking with the breaking of the drumbeat spell. He swallowed hard. "Can I beat the drum?"

The sergeant's face came even closer. "Not just the drum," he said. "You can beat the British."

Ned put his hand cautiously on the drumhead, stroked the skin. Then he picked up the coins. The sergeant smiled. A corporal entered Ned's name in the recruiting book. A few minutes later the squad started to march again.

For a few minutes Tom panicked. He ran up and down the street outside the commissary, pushing people out of the way, shoving one man over, scurrying about as if Ned were hidden in the air somewhere and all he had to do was go fast enough, catch him on the hop, turn an invisible corner.

But then, after a while, he pulled himself together, made himself think. If Ned was lost, he'd find him. Ned was somewhere in the city, he couldn't have been spirited away.

Tom stood quite still, made himself get calm, tried to *feel* the way Ned had gone. He remembered how the Indians up the Hudson could follow forest trails that white men couldn't see. But white men had their gifts too. You could put yourself in someone's shoes. He closed his eyes.

Ned. Fourteen. Bored. Wandering off somewhere. Getting lost. All alone in the city. Where would he go? Home. Where was home? The boat. Where had the boat been? The wharf. By the Sugar House. It wouldn't be there now, but the place would still feel like home.

He ran down the streets they'd come by. When he passed the brothel district, the whore was still on the balcony, watching the passersby. The street was much quieter now.

"Ya seen a young boy?" Tom asked.

"This town is full of young boys," she said disgustedly. Then she grinned, gap-toothed. "Ya coming up?"

Tom hurried on. The whore shouted at him. He came back down to the wharf and looked about. No Ned. Then he heard something faint, approaching from the distance. The dry sound of drums and the screeching of fifes and whistles. He'd heard it before, when they were going up to the commissary. Oh, God, he thought, not that. Let it not be that.

The band came around the corner, a block of boys in step, playing their instruments, then the rabble of the men they'd pulled into their snare on the way. Just as he'd known Ned wasn't outside the commissary when he was going through the yard, now he knew Ned would be here, with the recruiting band.

And there he was, right by the drummers, a little boy following the music. Tom pushed his way over to him. Ned looked up, unsurprised at seeing him appear. He had something in his hand but he kept his fingers closed on it. Tom remembered the game Which Hand? you play with babies, and his heart sank even more.

"What's that?" he asked.

Ned opened his hand. "Five shillings, Pa. It's for you."

Tom looked at the coins in horror. It was all his fault. What could you expect? He'd been complaining before he went into the commissary about having nothing. Ned was a good boy, he'd done his best. Sold himself for five shillings.

Ned caught his father's expression. "And a hundred and fifty acres of land when the war's over," he added proudly.

Tom thought of the oily Corty: "The notes in your hand are worth more than gold." This war so far was more like trading up the Hudson than anything else, except that Tom was always coming off worst.

"What you done now, Ned?" he asked quietly.

He followed Ned's gaze to a little folding table the recruiting sergeant had set up. He was standing behind it with a row of recruits lining up in front. A corporal stood at each side of the table, on guard. There was a great house upstate that Tom sailed past as he went up and down the Hudson, with a long carriageway and a statue on each gatepost, and the guards looked a bit like those statues, except that it was a different sort of entrance altogether.

"I joined up, Pa."

"You what?"

"Joined."

"No you ain't."

He grabbed Ned's arm and took him over to the desk. "There's been a mistake," he said to the corporal. "My boy says he's joined."

The sergeant gave him a long look, an angry grin on his face. He picked up his book from under the quill of the newest recruit and held it up to Tom. He stabbed the page with his finger. "He has," he said.

"I say he ain't."

The sergeant turned the book around, to look at it himself, as though he wanted to double check. He nodded at what he saw, and turned the book back again. He passed it to Tom and once more pointed at the page. "There's his name. Ned Dobb."

I know it's my own boy's name, and I can't even read it Tom thought. The page was full of scrawls, some of it splotched by the earlier rain. Every time they take what is mine, he told himself, they give me writing in exchange. Tom felt anger burning up in him, and tried to hold it back. He was a man who lay low and didn't cause trouble. He'd had trouble enough in his life, from the beginning of it.

"I know his name," he said quietly. "I'm his pa. He's not of age. Ned's just a boy."

The sergeant shook his head. "He's old enough to write his name, he's old enough to join."

Tom handed the book back. "There's been a mistake," he said.

The sergeant shook his head once more and put the book back on the table. Tom took Ned's hand and began to back off, meanwhile keeping his eye on the sergeant. It was like backing off from an animal. Keep your eyes firm, and it might not notice how easy it was to get the rest of you. He spoke as if they'd agreed. "Say good-bye, Ned, and come on."

"Take him," the sergeant said quietly.

The corporals weren't guarding an entrance, but an exit. They grabbed Tom's arms. He tried to struggle, but they had him tight. He kicked at their legs as he shouted at the sergeant, "Ya bastard. What ya want him for? Just a kid. It ain't his war."

The sergeant stabbed his finger at the recruits, just as he had at their names in the roll book. They were grouped behind the band, and they looked back toward the argument with slow curiosity, like cattle.

"See them there? All somebody's kids. But they're willing to die fighting tyranny. They're willing to pay liberty's price. Go on, ask your boy whose war."

Tom looked at Ned. Willing to die, said the sergeant. He was fourteen, he'd only just begun to live. Ned was embarrassed under his gaze. "I can learn to be a drummer, Pa," he said, as if that were reason enough for everything.

"God, Ned." Keep calm, he thought. Don't show anger, nor fear. Keep to reasons. Argue for Ned's life with a smile. "Sergeant, ya must be a family man. Me, I've had a wife and three children dead."

He had never said it to anyone before. Not a soul. No one in the world knew, save Ned. Nobody was to be told. Saying it made him think about it, made it happen over again. It must never be said. Except now. "Ned here's all I got. I don't want to give him up."

The sergeant didn't respond.

"He didn't have my permission," Tom said.

"It makes no difference. He's had the five shillings."

Tom took the money from Ned and held it under the sergeant's nose. "Ya can take it back."

The sergeant slowly shook his head.

Tom spun around, caught one of the corporals off balance, yanked himself free from him, then was caught in the small of the back by the other one and flung to the ground. The men kneeled on him. The sergeant bent down.

"You try that again. I'll run you through," he said.

Tom got to his feet. He pleaded, "Don't take him."

The sergeant looked him up and down, as though inspecting him for dirt from the roadway. "Sons go to war because fathers don't."

"You bugger," Tom whispered.

The sergeant silently pushed the roll book toward Tom, open at the page, a dipped quill lying on top of it. Five shillings lay beside it. The soldiers released his arms and Tom picked up the quill. Tongue probing his cheek, he slowly made his name from memory, as Ned had taught him.

"Ya bastard," he told the sergeant as he did it. He couldn't read what he himself had written.

Daisy hurried home through the dark streets. She was drenched. But what a day it had been! She'd been witness to the revolution. More than that, she'd actually taken part. She remembered that man and his boy who'd hung back. People like that didn't understand the war was being fought for them. Not just on the matter of trade, though that too. The man was a trader himself. While Britain restricted commerce, everybody suffered. Her father had said it over and over again. Both the successful merchant and the man in the street, or on the boat.

But the trade side of things was only a tiny part. The war was really about independence, both of the country and of the individual. It was about giving people like the man and the boy the right to a free human existence in which their liberty would be guaranteed, and opportunities for them to improve their station in life would be given.

Of course, it was hard for them to see that fact while their boat and goods were being requisitioned—to realize that short-term hardship would result in the long-term betterment of their lot. It was natural that the man had felt bitter, snarling and hitting out as his things were taken. He'd frightened her, almost. Of course, she'd always been protected from the life of the streets, where feeling held sway over reason. That would be another beneficial consequence of this war—greater equality of social status.

She arrived at her house. Lamps were lit in the drawing room. Her family must have eaten supper and were now spending the evening in there. It would be better if they didn't see her in this saturated state, Daisy thought. In any case they would be angry and worried because she'd been away for so long.

She made her way around the side of the house, toward the kitchen entrance. It was a trivial consideration really, about which she felt some shame, attempting to avoid or delay a family argument while brave men were preparing to fight the British and decide the fate of New York, and of all the continent, perhaps. But she didn't want to be prevented from thinking about the exciting events of today and the great ones to come by petty squabbling with her parents and sisters.

She opened the kitchen door. Cuffy looked up from cleaning the dishes. Her mouth gaped open in surprise at the sight of Daisy's clothes, her hair disheveled, her bonnet gone. She was just about to exclaim when Daisy put a finger warningly over her own mouth. Cuffy contented herself with raising her eyebrows in her comical way. Daisy hurried past her, crept through the hallway, and went up the stairs to her own room.

She opened the door. Cuffy must have been up to light the

lamp. For a moment she stood in the doorway, looking in. Her belongings seemed cosy and welcoming in the soft glow: the case of books, the doll's house she'd played with as a child, the clutter on her dressing table. Ben Franklin smiled at her like a kindly uncle from the wall. Rain beat against the window. From faraway came the muted shouts of the mob. It had been raw on the streets, dangerous, exciting.

She looked at the pile of pamphlets on her bed. Reading about these matters was a different thing indeed from living through them. But now she had done both. She had stepped down from her carriage, left her mother and sisters behind, run with the people. For the moment at least it felt good to be back, to recruit her strength and her principles in this quiet place while the city prepared for war.

She stepped in, closed the door, turned around and gasped. Her father was sitting in the low chair by the wall. She almost cried out in shock at seeing him there, but bit her lip to prevent it, immediately disgusted with herself. Men were being recruited to face the British, and here she was, in her own bedroom, gasping in fright at the sight of her father. A naughty girl who'd been out late and got her dress wet.

And then he smiled at her. He was a man who was often preoccupied, weighed down by the cares of business. Sometimes he was grim, occasionally almost sullen, from time to time bad-tempered. She loved to see him smile. His smile made him handsome.

"Papa," she said. Suddenly she almost wanted to cry. She seemed to have gone so far today, and now she was home.

"You're very wet, Daisy," he said gently. He stood up, came over, and rested his hand on her shoulder.

"I'm sorry, Father."

He pressed his face closer to hers, a hand on each of her shoulders now. His smile receded. "I told you not to go out there, Daisy. Not to leave the house."

"I was in the carriage with Mama . . . and Betsy, and Amy. We were coming back from the Rennslers."

"Daisy, that is not the point. You left the carriage. The others stayed inside."

"But, Father, I—"

"When you have a daughter of your own, you'll understand."

She'd been going to say something about why she had left the carriage, about the principles of liberty and independence, about her desire to take whatever course was open to her, a female, to contribute to the defense of New York. She felt a spurt of resentment at the way he'd brandished the word daughter at her instead.

As if by association her father stepped over to her doll's house and patted its roof. He turned back toward her, and there was the smile again, lighting up his face. Then he bent down and began poking his big fingers into the rooms, rearranging the furniture. Outside, the sounds of the mob were closer; suddenly there was the high-pitched tingling of a nearby window being broken. Daisy gasped and raised a hand to her neck. Her father looked up toward her and smiled.

"Don't be confused by those people out there," he said. "Family against family. It's easy enough to break down barriers, destroy dwellings, wreck things. Building is more difficult. It needs tolerance. Working together."

Daisy began to walk toward her window. Her father grasped her arm as she passed him, and then he was holding her, as he did so rarely, her head resting on his broad shoulder.

"You'll see what I mean," he whispered softly, comfortingly.

The recruits didn't begin to earn their drumhead money for nearly six weeks. They drilled, had musket practice, sat in camp and drank. At least it was somewhere to stay, and food provided. As he ate, Tom would wonder whose food it rightfully was and what they'd got for it on their chit.

Often the troops would go down to the old Battery and look across the harbor at the British fleet. It grew day by day. By August 22nd there were over four hundred ships anchored there, the biggest fleet ever seen in colonial waters. On that day transports began to ferry troops across the Narrows to Long Island.

It was what the American recruits had been waiting for, in fear and trepidation. The pincer movement on New York had begun.

A few days later, at dusk, Tom, Ned, and the others were marched down to the wharves, not far from the Sugar House, where a flotilla of small boats was moored waiting for them. Their longboat was probably there.

It had been a hot day, but turned to rain as night came on.

The water rose and fell in flattened waves, catching the light from the pitch-wood fires that burned along the side of the wharf. There was darkness, fine silvery rain, dim rolling smoke, the greasy water, and pools of illumination from the fires. Quartermasters doled out supplies as the new recruits shuffled up. Leaflets rippled off stacks in the faint sea wind and slithered along the soaked planking. *Common Sense*.

Tom and Ned waited in the ranks for their turn. Tom was in deep gloom, as so often in the last few weeks. Ned, aware that it was his fault, tried to show his father the bright side. "We'll get three hundred acres of land, Pa. We're rich. Merle's gonna show me how to drum. And we still got the ten shillings."

Three hundred acres when the war ended, ten shillings now. Yes, Tom thought, this war was like a business. Profit and loss. Profit in two weeks, four, in the life everlasting. Loss now. The line moved slowly toward the quartermasters. Each man in turn was being given one musket, one hat, two flints, six cartridges, one kettle of fish.

"Stuff stinks," Tom said.

The boy ahead was complaining: "Said I'd get shoes."

"Shoes are waitin' for ya, fart catcher. Over on Long Island. Brits got shoes all sizes . Ya heard of dead men's shoes?" The quartermaster cackled.

Tom and Ned were beside a pair of open casks; hard biscuits, dried peas.

"Grab 'em, Ned," Tom whispered. They stuffed their pockets. "Ya got to suck them peas, Ned," Tom explained. "Don't bite 'em. Break a tooth." He bent down, picked up a pile of leaflets, passed them to Ned, bent again and got some for himself. "Fuel, son," he explained, stuffing them in his breeches' pocket.

At last they were in one of the small, rocking boats, pressed in among the other recruits. A girl tried to sneak down the wharf steps but was yanked unceremoniously back by yet another sergeant.

"Abby!" her boyfriend cried, sounding frightened and forlorn, though he was a big strong-looking lad.

"I'll be waiting for you, Bill," Abby called back. A pause. "In the hay," she added. The recruits all laughed. Abby laughed too. She stood on the wharf, waving to Bill, as relaxed and jolly as if she were waving him off to his field or workbench.

Then a very different female voice spoke in ringing tones: "God bless you all." Tom looked farther along the wharf. There was the Liberty Woman, approaching along the dockside. The other women were with her, cheering. They must have been here all day, he thought, watching the soldiers being sent off to Long Island. There was the rich one. That bitch. Her bonnet was gone, her hair flattened to her head with the rain, and her gown sodden, but she still gleamed in the light from the fires, unsoiled.

They began to row the rainy Narrows toward Long Island, and the rich girl, the Liberty Women, the fires, the racket of the city, faded away.

The rain had stopped, the river glassy now, though the whole boat rocked as inexperienced men rowed badly. Tom watched them, lips pursed, from the huddle in the bow. Every now and then the oars would clatter against those of vessels nearby. Ned and Merle were sitting opposite Tom, Merle's drum wedged between his legs.

"Beat daddymammy," Merle said. He beat half a roll, just using the right stick. "Daddy." Then he beat the other half. "Mammy. Now put them together." He beat the whole roll. "Daddymammy. You try it."

He passed the drum to Ned, who rested it awkwardly between his knees and with a nervous smile lifted the sticks. Tom felt a pang as he watched his boy, so self-conscious and worried at learning to bang a drum, while a battle waited for him in the morning. A child with a new toy. Ned took a deep breath, brought his sticks down with all his strength, and gave the drum an enormous pounding, making up in volume for his inability to merge the beats together. Then he finished, laughing, embarrassed. But the rolling went on.

"Cannon, Ned," said Merle quietly.

Tom turned toward Long Island. There were sudden yellow flashes over the black hunched shape of the land, strangely out of time with the ebb and flow of the sounds, like Ned's sticks, and the crab catchers' oars. Everything about this time and place was rough, jerky, uneven. He turned back, in time to see Ned yawning.

"I'm tired, Pa," he said, surprised.

"It's the scares, Ned," Tom said.

Ned smiled as he had when he was about to play the drum. For a moment Tom could hardly speak. He had his own

scares, but it was the boy's that made it so bad, that made his
throat tight. He swallowed, and leaned forward. Ned's hat
was too big, and he pushed it up on his forehead. Then he
held Ned's knee and spoke quietly, earnestly, gave him the
only thing he could: "Hear what I say, Ned. Stick by the
officers." Ned looked back in puzzlement. "They never risk
hurt," Tom went on, ignoring the boy's surprise. "Look out
for yourself first." He reached over and pinched Ned's cheek.
"We come this far."

   Ned licked his lips, confused.

4

___

The Battle of Long Island was fought on August 27th 1776. The rebels, under the overall generalship of an old Indian fighter, Israel Putnam, had strongly fortified the village of Brooklyn itself. Then two large units were sent forward to guard the left and right flanks of the approaches to Brooklyn, and a line of men was put between them, along the Heights of Guan.

Unfortunately for the rebels there was a weak link in this defensive chain. On its far left only five men had been assigned to guard one of the approaches, Jamaica Road. Even worse, that fact had been reported to General Henry Clinton, second in command of the British forces. He secretly sent a small battalion forward to capture the men and also to take some rebel scouts who had been positioned on nearby high ground. The British forces were then able to break through the defensive line and tackle the rebels from the front and rear simultaneously. The Americans fought bravely enough, but outnumbered two to one, and now outflanked, their task was impossible. General Washington, on seeing both the heroism of his troops and the scale of the catastrophe that had overtaken them, exclaimed, "Good God, what brave fellows I must this day lose!" The rebels had 1500 casualties out of a force of 8000; Howe, with twice that number on Long Island, lost merely 400.

The one consolation for the Americans was that at least Washington managed to get his troops off the island. In a remarkable amphibious operation he ferried his army back to Manhattan in the space of nine hours, at night, undetected

until it was too late by the British. The weather had turned
once more. Rain, followed by fog, added to the protection of
darkness. As he boarded the last craft, with the British now
entering Brooklyn, Lieutenant Benjamin Talmadge looked up
the ferry steps and suddenly realized that the tall silhouette
he could just discern through the swirl was that of General
Washington. He had supervised the whole operation, ignoring the risk to himself.

The men were scattered over large wheat fields, with woodland to one side. It was strange to catch blue glimpses of men
as they lay amidst the crop, dark flecks like weeds amid the
yellow grain for hundreds of yards. The stalks rippled around
them when they moved, as though caught by random breezes.
An open space had been cleared nearer the roadway, and a
huddle of tents set up to house the wounded. Men lay on the
ground all around, on pallets, cloaks, and the stubbly soil
itself. Women were wandering about from one to the next,
looking for their particular men. In the tents lay the more
bady wounded—Daisy could see them through the openings,
lying in dim light. She went up closer to one of the tents and
peered in. The boy lying nearest the opening had obviously
been wounded in the head, a soaking bandage wrapped tightly
round his temple. He was looking straight up, his eyes
rolled back, so that mainly white showed. The coat on which
he was lying had been pushed up, and one of his legs was
moving compulsively back and forth over the soil, so that his
heel had already dug a deep groove in it. Daisy slipped in
and pulled the coat down, but the man's heel immediately
caught it and brought it back again. He was completely
unaware of her presence. She tiptoed out into the light again,
and feeling suddenly dizzy, raised her hand to her mouth.
The clean scent of her cotton glove made her realize how
sour the air was—it smelled of meat. There was subdued
moaning everywhere, and the quiet tones of girls who'd
found their own soldiers and were comforting them. From
the biggest tent, set to one side of the others, the noises were
louder—a pleading, whimpering sound like that made by a
small dog, and robust, booming, no-nonsense tones which
Daisy suddenly recognized.
She hurried over to the tent and went in. Sloan was there,
his back to her, leaning over a bench on which lay a young

boy. He glanced around as she came in, and she saw he was transformed from the Dr. Sloan who attended her family in swallowtail coat and neat wig. His receding gray hair made his pink face seem bigger and coarser than before; he was wearing an apron and boots like a tradesman, both blood-stained, as if he were working in a slaughterhouse. He screwed up his eyes when he looked at her, as though he had difficulty seeing her in this place.

"Daisy McConnahay?"

"Is it you, Dr. Sloan?"

"What in blazes are you doing here?"

"I've come to help," she said vaguely.

"This is no place for you. Go home to your mother and sisters."

She knew he was right. This was a man's place, and she was a girl. And she wasn't a girl like those outside, searching out their lovers in the cornfield. This place belonged to the common people, and she was a merchant's daughter.

Suddenly the boy cried out and began to writhe in a spasm of terrible pain. Dr. Sloan turned back to him and held him down. "Go home, Daisy," he repeated.

"Let me help," she said, and went up to the end of the bench where the boy's head and shoulders were propped on a cushion.

In the tent she walked into a wall of stench and almost retched. If the smell outside the tent was that of meat, this was of meat gone bad, a smell that wasn't simply disgusting, but frightening too. The smell had a sinister, secret familiarity about it. But in the center of the cesspit was the boy's face, a child's, thin and big-eyed with agony. She wiped the sweat from his forehead with the sleeve of her gown.

"Give me something for a tourniquet here," Dr. Sloan asked abruptly.

Without even thinking, Daisy slipped off her shawl and passed it to him. He twisted it tightly around the boy's thigh. "Hold it in place, will you?" he asked her gruffly.

She moved up to grip it as Sloan picked up an instrument. Suddenly Daisy realized it was a small saw. As he began to work, she turned away, but she could still hear the sludgy sound of the boy's flesh being cut as the saw bit into the bone.

When the leg was gone, she heard through the boy's endless scream the doctor's dry tones: "Thank'ee, Miss

McConnahay." She went up to the head of the pallet on which the boy was lying and wiped his face with her sleeve, then raised his head and gave him some water to drink from her flask. He gulped it down, and when he'd finished, she pressed his head to her breast and comforted him.

Then she was outside once more, with the tents, prone soldiers, and wheat fields swirling crazily around her.

Abby had almost kept her word to Bill, her lover. They embraced, if not in hay, at least in wheat. Not far away lay Ned Dobb, and beside him, stiff with his wound, his father. Suddenly standing over them was a lady; not a woman, a lady. She stood looking down, swaying like a tree in the breeze, the soft stuff of her gown drifting over her like the wind rippling over wheat. She was in gleaming whatever-it-was ladies wore, muslin or satin or something, but she weaved about in the corn just the same. Perhaps she belonged to the officers. What made the whole thing even stranger was that Ned half recognized her. She was a dreamlike woman. No, a nightmare woman, for Ned suddenly realized there were tiny flecks of blood on her gloves and sleeves.

Tom hoisted himself on his elbow. Lying in the wheat was like lying in yellow water, and he screwed up his eyes against the dazzle of surface light. He recognised her at once. The rich woman at the docks. The one who'd taken his boat. The bitch.

"Ya got eats?" he asked.

"Yes," Daisy said. She took some bread from her bag and gave it to them. Then she took out a flask of water and knelt to pass it to Tom.

"You're hurt," she said. She pulled his shirt open, and gasped as she saw the red welt on his chest.

"Chainshot," he said gruffly. She began to dab at it with the cloth he'd been using to staunch the blood.

"I can see the links," she said. As she washed it, she glanced up at his face. "What was it like?"

"The fight? Ya wanna know that? Why'd you wanna know that?"

"Please."

Tom thought. He didn't want to say. He couldn't say. How could you describe it? But at the same time, he should. She ought to know. She'd taken his boat, everything. She'd been the reason Ned had joined up, and that he'd joined up. She ought to know what she'd done.

There had been the waiting first, as the sun slowly came up. Hours of waiting so that you almost longed for something to happen, Ned and Merle giggling and whispering together like a couple of children, Tom feeling his nerves stretch tighter and tighter. And then it was dawn, birds began to call and flap across the water, a quiet dawn like so many he had known on the river. And still nothing happened, and Tom even began to get a faint hope, more painful than his fear, that nothing would happen, that the generals and politicians had come to some arrangement and decided not to go into battle. Then it began to hail.

Musket balls peppered the marshy vegetation all around. You could not picture individual people firing the individual muskets; the bullets simply rained down out of a clear sky. Men all about began to fall. Soldiers appeared, running toward him.

"Fella next to me said, 'Here they come, them's Brits.' But they was us."

"Us?" Daisy asked.

"Running away."

There was silence.

"And the British came?"

"Didn't even see them."

"They shot chain and grape," Ned said.

The chain came across the ground as the musket balls had come from the air, of its own accord. You saw the cattails whip over, and suddenly a soldier nearby had no leg. A man near Tom fell in two, sliced through the middle, and the spent chain wrapped itself about Tom's chest.

"It was my first battle," Ned said.

"You're both so brave," Daisy told him.

"We run," Tom said.

Daisy looked at Tom. Suddenly she brought her face close to his and put her arms round him. The unexpected pressure pushed Tom backward, and they were embracing and laughing in the corn. Ned looked away in disgust.

"Say your name," she asked.

"Tom Dobb. What's yours?"

"Daisy. You fought for the cause. You fought for America. You're both so brave."

They looked at each other for a few moments longer. Daisy blushed deeply. "You're both so brave," she kept saying.

Then Ned was crying out, pointing. Across the fields horses were shattering the wheat, galloping towards them, the mounted officers beating the grain for men, like hunters beating for game. A bulky man with gold epaulettes on his blue jacket, mounted on an enormous white stallion, was careering right at them. Bill disentangled himself from Abby and rose to his feet.

"It's the general," he suddenly shouted. "General Washington."

As he neared, Ned could make out the tears running down his cheek. He was slashing stumbling soldiers with his riding crop. "Form and march, you cowards," he kept shouting. Then he was on them. The crop whirled, struck Tom so that he fell as if shot, and he thundered onward.

Daisy, shaking, helped Tom to his feet again. There was a red welt across his neck and shoulder, almost crossing the lines of chainshot on his chest. Other officers came up, forming men into squads. Tom and Ned were suddenly part of a marching unit again, and Daisy was watching them as they went. She found herself clustering with the other women whose men were marching off to battle yet again.

Rows of red British, the dry sound of their drums, the union jack garlanded with gold, vibrant battle flags fluttering with the contours of the late summer breeze. The men stand erect as Sergeant-Major Peasy inspects. He is dressed like them, except that his hat is set straight across his head and he wears a long cape that gives him a brooding, secretive quality. He is heavy featured, with protuberant eyes, a triangle of bristle near the right side of his mouth, and a thoughtful, confident, merciless face. He is large—taller and weightier than most of his men, with a measured stride that shows no hurry. A tradesman, solid stock, who could have been a cooper or a blacksmith and would have produced his wares with an economy of well-directed force, but whose trade is war instead. The drums roll dryly.

The American lines zigzagged across the fields. It was very much a defensive stance. The first line of troops were deployed behind a fence; the second along its shallow ditch; on the slope behind, the reserves milled confusedly. Otherwise everything was still, except for the iron kettles, looped on straps and resting against the soldiers' backsides, rising and falling as the soldiers along the fence breathed. Beyond, Merle seemed a toy soldier, his drumsticks poised against the sweep of sky.

The British began to approach slowly, methodically, in step, the only irregularity the occasional flash of a bayonet catching the sun.

Tom and Ned were in the ditch. Tom drew a handful of dried peas from his bulky packet, showed them to Ned, who shook his head, and then gobbled them himself, the peas rattling against his teeth as dryly as the British drums, which were getting ever nearer. A little way along the ditch a boy yawned. Tom eyed him mischieviously, spat a pea which caught the lad on the cheek. The boy poked his head up, and instinctively looked toward the British lines, as though the pea had been a diminutive green musket ball. Then, puzzled, he looked along the ditch. Tom smiled, winked. The boy suddenly laughed.

The British approached down the slope in long even lines, their muskets held upright, their knees high as they marched in double time, keeping step. The Americans waited nervously as they got nearer, and then, unable to bear the suspense any longer, began to fire. They fired wildly, and the British didn't even hesitate in their march. The few who were hit fell, and as if according to a drill book, were replaced at once by soldiers from the line behind. Their muskets remained upright. Peasy, now carrying a long lance, called the cadence and made comments as he trotted beside them: "Be brave. You're British soldiers. Best bloody regiment in the world. These Americans are animals."

The British drumroll accelerated. Peasy barked commands. His troops magically shuffled from block formation into three tight lines—the first kneeling, ready to fire; the second taking aim; the third with arms at the ready. American muskets stared back from the interwoven branches of the fence, no heads daring to look up and view along the barrels, which were therefore not in parallel, a kind of musket squint.

"Fire," yelled Peasy, and the fence boughs splintered and holed as if abruptly diseased. American soldiers sagged against them or back into the ditch, dead out of nowhere. American muskets fired back obliquely.

Peasy cranked his troops through their motions: "First line

to the rear. Second line to the front. Third line to the ready."
The second fusillade blasted. Then the third. Then the fourth.

Suddenly the British pipes and drums played charge. The
three lines unfolded into one. Peasy superintended it at an
unhurried trot, grooming his troops, forming them up, ca-
ressing them; above all giving them the rhythm of his strength
and vigor, his economical, unhurried inevitability; his solid
legs and whole red form, pumping consistently like a juicy
heart. The bayonets were lowered in one flowing movement
along the line.

Merle beat Fix Bayonets, and the rebels responded—as
best they could. Tom's was twisted like a corkscrew. Ned
didn't have one. The British charged. Their bayonets appeared over the top of the fence, explored its inner face,
trimmed rebels away as a butcher's knife trims meat. The
rebels retreated into the ditch. The British broke through the
fence and marched on in formation. The two lines of rebels
were tangled in their ditch, smoke billowing over them as
they panicked. The rebels were killed in rows, Peasy super-
vising as a butcher might supervise his slaughterhousemen,
with no excitement or animosity, simply a desire that the
beasts should be killed quickly and comprehensively.

The Americans began to run, and the British ran after
them. The killing penetrated deeper and deeper into the
retreating rebels. Ned was trying to load a musket many
times too big for him. Tom dropped his own musket, grabbed
him, and tried to pull him away. Ned wouldn't come. Ahead,
a flag bearer had fallen. Ned struggled from Tom's grasp and
darted for the fallen flag, straight at the slashing bayonets.
Aghast, Tom watched his son retrieve the flag, then ran to
him and pulled him back. Along with all the rest they headed
for the woods.

Then Peasy was coming for them, at an angle. Ned froze.
The lance was leveled, and Peasy ran as if he could run
through a wall, run forever. Ned watched him in terror,
unable to move, as Tom had seen animals wait when they
knew they were going to die. Tom took the flag from the
boy's hand without Ned even noticing, and as the lance
thrust forward, dropped the flag over the end of the lance
and yanked hard.

"Run, Ned, run," he gasped.

Peasy's eyes flicked quickly, calculatingly, from Ned to
Tom, but there was nothing he could do. His lance was

tangled, and by the time it was clear, Tom and Ned were with the other rebels in the woods and the British jeered them from the field.

The sergeant-major, cursing, disentangled the flag from his lance. Then he turned back to the business of killing. Across the whole field Americans were scattering, running confusedly about like a nest of disturbed insects. Others lay still on the meadow as abandoned kettles rolled about the grass like blackened skulls.

In the woods the battle was over. There were only runners. Tom made Ned run between the huge trees, deeper and deeper, until they had separated from the other fleeing rebels and the noise of the battlefield was a subdued murmur almost beyond hearing, like the sounds of the earth, and they couldn't make out the screams of dying men any longer. Then Tom slowed them to a walk. As he recovered his breath, he could smell greenery again, as he had when lying on the meadow behind the ditch. The light here was green also.

Eventually the trees began to thin away, and then they were on farmland, with the fields gently sloping down toward the smoke of a distant town.

"New York," Tom said.

"They say the army'll get off the island. Go west."

"We're going home."

Tom had taken off the white straps of his uniform and made Ned do the same. He'd thrown them away along with Ned's hat. The logic, from his point of view, was simple enough. The need that had taken him into battle took him out again. The need was to protect his son, all that was left of his family. And a family needed a home. Their home had been the boat, which the war had taken from them. It had been taken in New York, so New York would have to be their home for the time being.

"We'll go underground," he said. "Work rope or somethin'."

New York was a city of fear. Loyalists hid in their shuttered and barred houses, terrified that the rebels would exact revenge for defeat. Rebels milled in the streets, angry and frightened. Two soldiers hung from a lamppost in Wall Street, *Deserter* scrawled on signs pinned to their chests. Many people were still struggling out of the city, loaded down with their possessions.

Tom and Ned scurried into New York against the tide of escaping people, taking the narrower, dingier streets and heading toward the docks. A little farther down, near McConnahay's Sugar House, was a large shed. Tom and Ned disappeared beneath it.

5

Daisy ran.

She had been awakened by cries and shouts from the street, and had gone to her window. People were running, waving banners, calling each other, pushing and shoving. Daisy herself almost called out. She wanted to raise the house, to sing and celebrate. And then she suddenly realized what the mob was saying: "We was beat."

For a long time she stood, watching them silently. She didn't experience any sorrow about what must have happened, nor any fear for the future. She was numb, sleepy. It was as though her mind, having crawled toward wakefulness and found the weather unkind, had turned back and escaped to its burrow again.

Then, suddenly, she woke for a second time. She rushed over to her wardrobe, pulled out the first gown she caught hold of, flung off her shift—her fingers clumsy with hurry—and struggled into her clothes. Then she ran.

Betsy and Amy scrambled after her down the stairs. They guessed from her haste that she was headed for the street. Betsy was screeching "If you go out there, Daisy McConnahay, you're a fool! Those people, they'll . . . they'll rape you!"

Her mother appeared in the hallway below and joined the chorus: "You're not going out in that street today!"

"Don't you know what's happening out there?" Daisy said.

"I know exactly what's happening out there. There's madness out there."

"I must speak to Papa now."

"I forbid you."

47

Daisy stopped, tried to calm herself. She felt strangely comforted by her mother's worry. With disaster on the battlefield and chaos in the streets, your family was what you had to fall back on. Behind her mother's anger, and behind those matchmaking ambitions that Daisy found so contemptible, there was love. And behind her Loyalism, another loyalty.

"I must see Papa," Daisy repeated gently, and kissed her. Then she hurried on her way. Behind her Betsy repeated dire warnings, and Amy cried "Daisy!" both their voices strident with envy.

It was a different mob from before. People were running with their possessions on their backs. One old man staggered down the street under a large, highly polished table, like a frantic tortoise; women carried their clothes wrapped in shawls or tablecloths. Daisy grasped the sleeve of one of them. "Where are you going?" she asked.

"Out," the woman replied. She had a yellow, hollow-looking face. "Away. They said we got to go."

"Who said?"

"They said," she replied stubbornly, and hurried off.

A soldier was coming along the street, his blue coat in tatters, limping at a run in the opposite direction from the flow of the crowds. She headed him off.

"Where are they? Where are the rest of them? Of you?"

The soldier stopped, wiped the sweat from his face with a cuff. "I snuck off, I gotta see my family." And he began his limping run again.

Daisy thought to buttonhole somebody else from the crowd, then changed her mind. Once again she ran, this time to the commissary. The yard gates were shut, she shook them and called.

At last a voice from behind the fence, familiar and unfriendly, said, "The commissary's closed."

"It's me, Sam. Daisy McConnahay."

There was a clatter of locks and bolts, and the gateway opened to reveal a black face and grizzled hair.

"Let me in, Sam," Daisy said.

He stood to one side, and she went on. The courtyard was full of slaves. They were loading supplies into boxes, hammering heads on barrels, tarring over the U.S. stamp on all the cases of provisions. Daisy watched the activity in horror. They were packing up the new United States.

"Sam, I want to see my father. Is he here?"

"He's busy, ma'am. He said he wasn't to be disturbed."

"Open the door, Sam."

Sam scurried across the courtyard and opened the door. She went through. She had got in. What a battle to win, what a soldier she'd make! Able to command her own family's slave! Across the hallway, beside the auction room, was her father's office. Daisy strode straight in.

Her father and some of his merchant friends were sitting in easy chairs before the empty fireplace. She recognized Mr. Rennsler, Mr. Stuke, Mr. Lane, Mr. Burnell—the commodity dealers who ran New York. They were absorbed in their discussion and didn't notice her come in.

Mr. Corty did. He rose from his seat by the others and came over to where she stood, near the door. Although he was a plump man, he had a gliding, silent way of walking. With the strange combination of deference and arrogance characteristic of him, he put his finger to his lips to bid her to be silent.

Her father was waving a broadsheet contemptuously, and she could just make out the gist of what he was saying.

"Evacuate, it says . . . Washington's beat for good . . . they're going to run his arse out of Manhattan . . . lordships coming in . . . eat goddamn anything we hand 'em . . . wonderful opportunity for our city . . . them maggoty pork and beans."

Daisy stared hard at Mr. Corty. He smiled back, more tentatively now. "I wish to speak to my father, Mr. Corty," she said, more loudly than last time.

"He won't like it," Corty replied, turning toward the merchants. At that moment her father looked up. He saw Daisy and got to his feet. He was big and unsmiling.

"What are you doing here?" he asked as he walked over to her.

Daisy looked at his powerful face, and tried to stop herself from trembling.

"I've come to ask you, Papa, to . . . open your doors."

He looked, or pretended to look, puzzled. He pointed at the office door which, if not fully open, was at least ajar.

"The army, Papa. The soldiers."

"Ah, them. Mr. Corty, take my daughter home."

"Yessir, Mr. McConnahay."

"You must help the soldiers, Papa. I've seen them on the field. There's so many wounded." And that was before, she thought. Before whatever happened yesterday. Before General Washington issued his evacuation order. Those poor men, exhausted, wounded, had fought again since she'd last seen them. And boys.

Her father was gazing at her, merciless, adamantine, amused. She thought back on how she'd taken Tom's boat, and his supplies. Just like that. Just by demanding them in the name of the United States. The man had struggled and complained, but in the end had given in, and even enrolled in the militia. He'd been recruited to the cause. And now here she was, trying to get supplies from her own father and not moving him. She could see his three daughters in her father's face. All those chattering women, all that frippery and expense, the prospect of silly intricate courtships, the cost of weddings. That was all women were good for. That man and his boy had had to face a real enemy—the might of the British army. Their defeat was honorable. She couldn't even cope with her own father on this tiny battleground where, as a female, she could wage war.

But at least she would make a fight of it, she thought, as Tom and Ned had had to. She stopped pleading and became angry; not petulant like her sisters, but angry. She said each word with furious clarity: "They fought and suffered for you. And all you can do is think of ways to feed the enemy. Don't you have any pity in you?"

One of the merchants, she couldn't tell which, called out: "That's no way to treat your father!" And to Joe said, "Why do you allow it?"

Her heart pounded as her father stared at her. Then suddenly his face broke into a smile again, the smile that made him look so young. "Allow it?" he asked. "I love it. This is Daisy McConnahay talking. My daughter. My girl." He laughed, and looked at her with love. She stared back, bewildered. She could not tell whether she had won or lost. "Sure," her father went on, "when you're young, it takes a cause to find any sense in this world at all."

Perhaps it was a trick. She picked up her only weapon once more, her anger. "Don't treat me like a child, Father."

"I wouldn't do that, Daisy. Not you. I know you too well."

"Then give out some food! You feed them, or you'll be damned!"

Her father turned to his assistant. "Mr. Corty, how much salt fish do we have in the warehouse?"

Corty busily consulted a notebook he'd drawn from his pocket. "Two hundred and fifty barrels, sir. I have a note of it here."

Joe turned back to Daisy and smiled at her once more. "Then set aside fifty barrels for our boys returning from the war."

She thought, So that's a fifty barrel smile. And then she thought, But I won. I won something. I fought my father and he didn't defeat me completely. He let me win fifty barrels' worth. Suddenly she felt an immense gratitude to him, and went into his arms.

"Oh, Daisy," he said. He sounded sad. "It doesn't matter a damn who deserves to win. It's who *does* win. You remember that, next time you're out there screaming *liberty*." His voice was still gentle. She wept in his arms.

When she'd left his office, the Sugar King turned to Mr. Corty. "Make that ten barrels," he said.

The British marched into New York. They assembled on the Bowling Green to salute their generals; the townsfolk crowded in also, to listen to the conditions of the occupation being proclaimed. Loyalists cheered, rebels stood silent. Tom and Ned watched from the corner of an alleyway; they were chewing lumps of bread. The prisoners taken in battle were lined up on one side of the square, looking shamefaced and tattered, trying to avoid the eyes of both sides. Suddenly Ned spotted a small figure in among them: Merle. Immediately he left Tom, who grabbed unsuccessfully for him, and ran around the edge of the square, pushing through the crowd.

Ned poked his head around the legs of guarding redcoats. "Merle!"

Merle's head slowly turned. His eyes rose to Ned's. Blood had streamed from the corner of one of them and dried across his cheek.

"It's me, Merle," Ned said. A redcoat cuffed him without malice, as one might a pestering insect.

"You got away?" Merle said.

Ned swallowed. "We did."

"That was lucky, Ned," Merle said. There was no sarcasm in his voice. "You got something to eat?"

Ned passed over his chunk of bread. "I'll get you more,

Merle." A redcoat hand shoved him back. Merle's attention was fixed on his piece of bread.

Standing to one side of the main crush of the crowd were the McConnahay girls. Betsy and Amy were triumphant, as though the war had been between them and Daisy and they'd been victorious.

"Where's your glorious revolution now, Daisy?" Betsy asked. "They ran like skunks."

"There's Father with the general," Amy put in excitedly.

"And the cream of the British army!" Betsy said. "They'll be drooling at our feet!"

"You disgust me," Daisy said. An urchin pushed against her as she was speaking, and then ran on. As she watched him go, she realized it was Ned Dobb, and she ran too, leaving her gloating sisters behind.

The boy nosed his way through the crush of increasingly ragged people like a small animal; squirming between legs, elbowing, shoving. Nobody even noticed him. They noticed Daisy, and gave way to her, so that a small channel seemed to appear before her in whatever direction she chose. She was able, holding her skirts as she ran, to keep up with the boy, until suddenly he disappeared into an alleyway that led off the square. Daisy turned into it and there, squeezed into a doorway, stood Tom Dobb.

Tom was watching an English sergeant-major who was patroling the edge of the crowd. He was a big man in a cloak, with a triangle of bristles to one side of his mouth and hard, bulging eyes which roamed ceaselessly among the people, restlessly searching. His eyes probed nearer Tom, then went away again, as if losing the scent; then, led by some instinct, back once more, never quite focusing on Tom, but drawn repeatedly in his direction. Tom remembered how he'd careered across the fence with his troops, the repeated obstinate stabbing of his lance. Then suddenly Ned was swirling round the corner.

"Merle—" he said.

"Get in," Tom snapped, interrupting him, grabbing his collar and pulling him into the doorway. He peered around. The sergeant-major's eyes were still there, not quite focusing on them. And then Daisy was there too, her long brown cloak like a banner in the crowd. The sergeant-major glanced at it, then away. He wasn't interested in the likes of her.

"Tom Dobb," Daisy said.

Tom grasped her arm, pulled her into the doorway too, pressed her back against the wall.

"You ran?" she asked in astonishment. Tom realized she knew what had happened. Of course. If he hadn't run, he'd be over there with the prisoners. Or dead.

"We all ran," he said. "Everybody ran."

"You ran," she repeated, unable to take it in.

"It was skat or get cut. So I ran."

"I thought you might have stood your ground, Mr. Dobb."

She was speaking like a lady; like the lady who'd taken his boat. "It ain't my fight," he said.

"It's *our* fight. All of us." She pointed at the rows of redcoats. Immediately Tom pulled her arm back in. She struggled impatiently to free it. "For freedom," she said, her eyes snapping fury.

"I was free already," Tom whispered, "until you all came."

Suddenly her hand was coming at his face. He caught it and held it hard. He watched her in contempt. She'd taken his boat, the only home he could offer his son. She'd caused Ned to enlist, at the age of fourteen. Now she was trying to hit him because he hadn't let Ned die. And soon she'd go back to some rich household and slaves would give her her dinner. And afterward perhaps she'd read some more books about freedom. The bitch.

"I can run too," she said, and suddenly she'd wrenched her arm free and was running back through the crowd, toward the other side of the square. Tom cautiously peered around at the place where the sergeant-major had been, but he was no longer there. He turned back and glanced down at Ned, but Ned avoided his gaze.

Tom and Ned picked their way through the riffraff of the docks, the sluts, drunkards, thieves, blacks who were washed up here by the tides of the city just as dead fish, slime, old spars, and sodden rugs crusted the sides of the quay. On the ropewalk the ropemakers plaited their hemp into rope as they had before. Tom ducked underneath the walk and Ned followed.

In was a dim green world, but different from the green of the forest: the green of half light, of decay. Foul water lapped the dockside just below. Tom and Ned squatted against the clapboard of the warehouse and peered out over the river and alongside the docks. Tom's heart froze. There, about halfway toward the Sugar House, was a bulky, heavy-striding figure in a cape, prowling backward and forward as before, like an animal trying to scent its prey.

"That man," Tom said, almost to himself. Then he clutched Ned. "He'll get you. He'll hang you. Hear me, Ned?"

"I hear you, Pa," Ned said, irritably pulling away from him. Tom caught hold of the boy again.

"Ned."

Tom twisted the boy's face so that he could see the sergeant-major. "That man."

"I heared ya," Ned said, and again struggled free.

Ned went back to where a gang of boys was squatting. They held clay pipes and the smoke, in this green light, made the group look sinister, even fiendish. They were the boys Ned had seen marauding the streets on the day he joined up, the self-styled Mohawks. One of them, obviously the leader, looked up and motioned Ned to sit by him. He handed Ned the pipe. He was a tough-looking boy, with short hair, alert red-rimmed eyes, sneering mouth, ragged clothes. He didn't seem so sinister close up, nor did his gang. It was like sitting in a cluster of scarecrows.

"So ya went to war," the leader said.

"Yeah," Ned replied, spluttering on the pipe.

"And you run."

Ned looked back at him cautiously. "Yeah," he whispered. The leader grinned. "That's the stuff."

Ned started with surprise.

"Do more good being alive," the Mohawk said. "And free."

Suddenly, above them, there was an enormous noise. The Mohawks and Ned looked up, startled. Then they realized it was enormous because it was close, just overhead, the tramping of feet. The chief Mohawk said: "It's the prisoners. They're being taken to the Sugar House."

Ned crouched under the ropewalk, listening to the feet. Merle would be among them. Then the sound was gone and the prisoners came into view on the dock. He glanced back at the smoking Mohawks and at his father, crouching deeper in the dimness. Perhaps they were right. Compared to what the Sugar House must be like, this was freedom.

6

New York burned. Five hundred homes were destroyed in the early days of the British occupation, over a third of the entire city.

No one ever knew for sure who, if anyone, had started it. Certainly patriots had assisted in its progress. One of them, caught cutting the handles of water buckets to make firefighting more difficult, was hanged from a signpost at the intersection of two roads.

Daisy watched the hanging. She was still a "woman of the streets," as Betsy waspishly described her. Of course, the streets were very different from those heady days before the Battle of Long Island, or even from the panic-striken ones immediately after it.

Most of the rebellious inhabitants of New York, and in fact most of the timid ones, had fled the city. But despite the huge influx of British soldiers, many of the houses were empty. Those that belonged to known rebels had the letter *R* daubed on the front door, not so much as a badge of shame— since the owners weren't there to see it and probably wouldn't have felt ashamed if they were—but as an invitation to any passersby to enter and help themselves.

The mob had dispersed. Daisy nevertheless made visits to friends she knew who supported the revolution, and visited the inmates of the Sugar House prison as often as she could. She felt somehow responsible. After all, the Sugar House was her family's property, and now its gloomy recesses were stocked with her ragged countrymen. Even worse, these men who had been defeated in battle were soldiers of the new

American state. An army was only as strong as the cause it represented: if its organization, resources, morale, and above all, its principles, were adequate, it would prevail. And while Daisy's sex prevented her from being a soldier, it didn't prevent her from taking some responsibility for these less tangible commitments. The deserters, as far as Daisy was concerned, were another matter altogether—they had betrayed their cause. But the brave men who had fought until wounded or captured, the silent ones who had already given their lives to the republic, these men were owed something. And Daisy did what she could, foraging supplies from the stock of her mother, and when she could get near enough to them, of her father, to repay a tiny amount of that debt.

In the same spirit, she watched the hanging.

She'd never seen one before. In the old days, before the war, there had been the spectacle of judicial hangings, much enjoyed by the common people. But to attend would have been, for Mrs. McConnahay, vulgar, and for Daisy, unspeakable. During the troubles that preceded the war and all the hectic days when the fighting for New York had taken place, a number of informal executions had taken place. Daisy had seen bodies hanging in the street, swaying with the eddies of the wind. But this was the first time she'd seen a man killed.

A rope was flung over a signpost. The prisoner was trundled up on a cart pushed by two soldiers. His arms were bound and he was standing upright, staggering as the cart bumped over cobbles. He was shaking, but his features did not express fear. Instead he looked upset, and terribly sad. The rope was put around his neck, and the cart was jerked from under his feet. Daisy wanted to look away, but forced herself to watch. The man tiptoed in the air, his feet feeling for the ground only a foot below him. So near, so near. In front of her eyes the man was dying for an America that had also been so near, which had coalesced into a Congress, a Declaration, an Army, and which was now being destroyed again by the pitiless might of the British. The poor man struggled for several minutes, while Daisy watched. When he was at last still, the cart was trundled back once again. The body was cut down and flopped onto the same planking on which it had been upright minutes before. But even now the matter wasn't ended. The rope was tied around the corpse's ankles, and it was rehung, the neck elongated and bent, the head horribly askew.

* * *

Autumn deepened. So, on the whole, did the predicament of the American army. Washington took many of his troops from Manhattan to White Plains, but was soon pursued and dislodged by Howe's forces, which then returned to Manhattan and defeated the remaining American forces on the island—nearly 3000 of them had been left in and around Fort Washington—and killed or captured them all.

The American army was now badly divided. Approximately 3000 troops under the command of General Heath were stationed at Peekskill, sixty miles up the Hudson from Manhattan, and they were guarding the southern access to New England; 5000 men under Washington himself had crossed the Hudson farther south and were now positioned around Hackensack; while another 5000 under General Lee waited at North Castle, just above White Plains. Washington had committed the strategic blunder of splitting a force that was weak enough to start with. Winter was not far off, some of the short-term enlistments were expiring, and men had deserted in droves and were still doing so. Lord Cornwallis took full advantage of the situation, defeating the Americans at Fort Lee and harrying their forces across New Jersey. Desperate for local troops, Washington made a personal appeal for more New Jersey militia. He failed to achieve a single enlistment. He pleaded with his own subordinate, General Lee, to bring his forces down and join him, but Lee hesitated and when he'd finally begun to move south, was captured by a British patrol at White's Tavern, near Veal Town.

Eventually Washington reached the banks of the Delaware, opposite the town of Trenton, which was garrisoned by a Hessian regiment of about 1000 men. After dark on Christmas night Washington once more demonstrated his skill at ferrying troops, getting his whole force across the icy Delaware under the cover of darkness and bad weather. The Hessians were taken completely by surprise and overwhelmingly defeated, mainly by hand-to-hand bayonet fighting in the streets. For the British it was a pinprick: "The only disagreeable occurrence that has happened this campaign," as General Howe expressed it. For the Americans it was a small ray of hope. However, it was time to winter the troops now, and any evaluation of the campaign that had just finished would establish the almost complete supremacy of the British. They had won every battle that counted; they had taken New York and were threatening Philadelphia. The American army, now wintering near the small village of Morristown, New Jersey, consisted almost entirely of amateur soldiers. The army was inadequate, despondent, and acutely prone to desertion. It was a cold winter in New York.

Daisy watched from her bedroom as the muddy streets became white with snow. Then the carts, soldiers, horses, and passersby churned up the snow and returned the streets to their usual filthy state again. Most of the refugees in the fields, woods, and villages of upper Manhattan and the mainland had returned as the air grew colder, the wind sharper, the welcome from sympathetic country people thinner. The rebels hoped that their faces had been forgotten; the timid that the occupation had now gone on for long enough to have run out of malice and achieve stability.

The snowy streets began to seethe and pulse with people again. Many found that they had nowhere to live anymore, because British reinforcements had arrived as well and New York was bursting at the seams. Their homes had gone in any case, looted for spoils and then dismantled for kindling to keep the British garrison heated during the worst of the winter. Even in the streets that had escaped the fire, many houses were missing and the rest were seedy, impoverished, and unkempt, the gaps between them like those in a bad mouth.

The McConnahay house, like those of many of the merchants, had remained intact, indeed prosperous, and as the city declined, Daisy grew increasingly ashamed of its prosperity.

One afternoon in the early spring of 1777, she returned home from a visit to the Sugar House prison. The snow had begun to thaw at last, and the softening streets soaked her feet and dirtied the lower part of the anonymous brown cape she had taken to wearing since her elegant dresses had come to seem shameful, and the liberty sash forbidden. She walked wearily up the path to the house and went in through the kitchen door, as she had done since that first day on the streets.

Cuffy was there as always, tending the fire in the stove. She looked up and grimaced her disapproval at Daisy's state.

"Miss Daisy, you're soakin' wet!"

"I'm all right, Cuffy."

"You better change before you see the mistress."

For months Daisy had gone her own way in the house, avoiding the rest of her family as much as possible—her mother and sisters at any rate. Her father was his usual self, cheerily affectionate when he noticed her at all, making it clear he was always happy to forgive and forget Daisy's moment of silliness.

"Why does my mother wish to see me?" Daisy asked.

"You better change first," was all Cuffy was prepared to say.

Daisy went through into the drawing room as she was.

It was a room of lace and silk, of family portraits. Portraits of spaniels too. The real things reclined, equally inert, upon the deep-piled carpet. A fire blazed in the hearth. In the middle of the room, perched upon high chairs with sheets swatched about them, like babes waiting to be fed, sat Betsy and Amy. Each had a sort of tower balanced on her head, perhaps two feet tall, made of wicker and straw, through which a French hairdresser teased and enticed the long blond hair that had been chosen for the occasion into an endlessly elaborating upward flow. Both hairdressers were commenting effusively as they worked, trumpeting their own sensitivity, piquancy, and genius in transforming these charming ladies into labyrinthine beauties as the imperfections of nature were made to give way to the unchallengable authority of Art.

Martha McConnahay was more informal in shift and indoor cap. Her toilet had not yet begun. Meanwhile she scrutinized the rouging of her daughters' cheeks, performed by young apprentices of Marcel and Pierre, who were still unsophisticated enough to be responsive to her tart criticisms. Curling irons hissed and steamed. Martha's wig, perched on a stand, awaited her in a corner.

"C'est formidable," she told Pierre as she admired Betsy's hair.

"Eet ees," Pierre answered serenely.

Nobody seemed to notice Daisy's entrance. She stood watching these activities, open-mouthed. She thought of the huge dismal interior of the Sugar House as she'd seen it only an hour or two ago, the looming molasses-blackened walls and pillars, the dark shifting carpeting of prisoners on the floor, the blank volume of dim air above them, the smell of McConnahay sugar and soldier's dirt, the damp cold of the atmosphere. Here it was hot and smelled of essence of roses, hair powder, steam, and spaniels. Pierre, and then Marcel, getting higher in their hair edifices, mounted stools.

Cuffy came in. She had put a clean white apron over the kitchen dress, and carried a tray of bonbons. Martha clucked in automatic disapproval, either of her tardiness in bringing them or because she'd brought them in at all. She took one all the same, popping it into her mouth and wincing as the sweetness hit her bad tooth. She turned back to Cuffy and glared at her. Cuffy, misunderstanding, proferred the tray. Martha, suddenly furious, banged it from underneath, and bonbons flew through the air and scattered over the carpet. Cuffy looked straight back at her, careful to show no emotion. Then she bent down and began to put the bonbons back on the tray.

Martha meanwhile had become aware of Daisy's presence. Her gaze traveled down the plain brown cloak to the mire and wet that fringed the lower part of it. She was still coping with the bonbon in her mouth when Daisy spoke: "My God, Mama, what's going on?"

Martha smiled. She stepped over and took her arm. "Now before you start, Daisy—don't," she cajoled. For months she had glared silently at her, when she'd been forced to notice her at all. Now she'd obviously taken a leaf out of Joe's book. Her tone implied that Daisy had a tendency to be a little difficult, a little silly, no doubt the result of her being a young person. A girl. "There's the chance of a lifetime here tonight for your sisters—and for me. If you set about spoiling it, well . . ." She took another bonbon and squeezed the powdered jelly delicately between forefinger and thumb. She surveyed it, and then Daisy. Then in a half jocular, wholly threatening tone, she went on: "If you set about spoiling it, I'll have the skin off your back."

Amy, unreal in clouds of powder, thunderously sneezed.

"Oh, be quiet, Amy!" Martha said wearily, as though yet another daughter was deliberately making a fuss.

"Spoiling what, Mama?" Daisy asked.

"Lord Hampton and Lord Darling are coming here, my dear."

Daisy stared at her mother in amazement.

"Two young officers the general's asked us to billet. You know what it's like finding accommodation in New York these days. We all have to make our contribution." Martha, having covered what she regarded as the logic of the situation, allowed herself to succumb to its excitement. "Nobility, Daisy! Nobility. And both of them unmarried! They're fox hunting today. Would you believe it, fox hunting! They'll be along when they've finished. Lord Hampton's the nephew of Poppy Hessup who, I'm told, stands very close to the queen's chamber."

"No doubt," Daisy muttered. She turned away from her mother's eager face, the deadpan of her painted sisters, and found Cuffy's eyes above the tray of bonbons. Cuffy looked back, knowing, silent, sympathetic.

"Daisy, I'm warning you," Martha said, noticing the interchange. "We all know your views on the subject, but you'll keep them to yourself tonight, do you hear? Just make yourself look . . ." Her eyes appraised Daisy's cloak once more, flicked to her sisters and back again. ". . . Nice. And for once try to behave like a respectable member of this family." She picked up a doll from the dresser. Its hair was ridiculously high and ornamented. "Now that *is* you. Get yourself dressed up for a change." She handed Daisy the doll and hurried over to a long table where a gown was laid out. She passed this to Daisy.

Daisy sighed, shrugged, and turned to leave.

"And clear your room while you're up there of all that poxy rebel patriot stuff!" her mother suddenly called out. "Lord Hampton is to sleep in there."

Daisy had frozen in midstride. Very deliberately she placed her foot on the carpet, stood, turned, and faced her mother once more. She could feel her cheeks burning. "In my room, Mama?" she whispered.

"Yes, your room, Daisy. Lord Darling is going into Betsy's room."

Still unable to comprehend how her mother could be saying such things, Daisy looked at Betsy, who looked back and chortled with glee, much to Pierre's chagrin.

Martha had tormented her enough. "You girls will all sleep together," she concluded.

Daisy blushed again, separately from her previous blush. She surveyed her smirking sisters. Sleeping with *them* would be a desperate enough fate. But how dare her mother, how could she . . .? Did she imagine this was all some sort of game, the occupation of New York, the battles, the dying and wounded? People had been hanged for trying to dislodge the

British from New York, and here was Martha McConnahay
not merely giving them lodging, but using this treason as an
opportunity for teasing and playing coy tricks upon her daughter. The enormity of her behavior took Daisy's breath away.

"But Mama!" was all she could say, her voice a furious
whisper.

Her mother picked up a glass of wine and stared her down.
"Sacrifices, Daisy," she said, "We all have to make them."
She grinned contemptuously. "There is a war on, you know."
She sipped her wine.

Daisy strode out.

She lit her lamp and looked at her little room. Ben Franklin on the wall, Tom Paine on the dresser, a small American
flag; her intimate things, hairbrushes, doll's house, wardrobe
of clothes, her drawers of underclothes; her bed. She imagined a British officer, a lord, taking over this room, and felt
violated, as though her thoughts and her person were to be
taken over too. Her mother's joke contained more truth than
she knew.

Agitated, Daisy walked over to her window and peered
from behind the curtain, as she did so often. The street was
almost deserted in the chilly afternoon, only the occasional
passerby, hunched against the cold. A carriage went by,
harness bells jingling. You could almost think New York was
a normal town. But over there, where the buildings were
more thickly huddled and the dark river caught an occasional
gleam of light, it was a different story, with the teeming,
secret lives of the wharves, the deserters, vagabonds, whores,
thieves, and the Sugar House nearby, in its blank despair.
And farther on still, the English garrison, those endlessly
drilling soldiers, row upon row of white tents positioned over
the fields. They'd looked to her, as she'd peered at the camp
from a safe distance on one of her restless, directionless
walks, like rows of shrouds.

But the war was a long way from this street. It hadn't
always been. She remembered the cartloads of furniture trun-
dling past as the people fled, men limping along the roadway
with their lives and livelihoods on their backs, women holding babies, some so young they had been born as American
citizens, now already dispossessed. So much struggle and
suffering had taken place so recently; so much continued
close by. And yet you'd think for all the world that this was a
peaceful scene.

Daisy stepped back from the window, went to her wardrobe, carefully inspected all her gowns, chose the most showy and up to date, and with utmost care and seriousness began to dress herself up to fashionable excess.

7

Small, pink, squealing, the porker ran for its life over a boggy field. Squealing, the boys ran after it, stopping at intervals to grunt at each other, leap about in piglike terror, flap imaginary pig ears, snort and giggle. Some distance away, but getting closer by the second, soldiers squished across the mud after the boys, crying out, as if anyone were interested in the information, "Our pig! Our pig!" Behind the soldiers Dick, leader of the Mohawks, was quietly creeping toward an ammunition chest, left open as the soldiers' attention was distracted by the commotion, and helping himself to a grenade, which he concealed in a small canvas bag he'd had the forethought to bring with him.

Just as the soldiers neared the rest of the boys, the boys decided to concentrate on the chase again. At that moment a trumpet blew somewhere and, cursing, the soldiers went back toward the camp and began to form ranks. One of the boys whooping in triumph, dived upon the careering porker, and the two of them slid together across the gluey field. In the distance an officer shouted at his men. Goods were piled up in carts, stacked in crates. Tents were pulled down and folded up. This particular battalion was preparing to move out.

In the rope shed by the docks Tom Dobb was warping a thick hawser. Stripped to the waist, he was heaving at a huge wooden beam that twisted hemp cords into rope. His body was glistening with sweat, despite the coolness of the shed. Then he stopped, head cocked, as footsteps ran along the ropewalk outside. They were too frequent and light to be the tread of soldiers. As Tom watched, Ned rushed into the open doorway. He was covered in sweat and mud. He'd been gone for hours, without having told Tom where he was going, or why. Recently he had spent a lot of time away, running the streets with the Mohawks, perhaps going even farther afield. The streets were dangerous. If the Americans could take a young boy like Ned to be a soldier, then by the same token the British would have little hesitation in making him a prisoner—or even worse.

Over and again, as he yanked the beam around, Tom had imagined how it could happen. Two or three redcoats sauntering out of some groghouse and wandering the streets, bored with the long winter in New York, looking for excitement. Ned comes past. They grab him by the ear, tease him, bully him, ask him questions. He blurts something out, some fire and brimstone taught him by Dick and the other Mohawks. Once, on the wharves at night, he'd heard Ned abusing some soldier who was occupying himself with a whore in the bottom of a moored boat: "You damned rascally scoundrel lobster son of a bitch!" Luckily the soldier was too busy trying to cope with the coldness of the night, the warmth of his welcome, or the frantic rocking of the boat, to take any notice other than spitting a quick curse back over the dock.

Sometimes Ned and the other boys were gone for so long that Tom suspected they'd left the confines of the city altogether. These possibilities were even more terrible. If they were roaming the countryside, there were all sorts of irregulars, foragers, ruffians, and cutthroats who could kill them or drag them away. Some of them even put on a pretense of principle, claiming they were fighting for independence when in fact they were out for as much rape and pillage as they could find. The country people, he'd been told, called them *cowboys*, because of their habit of slaughtering and eating all the livestock they could get their hands on. Even worse than the cowboys was the garrison. If those boys hung around there, they could be shot as looters.

All in all Tom was unhappy that Ned had been away so long, and he expressed his feelings by becoming more taciturn. He concentrated on manhandling the winding beam, ignoring the arrival of his son.

Ned didn't even notice. "Pa," he cried as soon as he made out his father in the dimness. "We stole a pig."

Tom stopped for a moment, looked at him unsmiling. Cowboys. Pigboys, anyway. But they could have filched a pig from the streets. Even now, after the long winter, you could see an occasional skinny one rooting for garbage on the streets.

"Then we eat," Tom said, turning back to the beam.

Ned's face fell as he suddenly remembered. "It got away. I fumbled it."

Tom turned back to him. He almost wanted to smile. The young warrior and would-be rogue couldn't keep hold of a stolen porker. Then Ned continued, and Tom's face clouded again.

"Dick's getting a grenade. Us Mohawks gonna blow a hole in their mess. Get some eats to Merle and them."

"You ain't no Mohawk," Tom said roughly.

"I am now, Pa. They elected me to the gang."

"What you talking . . . you ain't no Mohawk." Mohawk, he thought, Mohawk. My son an Indian.

He'd asked Dick once why he called himself a Mohawk. Dick was surly and suspicious at first, but finally explained. It was because of the Boston Tea Party. Tom had heard a lot of talk about the Boston Tea Party, both upriver and on his visits to New York. It had to do with starting off the war. Everybody seemed to know all about it. Often Tom felt that other people were in on a secret he didn't share. He wasn't curious enough to ask, and he didn't want people to think he was ignorant. And anyway, it wasn't his war. But sometimes he thought how strange the name was. The Boston Tea Party. How could a tea party help to start off a war?

Dick told him how. As soon as Dick said it, Tom thought to himself, I mighta known. Business. It was always business. Business, trade, commerce. At every step in this war you came across one of those words or another. There was a tax on tea. The British had ordered it. The people of Boston wouldn't accept it. They weren't going to pay tax if they couldn't sit in Parliament. So, Dick said, they formed up into Sons of Liberty. These were gangs, like the Mohawks, he said. Then when the ships carrying tea came into Boston harbor, they stripped off, browned their skins with paint, put blankets around their waists, and raided the ships, throwing all the tea overboard into the harbor. Tom thought straightaway of the shippers' feelings. They'd taken that stuff all around the world, from India, only to get a gang of roughs, dressed up to make your blood curdle, spoil it all by dumping it in the water, after you'd taken the trouble to keep it dry all that time. Just like them women taking his boat. Liberty Women, Sons of Liberty, he thought scornfully. More like merchants, or the hirelings of merchants. Sons of merchants. Merchants who didn't like their prices going up. He thought of that crew in the commissary. Mr. Corty, Mr. McConnahay. Those were the Mohawks, not the likes of Dick and his tattered crew. But Dick didn't see it like that. The Boston Mohawks were great heroes, and his gang was named after them.

Tom had tried to talk sense into him. "You don't want to be a lot of Indians," he'd said.

"That's another thing," Dick had said. "We want to fight like Indians. Not standing in the middle of a field, being shot at by musket balls. Indians fight while nobody can see them. They jump out from hidden places in the rocks or the woods."

"There ain't no rocks or woods in New York," Tom replied.

"You can still fight and nobody'd see you," Dick said.

They're just a gang of roughs, Tom thought. Ned wasn't a Mohawk. "You ain't blowing no grenade," he went on. "You seen them bodies floating in the river, big and swelled up, the birds picking them. Them are boys like you, got themselves shot. D'ya wanna get yourself killed? D'ya wanna end up in the river?"

Before Ned could reply, there was a commotion in the doorway and redcoats were trooping in. There were four of them, obviously looking for someone. Tom pulled Ned toward him. Fool boys, meddling with grenades. There could be hell to pay. He turned toward his beam, began to lever it around. Take no notice. Show no interest. Mind your own business.

The redcoats thumped their way up to the far end of the rope shop. They were picking and shoving among men as if they were farmers handling cattle. Tom continued working. He gave Ned something to do. You must never let them catch your eye, he thought. If they do, you're sunk.

They were getting nearer. They grabbed Clowski a giant of a man, an immigrant from somewhere in Europe who could hardly speak English. Tom listened to him jabbering and the soldiers cursing him in reply. Then, suddenly, he heard a voice directly behind him.

"Here is a likely-looking customer," it said. A hand clamped down on his shoulder. Tom turned, slowly, slowly, don't look too eager, but don't be too unwilling. A poxy-faced, tough-looking British sergeant was there with a young corporal, and two privates holding some sort of contraption that Tom couldn't make out.

"Are you fit? Are you fit? How fit are you, eh? Corporal Birdsall, how fit is this man?"

"Come on, come on," the corporal said, grabbing one of Tom's knees, hoisting it up, shoving it down again. "Make time, get 'em up, get 'em up." He jerked the leg again, then "Up, up, up," he forced Tom to run on the spot, under the appraising eye of the sergeant, his knees pumping higher and higher, faster and faster.

Then, while he was still running on the spot, Tom saw his chance. The other rope makers, curious at the sight of whatever-it-was the soldiers were carrying, had clustered around it and began to poke at it. In his jerking vision, through a film of sweat, Tom got some sort of picture of it—a wicker and straw man, arms akimbo, dressed in a blue jacket.

"What are you all gawking at?" the sergeant asked the crowd. "Listen you dumb Yankees. This is the hare, and it's for the officers. . . ."

Tom allowed his running to move him forward gradually, towards the door of the ropeshed.

"This lure, or guy, as you might say, is for the officers, on account of they want a fox hunt. . . ."

The door grew nearer. Tom could see the wharf, the gray tacky waters of the Hudson, the dark form of Long Island.

". . . before they ride off to their bloody war, but there ain't no foxes in New York. I think you lot have et them all. . . ."

The doorway was just there. Just another couple of steps.

Without changing his tone, the sergeant said: "Come here you. Fetch him, corporal. Watch him."

The corporal ran over, pulled Tom by the arm and lugged him, still running in place, his legs pumping disproportionately up and down, back to the sergeant, who concluded: "So you got to drag the hunt with our ropy friend George Washington here. Right?"

Tom stopped.

The figure was a monstrous doll, wearing a cocked officer's hat with a plume. Tom stared at the blank face. George Washington. The wicker and straw emptiness stared back.

"Tell him the pay, corporal," the sergeant said.

"Yes, Sergeant Marley. The pay's two coppers."

"What do I have to do?" Tom asked.

"Bloody run, that's what you have to do," the corporal said. He put a penny in Tom's hand. Tom inspected it in puzzlement. "You'll be good at doing that, I'll be bound. Half now, half when you're done," the corporal went on. "If you live through it, that is. If you get any ideas of running off, think again. We'll go after you, and when we find you, we'll string you up." He nudged Marley. They both grinned. Even George Washington seemed to grin. The two privates who supported him didn't. They eyed one another and shifted uneasily, sensing the hostility of the rope workers, who clustered all around them now, aware that even if these people were deserters and renegades, they still belonged, insofar as they belonged anywhere, to George Washington's camp.

The corporal put his hand on Tom's chest and shoved him toward the side of the shed, where Clowski was standing. Tom in turn grabbed at Ned. He shoved the penny in Ned's hand. "Get us a sausage, Ned."

Ned pushed the money back at him. "No, I won't get you no sausage. You toady to these bugs like they was tin Jesus."

"It's to keep you safe, Ned. Come on."

"I can watch out for myself, Pa. It's you who needs to keep low."

"Ned, Ned, it ain't right to say that to me now."

"Ain't me hiding. It was you who run and me ya dragged."

Tom looked into Ned's bitter face. The boy looked straight back. His eyes were hard, unflinching. Hating him. Tom had never thought of it like that. It was you who run, and me you dragged. He'd been saving the boy, that's all, protecting him. Just like now. What was the point of going against these soldiers and getting beaten up, maybe killed? And Ned being picked on because he was his son. Maybe having to run instead. It wasn't fair.

It was too complicated to explain, and there wasn't time anyway. "Ned, Ned," Tom said, taking hold of him, "it ain't right, this—"

Ned wrenched himself away. "Take care of yourself, Pa," he said sneeringly. "Stick with the officers, Pa." Tom thought of that night crossing the Hudson before the Battle of Long Island; his fears for the boy, about what might become of him if he should be killed, his despair that he had nothing to give him except the promissory note and some advice that might save his life. And now the words were being thrown back at him. "Ya won't risk hurt, Pa," Ned said, turned, and ran.

"Ned! Ned!" Tom called.

"Hey, come on here," Marley said.

"I'll tear your bloody legs off," the corporal explained. "Do you understand?"

"Yeah," Tom replied.

"All right, let's go," Marley said. "Follow me. Let's go."

Marley went through the doorway. Tom and Clowski followed, surrounded by soldiers, as if they were prisoners. The denizens of the wharf and ropewalk, the pickpockets, whores, loonies, the homeless and the patriots watched them go, shaking their heads in sympathy and resignation. They'd seen this sort of thing before, the bloodybacks coming in, grabbing some poor soul for some reason or other, disposing of him in the river likely as not. At least it wasn't them, this time. The sympathy faded. They turned back to their work, or idleness.

Tom and Clowski, and George Washington, were taken to some scrubby fields north of the town where the British gentry and the New York Loyalists were on parade. Gleaming carriages were trotting up and stopping by the roadside. Diminutive black slaves, resplendent in turbans, maroon coats, and gold trousers, opened doors for the ladies, who stepped out in reverse, holding their skirts up to avoid any difficulty with the steps and to offer a glimpse of stockinged ankle and delicate pump to the passing throng.

Lord Hampton, in full-dress uniform and mounted on a chestnut mare, was talking to his comrades in the hunt. But when he saw ladies alight, he wheeled his horse around, cantered toward them, removed his cocked hat, bowed low and dashingly. The ladies dropped little curtsies in return, giving tinkling giggles as they did so. Hampton, well pleased, spurred back to his colleagues. There was nothing like a uniform to catch the eye of the ladies. And there'd be no shortage of *them* in his new billet, so they said—three plump chickens for him to pluck.

The looks of the McConnahay girls were the talk of the whole garrison. Offspring of one of New York's richest merchants too, old Joe McConnahay. Every comfort would be provided. A big house, no doubt, with plenty of nooks and crannies where he could play games with the girls, and with no competition from his fellow lodger, either. Lord Darling, as was well known, preferred to make his investments in another place altogether. A regular little harem was in prospect.

The two soldiers were being fastened to the dummy by means of drag lines attached to its arms. Hampton inspected the men narrowly. He was a judge of flesh, be it horse, female, or man. The bigger one looked to have the strength, but that meant nothing. He had a big body of his own to carry over the terrain, not to mention George Washington. The other one was a different kettle of fish altogether. He was ill fed, undersized, wiry, the sort who could go on forever. He would make good sport, the little one.

Hampton himself was master of the hounds. They were ready to go. The guy pullers were as ready as they'd ever be, swinging their arms against their chests because of the cold. They'd be warm enough in a moment.

"Now soldiers," Hampton called in the clear tones of authority, "run them bloody off."

With a few kicks and shoves from the soldiers who'd been holding their tether, George Washington and companions began to run over the fields and away.

Tom's left wrist was tied to the doll's right arm, which stuck straight out like a signpost. Clowski's wrist was attached on the other side in the same way. The hunt master, a mannekin with rouged cheeks like a girl, on a horse that was too big for him, called out in a thin, silly, lisping voice, "Wun them bloody orff," and after a few spiteful kicks and shoves, he and Clowski were haring over the hilly meadow with the stiff-legged puppet in between them.

Tom knew at once they made a bad team. Clowski immediately headed up the slope, following the soldier's instinct to gain height. But they weren't here to fight, they were here to run, and Tom knew how to run. You had to keep low, to avoid making a silhouette on the horizon. At the bottom of a valley you could merge with the detail of the landscape. More important still, when you were running from dogs, at the bottom of a valley you could find water.

But not while they were still in sight of the hunters. Don't go up or down while they could see you. Don't show them the way. He yanked on the drag, pulled Clowski back on a level course. It was like controlling a willful horse, and took as much strength as the running. It wasn't just a matter of direction, either, but of reining back. Clowski was running too fast. His legs were going like pistons and he was already taking short, rasping pants. There was no need to run like this while you were still in sight. They wouldn't start the pursuit until the quarry was lost to view—there'd be no sport. At the moment they were too busy prancing their horses in front of all those rich bitches in their finery.

But there was no holding Clowski back. It took all Tom's strength just to keep him level. The big man surged ahead, whimpering with fear and frustration at not being able to go any faster; Tom kept, as he had to, four arms' lengths behind.

At last the valley curved, and peering over his shoulder, Tom could no longer see the hunters and assembled onlookers. Immediately Tom put on speed and began to tug Clowski down the slope. Clowski resisted at first, and then, responding to the easing of the ground, began to go with him, to go faster, to go in front once more, to go faster, ever faster, toward the valley. Tom would have held him back if he could. It felt easy to run downhill, but it tired you out just as much as staying on the level; you had to move your legs as fast, and it was more difficult to place your feet. But there was no choice. It was like being tied to a rock rolling down the cliff, so Tom surrendered to speed, watching the rocky ground as closely as he could so that he could place his feet without stumbling.

As he ran he thought again about what Ned had said: "It was you who ran, and me ya dragged." The boy was right. He had dragged Ned through this war as he was dragging George Washington now. That was what his life had become. Run and drag. Run and drag. From the very beginning, from those early glimpses of horror in Scotland, it had been run, run, dragging the past behind him; run run down the Hudson, with the face of John Beeley running after him, the mouth bobbling blood and spit, the top of John's head a platter of blood; then, later, running from the fever death, the dead faces of nearly all he'd loved. Running always to the next refuge, dragging behind him what he could salvage, dragging his memories. And then this war. They called it a war for independence, but all he knew was that he had to drag his son through it. Like he was dragging this doll.

Georgie Washington. It didn't weigh much, but it hampered and harassed you.

In the distance, far back, he heard the thin tallyhoing of horns, than faint puppylike baying that grew and deepened by the second.

They were in the valley now, running over level sludgy fields. Clowski had begun to slow down. His chest was heaving and his head was beginning to bow. Mud grasped their feet as they ran. Tom glimpsed the brown pulsing of the dogs, a flash of red, as the hunters appeared round a distant bluff. But there was the sound of water ahead. Tom pulled the guy line and Clowski toward it. It was like walking with a ball and chain.

Then Clowski stopped. He was sniveling, exhausted. "Can't go no farther, can't go no farther," he was saying, gasping and irritable. He could no more be moved than, earlier, he could be stopped. There was a flat block of rock nearby. Tom kneeled down beside it. He motioned Clowski to do the same. Washington lay flat. Tom picked up a stone.

"Put your rope there," he told Clowski. For a moment, as the baying grew nearer, he wondered if he should free himself. No. If they found him after he'd ruined their sport, there'd be hell and damnation to pay. And if they didn't, they'd look for him until they did. That poxy Marley wouldn't give up. Tom would have to stay in hiding, he wouldn't be able to go back to the ropewalk, back to Ned. He picked up a stone and began to pound Clowski's rope against the flat rock. He'd made enough rope now, he knew how to break it. Maybe this same rope that tied them had come from the ropewalk. It was the women who made this thin rope, the women and the old men. Tom made thick hawsers for holding ships, not animals and people.

The dogs were clearly visible now, scattered over the meadows, still sniffing. Thank God they used their noses and not their eyes. They still didn't know how near they were. He beat the rope in a frenzy. You know how to make rope, you know how to break it. The threads pulped, frayed, gave. He gave the rope a jerk and it was done. Clowski, hunched, staggering, began to move off, like a hurt animal.

"You wanta go to the water. Them dogs have got your scent. They'll run ya down."

Clowski took no notice. He lumbered away, beginning to go toward the high land. The dogs saw him.

Tom ran across the rocky banks and into the water, ducking the lure and himslf and then making his way over the clutter of river stones to the far bank. He'd cut out some of the scent, and there was the cover of the trees alongside the water, so he moved more slowly, pulling the sodden doll along the ground behind him. Somewhere not far off, poor Clowski shrieked, amidst the yapping, as the dogs got him. You could hear the hunters cursing as they realized George had got away. They didn't call the dogs off Clowski; he was fair game now.

And then there was barking much nearer, this side of the bank. Tom looked back. He couldn't see anything yet, but one of them was over this side. It must have caught the scent, blown across by the breeze, or maybe he just wandered off from the pack and got here by chance. The doll kept snagging rocks, roots, tree trunks. Tom picked it up and put it on his shoulder. He'd dragged it so far, he'd carry it the rest of the way. He wanted the doll to get away now, that was the strange thing—ugly misshapen hobbledehoy as it was, he'd brought it so far, he wanted it to get away clean. He ran again.

It was as though he ran and the trees and the ground didn't move. Somewhere nearby a horn sounded a sharp little tune that Tom had heard before. It sounded triumphant and sad at the same time. Then he remembered. A British trumpet had played it before the battle on Long Island. Merle said it was called "Gone to Earth," a fox-hunting tune. The sounds seemed to be so much a part of his exhaustion and fear that he wanted to weep. The barking was right behind him, and he could hear the animal's breathing. Then the animal's muzzle was around his legs. He spun round to face it, and backed against a tree. The doll sagged beside him. The dog reared on its hind legs, put its paws on his chest, growled deep in its throat.

Then other dogs were bounding up, there was the muted gallop of hooves on soft ground, and the officer's pinched, cruel, silly face leering down at him. He was smiling. He waved a sword. Tom watched the silver of its blade as it winged toward him, and he prayed for Ned. What chance did the boy have, alone in New York with those Mohawk vagabonds? He'd dragged him all this way, only to lose him now. The sword fell.

There was a thump, the dragline was severed, George Washington lurched to one side. Hampton slashed it open with two quick strokes of his sword. The ribcage gaped, and the batting flowed out.

Hampton inspected his handiwork with some satisfaction, then turned to face Tom. "So ends," he said, in his high-pitched unpleasant voice, "this American dream."

Marley, good as his word, trotted over from behind the members of the hunt and passed the gasping Tom his penny.

8

Amy plinked a tune out upon the harpsichord. Her fingers were small and delicate; the playing was clumsy and hamfisted. Lord Darling sat beside her, eyes shut in apparent absorption. Indeed he was absorbed, but in the sounds created by his complicated digestion. His digestion had ample room to be complicated in. His bulk, splendidly packaged in a maroon weskit, rested upon his lap as one might rest a pet animal or a small child; and indeed from time to time, he patted it in a spirit of affectionate enquiry, eyes still shut.

It was pleasant sitting still after an afternoon's hunting, or rather, after an afternoon spent trotting in the wake of the hunt. Hampton's tomfoolery, of course, sending a couple of ne'er-do-wells over the landscape with some scarecrow in tow. Not a thought for anyone else's pleasure, of course. The fact that he, Darling, had to take part of the regiment north tomorrow on relief duty at the camp by Fort Lee obviously never crossed his mind. Make a manly show, and similar rot. And tomorrow night Darling would be under canvas after just one day in these splendid new quarters. In the meantime he proposed to make the soporific best of them.

To be fair to Amy, her technique, honed in competition with the hapless Fanny Rennsler, could actually achieve a slightly higher level of accomplishment, but was hindered by her inability to bend her head down sufficiently to watch her fingers travelling over the keyboard, or "see the notes," as she put it several times in a complaining tone to her companion. On each occasion Lord Darling offered a loud harrumph by way of sympathy and consolation, proferring the comment

76

without feeling any need to open those inward-gazing eyes of his. Indeed he was but poorly qualified for his role as music turner to the recitalist. Fortunately, however, for their mutual rapport, Amy couldn't in fact read music. Long hours with a languid music teacher had eventually enabled the occasional crochet to swim before her alarmed gaze; or a complicated shoal of semiquavers; or the leviathan of a breve would rise to the surface of a score. But as soon as the lesson ended the whole shoal, with a flick of their tails, would swim away. As a result Amy could learn only by ear, and confined herself, in her recitals, to well-worn paths. These, luckily, were what her listeners—insofar as they wanted to listen at all—wanted to hear. Her mother implied, with a wave of her arm—a wave that she had devised to indicate the latent accomplishments of her offspring—that if she should so desire, Amy had other strings, as it were, to her bow. Her father meanwhile found one tune pretty much like another and was seated at this moment, like Lord Darling, with his eyes shut; though in his case, no subterranean drama was being observed and no inner music being attended to. He was simply asleep.

In any case, Amy had other things on her mind, or at least on her head, than the intricacies of music. Her hair—that is to say, *the* hair—exhibited the full triumph of Marcel's technique. It was well over a foot in height, and looked like nothing more than a symmetrical sort of waterfall, except that, enacting the triumph of art over nature, it was falling upward. Perched atop these shaky foundations was an unlikely castle, built at a rakish angle, complete with drawbridge, banners, even sentries peeping from the turrets. Elsewhere the military effect was softened somewhat by the addition of flowers, ribbons, and various items of large and expensive jewelry.

But if Amy's head was substantially ornamented, her shoulders were not. Indeed her gown was cut so low that her bosom rested upon, rather than within, its bodice, and immodesty was only prevented by the fact that once it did begin, the gown proceeded in earnest, with much frothing of lace, spraying of ribbon, and marching of pleats. The wash of its embarkation was sufficient to conceal any youthful indiscretions, and prevent Amy's shame should Lord Darling be interested enough to open his eyes. But he wasn't, except at random moments to turn an irrelevant page; and she wouldn't have felt any indiscrete impulses if he were.

Betsy was similarly attired, although in her case her wig was a redoubt topped by a great cannon, its barrel elevated as though about to fire. As with Amy, however, the effect was softened down below, and in her case the picturesqueness of the foothills was being roundly inspected and much appreciated by Lord Hampton, who was sitting next to the fair Betsy. Perhaps he was shortsighted, because he came extraordinarily close; more likely he was drunk, since his head wobbled alarmingly as he did so, as if it had not been fastened on properly.

Lord Hampton was bewigged and berouged almost to the same extent as the adjoining Betsy, but he was pinch-faced where she was oval, and scrawny where she was voluptuous. At the other side of Lord Hampton sat Daisy, dressed like her sisters in the last extremity of fashion. In her case a warship was riding blond waves in full precarious sail, a union jack billowing from its stern. She sat upright, her hands on her lap and her eyes staring straight ahead; if they noticed anything at all, they would have been able to make out the nape of Amy's neck.

The threesome were seated on a couch, in front of which stood a small table supporting a decanter and glasses. At some distance opposite, Joe McConnahay lay slumped in his chair, engaging in his preferred mode of after-dinner recreation while Martha sat alertly in hers, watching every movement, every small item of activity in the room, and in particular the bobbing of Lord Hampton's head in the proximity of her daughter Betsy's bosom, and watching with evident approval.

Amy began to sing:

If buttercups buzzed after the bee

If boats were on land and churches on sea . . .

Lord Darling winced with surprise. One pair of eyelids opened and an eye peered out. Having made sure despite the sudden onslaught of Amy's voice nothing untoward had happened after all, it retreated once more, closing its lids behind it. Lord Hampton meanwhile made use of the fact that the room now had another focus of attention, to place his hand down the front of Betsy's gown and begin to caress her breasts directly. Betsy looked at him interestedly, and nestled closer.

> If ponies rode men, if grass ate the cows
> If cats should be chased into holes by the mouse . . .

And then Lord Hampton's attentions were temporarily arrested, as he in turn experienced a surprise.

Daisy hadn't altered her stiff posture when Amy began to sing. She had heard her sister sing before. But one of her hands moved, like a small independent animal, from her lap and over her thigh. It scurried across the small interval of couch, then very dexterously, under the cover of the table, it began to climb onto Lord Hampton's leg.

Hampton glanced down at Betsy's lap. *Her* hands were still in place. Best not to look. Carry on as normal. He began to move toward Betsy's breast again. The hand began to tiptoe up his thigh. You never knew with these ice-cold gals what was going on in their . . . great heavens, she is actually beginning to . . . of course it wasn't every day that an American female could get her charming little clutches on a true English aristocrat, blood will out, what . . . but this was really . . . spend the afternoon tearing over the fields after that guy, and here I am with a pretty little fox in pursuit of me . . . *and* aiming for my . . . personals. In her own father's drawing room to boot. Damned if the little minx isn't after my brush.

Daisy let her hand roam up his lordship's leg, and then begin to caress the hard-and-soft bumpiness of his groin, beneath its silk. Hampton pinked beneath his rouge. He manipulated Betsy with corresponding energy, and she gave him a surprised glance. Then she saw what Daisy was doing and glared at her in fury. Heavens, Hampton thought, what soirees these New Yorkers hold. They are almost more than a gentleman can bear.

Daisy's other hand, also as though of its own free will, rose to the top of her wig—concealed from Hampton's gaze by being on its lee side—removed the pin that held the union jack in place on her galleon, and returned, still unseen, with its trophy.

Now her right hand grasped its prey, while her left prepared the weapon. She thought, What a battlefield to fight on. Men go out with weapons to kill or be killed for the cause, while I sit in my family's house expressing my rebellion in the only manner open to me.

Amy was singing: "If mamas sold their babies to gypsies for half of a crown . . ."

Then Daisy struck.

Hampton shrieked.

He clutched Betsy's breast, as a drowning man might clutch a straw, with blind force, in a desperate attempt to transfer the unspeakable agony in his groin to some other object. Betsy gasped; her mouth opened wider and she in turn began to scream. Hampton, still aware, somewhere on the fringes of his distress, of the need for decorum and British reserve, reverted to a distraught whimper and buckled slowly toward the table, the flag still fluttering from his breeches.

Amy sang: "Then all the world would be upside down!" and at that precise moment Hampton's wig slipped off, to reveal a white, round, totally bald head, somehow more naked than Betsy's breast could ever be.

Then Daisy was rushing from the room; Betsy was reclining prostrate; Hampton, on his feet but still bent double, was muttering, "Damn'd Yankee bitch!" Martha was rushing between him and Betsy in agitation and confusion; while Amy, horrified at the effect of her song, had burst into tears.

Lord Darling opened his eyes. Noting that the entertainment appeared to have come to an end, he rose to his feet and began to bow politely to the ladies. Joe McConnahay, fatigued by a hard day at his offices, continued to snore. Hampton was repeating "Whore! Whore!" in a thin, despairing voice.

Daisy ran into her room. She tore off the monstrous wig, splashed water from her pitcher over her face and neck, and then looked wildly around, desperate to do something, something more, to cleanse herself. She tore at her gown, stamped with impatience when it wouldn't come off. She could still feel Hampton's shape on her hand, and she wanted to retch at the memory of what she'd done. Dressed up and painted to be his lordship's *whore*. Hampton had said the word. The tune of Amy's song thrummed through her mind, and with each note she felt the nausea come closer, as though each was another step through the vileness of the evening. The world turned upside down. Yes, it was well chosen. If mamas sold their babies for half of a crown. That surely was what her own mother had been doing. Making her girls into dolls for the English gentry to play with.

Daisy strode about her room spitting the words of the song out, trying to break them free of the lurching, nauseating tune. This was her war for independence, sticking a pin into the unmentionables of that man—of that unmentionable man.

She found herself shrieking with laughter. How he'd folded over! And the union jack, waving from that little redoubt! Nobody could accuse her now of being unwilling to run the Loyalist flag up its pole.

Then she felt sick once more, and bent over in her turn, waiting in case it came, her attention fixed with peculiar irrelevant intensity on her prettily patterned carpet. What a battlefield I have to fight on, she thought again, with paper flags and saucy bosoms and that dreadful music tinkling so that it seems to be music in my mind, the music of thoughts unbearable to think.

The thought that I hate my sisters. That I hate my mother and father. And that I love them.

The thought that I do not belong here but have nowhere else to go. They have not yet made an America for me to live in, and I believe they never will.

They, they. Always they. Why not me? Why isn't there anything I can do? That boy who lost his leg in the wheat fields. It was terrible to see it. Sad. To hear it, rather. The sound of it being cut, and the smell of meat. Perhaps he'd died afterward. But that was clean compared to what she'd been through. Even when he was screaming on that pallet, under Dr. Sloan's saw, he had more dignity than she had now.

She straightened up. Into her line of vision came the doll's house. She thought of her father in this room last summer, on the evening after the Declaration had been read out. She'd come back from her first day on the streets to find her father sitting here. He'd been so . . . so *fatherly*, she thought with bitterness. Firm and gentle. Rebuking her, then embracing her. Outside on the streets the mob had been shouting, smashing windows. She was frightened, excited. Her father played with the doll's house. "Don't be confused by those people out there," he'd said. "Family against family. It's easy enough to destroy. Building is more difficult. Working together."

She'd realized since what he'd meant. Keep what we've got. Try to grab more. Sell your pork and salt fish to the enemy. And your daughters. That was *building*. And meanwhile the poor benighted mob on the street had been breaking windows!

Suddenly she lifted up her doll's house. It was big and cumbersome and she staggered with the weight, but she raised it high, high in the air. It would be like destroying her own childhood, but it had to be done.

She flung it to the floor and watched it smash.

At that moment her mother walked in. Martha was still wearing her wig, and walked leaning forward, almost tottering, to keep it balanced on her head. She was red with fury.

Again Daisy wanted to laugh, though not at her mother. She'd been caught in the act. Thinking about the mob rampaging through the streets; breaking a doll's house.

Fighting her miniature war.

It was like when a child daydreams of some heroic adventure and is surprised by a grown-up while immersed in her toys.

"Well, I hope you're proud of yourself," her mother said. Daisy felt herself shuddering with buried laughter. "Did you hear what he called you? Yankee bitch."

She stared at Daisy, round-eyed. A woman who had hardly deigned to notice the turmoil of the last few months, except when the unruliness of the mob gave her a headache, now brought up short by Hampton's obscenities. Then the eyes filled with tears, and in a completely different tone she said, "Whatever you may think, Daisy, we have always loved you, your father and I. We had such high hopes for you, and you've never before given me cause to feel ashamed of you."

The change of tone was so unexpected that Daisy found her shudders of laughter shift correspondingly to sobs. It was like that day at her father's office, when he responded to her anger with love and pride. Then, though, she'd been able to lay hold of her anger again and use it to win a victory, albeit a small one. Fifty barrels of salt fish. But this time she was defenseless. She'd used up her stock of anger already. "That's not fair," Daisy said, weeping and putting her arms around her mother.

Martha embraced her in return, but Daisy was conscious at the same time that she remained firm. There was no give in her body. And after a few minutes she disentangled herself, holding Daisy at arms' length. Her wig towered absurdly, but it didn't make Daisy want to laugh anymore. Like everything about Martha, it was foolish but you couldn't ignore it.

"After tonight," Martha said, "You know where we stand, Daisy. You cannot belong to this family and fight on the other side."

"I know that."

"You must make up your mind."

Daisy looked straight back. She suddenly felt she was seeing her mother for the first time, with neither love nor hatred, bitterness or laughter.

"I have," she replied.

9

After Tom went off with the redcoats, Ned hung around the wharf for a while. He kept thinking to himself, sausage, I won't get you no sausage. His father had gone off with them lobsters for a bit of sausage. Running was one thing, running was just being scared. Running scared. But going off hunting with the Brits, that was turning traitor. For a sausage. Get your own sausage. His thoughts were so vivid he said the word out loud and a drooling old man, sitting on the planking plaiting rope, looked up hopefully. His eyes were moist and cloudy.

Ned hoisted himself down from the ropewalk and slipped underneath, to the dark corner where he kept his few things. He fumbled for the drumsticks Merle had given him and slid them inside his pants, held in place by the belt. Nobody knew he still had them except Merle himself. They showed he'd been in the army, which showed he was a deserter if you were a patriot, and a rebel if you were a Brit, so he kept them hidden. Even his father didn't know he still had them. Though it didn't matter what his father might think. His father was playing around with the Brits at this moment.

Ned walked stiff-legged out from under the ropewalk and along the wharf, through people fiddling with boats, making rope, begging, cadging, soliciting. Past a couple of redcoats slouching against the wall of a building.

He walked the streets of New York all the rest of that day. He kept away from places where his father might look, mainly keeping to the north of the city, where buildings gave way to unkempt, trampled-over countryside. That night he slept in a derelict shed.

The next day he made his way back toward the Sugar House. Merle would be expecting to see him. On the way he met Dick and some of the Mohawks, and sat with them for a while, squatting in the doorway of what had once been a shop. Dick gave him some food. He said his father had been searching for him all night. Ned said, let him search. He wasn't ready to go back yet. Maybe later today. Maybe tomorrow. He wanted him to know he was of age to stand on his own feet. Didn't need to hold on to his pa's coattail. Didn't need to stay by no officers. Dick nodded in support. Didn't need to toady for coppers. Didn't need his father should toady for him.

Then he went on toward the wharf, looking around to be sure his father hadn't come back yet. The Sugar House was more tattered than last year, the clapboard peeling and sad, planks crudely nailed over the windows to stop the inmates escaping. The old McConnahay sign hung from one hinge, ready to drop, and the Sugar King's name, in proud letters over the near wall of the building, had already faded. The letters, hard enough to pick out already in such a big name, all looked alike now.

There were always two or three soldiers guarding the doors, and several others ranged around the building, but they'd let you in to visit from time to time if they knew you, and they'd had plenty of chance to know Ned, because he visited Merle whenever he could. He got the nod from the corporal and began to go through the big doors. Then the corporal called out: "Watcha done?"

Ned stopped. He didn't turn around. "What?"

"You walking funny."

"I hurt my leg."

"Hurt ya leg? You Yanks run too much, that's why you hurt ya leg." He laughed. Ned limped on in.

America for Ned was a country of dim places. His burrow under the ropewalk was dark, with a dim green waterlight from the river as it lapped the dock pilings nearby; the ropeshed where his father worked was dim, the windows tiny and usually shuttered in the winter, since they mostly lacked glass to keep the weather out. And the Sugar House was like a vast cavern, the walls black with molasses, the timber columns supporting the roof becoming indistinct in the darkness above. The only source of light was a small brazier burning near the middle of the floor, and until his eyes grew accustomed, Ned could only vaguely make out the dark shifting forms of the men sitting and lying all over the floor of the huge warehouse.

The shapes gradually became more distinct. The atmosphere was fetid, a combination of the sugary smell of molasses and the sweat and dirt of the soldiers who'd been here for so many months. There was a melancholy hubbub of voices. Ned stood, not wanting to tread on anybody, getting used to darkness and stink. "Ned, Ned." He picked out among the tired voices, the long, familiar, comical face of Merle.

He was sitting propped against one of the pillars, near the middle of the room. Ned made his way over and squatted alongside him. He dug some bread Dick had given him out of his shirt and Merle ate it greedily.

"Some of the bugs is marching north today," he told Merle. Merle didn't reply—his mouth was stuffed full. "They say most of them is going to stay on here, and go south later." The campaigning season was coming on. For months the war had been locked away under snow and ice, you didn't need to think about what had happened for the time being. Just remember that Washington had got his men across the Delaware, through the dead cold, the boats crunching through ice, and then defeated the British at Trenton. Or if not the British, it was the British Germans anyway. But as the spring began to approach and the war came around again, people began to remember other things that had happened in the summer and autumn of 1776; the defeat at Long Island; Washington backing away off Manhattan, through New York, New Jersey; defeat after defeat, retreat after retreat. Crossing the Delaware and defeating a thousand Germans was neither here nor there. The American army had won nothing that mattered. They had lost New York, lost an immense amount of ground. The disappointments and disasters became real again as the snow thawed.

"They'll be going after Washington then," Ned said. "They say Washington's whipped."

Merle was swallowing his bread like a dog, without chewing it first. Ned could hear the movements of his throat, almost like retching, as he got it down. Ned's eyes were quite used to the darkness now. Behind Merle, on the pillar, he made out a pale circle of cleaned wood in the middle of the dingy black. He'd seen circles like that before.

"Lickin' molasses, Merle?" he asked.

"I got splinters in my tongue," Merle replied, and smiled his downturned smile that looked like a grimace.

Ned saw how frail he was. His own father went off some place, running for sausage, and Merle, honorably captured in battle, drumming away against the enemy as if you could beat them with drumbeats, standing there while they all run, his one drum banging away against all those approaching British drums, like the battle was just a battle of noise. But they'd lost that battle like they'd lost the other one. And so here Merle was now, rotting away in this Sugar House that belonged to some well-fed turncoat New York merchant, sitting in the dark from one year to the next because he'd fought bravely for his country. The only thing was, he was alive.

It was better than being on them prison ships. Ned had seen them wallowing in the harbor. Even the guards didn't dare stay on. They went on with food, unbarred the hatches, shoved the food down, and barred the hatches again. They just let the prisoners fight for it underneath. It was like being buried alive, buried in a box at sea. And they *were* buried at sea too. Every day a burial detail went on board the ships, and the prisoners passed up the bodies of the men who'd died in the night. The detail wore masks over their faces, but they still wouldn't go down to get them themselves—the prisoners had to pass the bodies up, which they did. They were glad to get rid of them. The detail just dropped the corpses over the side, without even a prayer. Ned had watched. Just lifted them over into the water.

He almost told Merle about it. It might make him think that what he was getting here in the Sugar House wasn't so bad after all. But it would make him scared too. He'd think, perhaps, *I* will be sent into one of them. Perhaps the bigwig who has the warehouse will take it into his head to keep sugar in here again, Ned thought, instead of rebel prisoners. No, it wouldn't do Merle any good to have that on his mind as well. If he thought he was being treated badly now, he could also think it might get better. If he thought it could be worse someplace else, he'd have the fear of it night and day.

"Ya bring ya sticks?" Merle asked.

Ned nodded. He looked around, to see if there were any guards in sight. No, only prisoners, and they took no notice

anyway. He put his hand in his trousers and eased the sticks
out.

"I got a new beat," Merle said. He picked up his own
sticks and began beating them on the floor, a swooping rhythm.
The way Merle played, as you listened to the intricate dry
sounds of his sticks, you could suddenly catch a tune in there,
notes going up and down.

"I like it, Merle."

"You try it."

Ned tried it. He was conscious at first of how bad he was
with the sticks compared to Merle, but after a while the beat
took the sticks in hand and he let them go with it. He played
faster, louder, and behind the rattle of the sticks on the floor
he began to catch, not Merle's melody—he couldn't play like
that—but something else, a deep throbbing sound, as if the
floor as a whole were beginning to vibrate, as if he were
playing the beat of this whole dark building with its forlorn
figures on the floor and the unreachable emptiness up in the
rafters. Then Merle joined in, and the sound surrounded
them completely. They saw nothing but their flying sticks.
They didn't see Peasy in the shadows.

The sergeant-major had heard the telltale rattle from the
Sugar House while having a word with one of the sentries at
the door. A drummer among the prisoners. He was always in
need of a good drummer. He cared for his boys as if they
were his own, Ben and the others, but they *were* only boys,
slight, frail boys, and the bitter winter, the shortgage of
supplies, the tent life, had taken their toll, breaking the
health of the weakest, searching them out mercilessly—that
weather-sergeant always on the lookout for weakness, always
the first and sharpest to penetrate the ranks.

Peasy had nursed them with the same care for detail, the
same unfailing devotion to duty, the same practical intelligence as he showed in working out the dispositions of his
battalion on the battlefield and in the same way he buried
them now—in short graves, but fully six feet deep. Dug neat
and clean, with sharp edges, corners on the right angle.

It wasn't that he was grieving in person—he'd been on
enough battlefields and in enough winter camps, in enough
hot places and cold places, to keep himself from grieving;
seen enough wounds and fever, watched enough deaths of

boys and men. He just wanted to do the work right. Before the digging began, he made the crosses, chipped out neatly with adz and sheathknife and burned the names on the crossbar: BOY JOHN aged 12, BOY DONNY aged 13. The graves were filled in neat, oblong mounds on the top, even though this was only a corner of a garrison camp, and one day, when the Americans had been beaten into sense, would just be the corner of a field.

Peasy knocked the crosses in with a mallet, then said "The Lord is my Shepherd" while Ben and the corporal stood with heads bowed. Then Ben looked at him, face pale, eyes wide with the fever.

"They're just sleeping, Ben," Peasy told him.

They'd been through this ceremony before. "Put to bed with a mattock," Ben said. He coughed, bowing down with it.

"Tucked in with a spade," Peasy said, finishing it for him.

"It's me next," Ben said.

"Not you, son. I drummed when I was a little boy. Just like you."

"And now you're a sergeant-major," Ben said.

"Like you will be, son," Peasy told him.

He'd strode off. No use in dwelling on it. That was the thing about doing the graves neatly. Once they were done, they were done.

But he could do with a new drummer. Why not? It would give some boy-prisoner the chance to get out of this hellhole, and what did it matter to children which side they were on? What did *they* know about it? The only thing that mattered was to treat them right, make a family for them. His battalion was marching today, so he could do with finding a drummer now. Give some boy the chance of fresh air, a soldier's life, sparse but decent, better than this dank sugarpit where the planking oozed rum and the whole place stank of sweetness, pee, and shit.

His dark cloak around him so that he was almost indistinguishable, dark on dark, Peasy stepped into the Sugar House, picking his way between prone straggling prisoners with his habitual care and precision. He stood, pressed in against the shadows of the wall, watching and listening. Two of them, by God, both playing like they were possessed.

They stopped.

"Ned, you played—" Merle said, and stopped. He was looking over Ned's shoulder. Ned turned to see.

It was like seeing an animal of the night when you were in the forests. You don't see it at first, but you can feel it's there, and then you realize you've been looking at it all the time, just thinking it was part of the forest or the darkness. Ned didn't see Peasy at first because his shape was too big, and in his cloak, too simple for an ordinary man. Then suddenly he understood. All that shadow was him.

The man's face slowly formed. His eyes were hard, and bulging, his features large, and there was a small triangle of hair by his mouth. It was him. The man with the spear, who had come toward him in the battle as if nothing in this world would stop him, as if he was Death himself. He was the man his father had pointed out from under the ropewalk: "That man. He'll get you. He'll hang you. Hear me, Ned?" Yes, his father had warned him about this man, saved him from him. As he thought of his father, Ned nearly wept. Of course Pa had run. If you didn't run you died. It was scat or get cut.

Ned ran.

Someone grabbed him immediately, another redcoat who must have been standing between him and the doorway. He twisted his ear and marched him back to the sergeant-major. Ned tried to explain he was a friend of Merle, that he was only here to bring Merle bread. The sergeant-major simply bent down and picked up his abandoned sticks.

"Listen, my boy," he said. "I'll get you a drum of your own." He nodded toward his corporal, who pulled Merle to his feet and then took him with one arm and Ned with the other. Ned struggled. The sergeant-major's huge face dropped from the rafters to him, as an owl drops. He grasped Ned's cheek, a sharp-nailed finger on his open eye. In a deep whisper he said: "Cross me and I'll pop it out of its socket."

Peasy watched as the corporal took the boys out. You had to know how to talk to children of that age, keep them in line. They'd soon get used to his ways, learn to be soldiers, become part of the family. And when he'd finished with them, they'd be good drummers too.

After her mother left, Daisy stood where she was for a long time. She could hear noises from downstairs, wailing from her sisters and Lord Hampton, and her mother's voice, raised at first—no doubt defending her daughter against the worst of Hampton's charges—and then lower, placatory. Papa grunted occasionally. No doubt, having been woken up from his sleep, he had found his way to the decanter and was trying to turn a deaf ear to all this female nonsense. And he held no brief for their lordships. She had seen that in his eyes over dinner, the expression of contempt as he watched Lord Hampton drawling, flirting, haw-hawing his way through the courses, boasting of how he'd spent the afternoon chasing some poor vagabonds over the fields on his horse. Her father was no more a Loyalist than he was a rebel—it was worth holding on to that, it made her feel less alone. The virtues he respected were those of sound common sense and industriousness; these were the principles of all successful merchants and tradesmen, be they British or American. He scorned the brainless dissipation of such as Hampton almost as much as he scorned the rabble-rousing of Tom Paine, who'd taken to selling revolution when nobody would buy his corsets.

About Betsy and Amy there was no point in thinking at all: they did not operate on the level of thought. All the more reason why it would be impossible for them to understand what she'd done and why she'd done it; all the more reason why it would be impossible for her to put up with their self-pitying babbling and resentment even for one night.
with their self-pitying babbling and resentment even for one night.

Daisy collected her few things, tiptoed down the stairs, and crept into the kitchen. Cuffy was still there, of course, stirring some chocolate which she was about to take into the drawing room in order to soothe the troubled nerves of those present.

"I am come to share your quarters, Cuffy," Daisy told her, "if I may. It is only for a night or two, until I can think what I should do."

Cuffy was startled, but she showed her into her tiny room, not much more than a larder which you reached by a door from the kitchen. Cuffy lit the candle. Daisy sat herself on the single horsehair mattress on the floor, and while Cuffy went back to her work, thought about the events of the past and tried to imagine those of the future. At last Cuffy returned, and they lay down together. Daisy blew out the candle.

"Won't Miss Betsy and Miss Amy wonder where you gone?" Cuffy asked.

"They'll just be glad I'm not with them," Daisy told her.

Nevertheless, every time there was a sound from elsewhere in the house, Cuffy started, as though in fear. When Daisy asked her what was the matter, she wouldn't reply at first. But Daisy insisted, and then she did.

There was nothing but Cuffy's black voice in the dark room. "I afraid if the master come."

She said nothing more. Daisy didn't reply. She was thinking of a scene many years before, when she was a little girl and had gone with her papa to the wharf right by their Sugar House. A slave ship was being unloaded, and an auction held. The Negroes were herded into a temporarily erected pound, and her father had walked thoughtfully around its perimeter, eyeing the wares. Finally he leaned on the fencing and motioned toward a lanky girl, quite naked, who was perhaps a couple of years older than Daisy herself. He'd opened her eyelids wide with thumb and forefinger, carefully examining her pupils and whites; he'd opened her mouth and inspected her teeth, carefully felt her stomach, slapped her rump. Then he turned to Daisy and said, "Shall we have her, as a present for Mama?"

She could even now hear her voice, as though it were the voice of another child: "Oh, yes, Papa! Let's have her!"

So Cuffy had come into the household. She was a quiet, good-natured, hard-working girl. Soon she seemed to be part of the kitchen itself; then part of the family. She and Daisy grew up together. Cuffy was reserved, sensible: in some ways Daisy felt closer to her than she did to her featherbrained sisters. Of course, she'd never forgotten that scene by the docks, but oddly, she didn't associate it with the girl she'd grown fond of. It was not a memory of Cuffy, but of her father, in which he showed himself to be a sound businessman and generous to Mama at the same time. A cosy memory. Now, suddenly, she saw it in a different light, and Cuffy's life—and her own—were rewritten at a stroke. He had chosen Cuffy as he might choose a consignment of molasses or a bolt of cloth. She was family property, to be used at their convenience, including his.

In the dark room Daisy felt that the separation from her family was complete. For the first time in her life she stood alone, with no friend to assist her except Cuffy. And Cuffy was a slave. At least, thank God, her father didn't come to Cuffy's room that night.

Cuffy rose at dawn the next morning to light the kitchen stove and begin to prepare breakfast for the family and its guests. Daisy remained in her bolthole until the house was empty. Nobody asked after her. Her sisters must have guessed she'd spent the night with Cuffy, but clearly were unwilling to demean themselves by discussing such personal matters with a slave. Only when at last her father had departed for his chambers in Wall Street, and their lordships, presumably reconciled with the rest of the family, had departed also, did she reemerge. Then she grasped Cuffy's arm, told her to leave her work and put on her cloak, and the two of them left the house to pursue that occupation of Daisy's known to Betsy as "walking the streets."

At first she had no clear idea of where they should go. But after a few minutes she found her footsteps leading her, as if of their own accord, in the direction of the Sugar House. She wished she and Cuffy had packed a basket in the kitchen before they went out, but no matter. She had found from her previous visits that the prisoners were grateful if you slipped them a few pennies; they could pass them in turn to the guards in exchange for some comforts, or gentler treatment.

When they reached the Sugar House, however, there was something of a commotion at the door, and the two women held back. A cart was in position on the roadway, and several soldiers were standing at the back of it, obviously loading something. Then Daisy realized it was two prisoners. They were being pushed up into the body of the cart among drums, chests, canvas bags, and other luggage that was already aboard. Two boys, that's all they were, one filthy and bedraggled from his time inside the Sugar House, dazed by the light and stumbling amongst the objects stacked about him, the other poorly dressed indeed, in an overlong man's jacket, but not so wretched as the first. Then Daisy realised she knew him. It was Tom's boy, Ned Dobb. She stood and watched, frozen with horror. She saw now that there were other boys already on the cart, three or four of them stacked in amongst the baggage. The soldiers had simply gone to collect more supplies from the Sugar House, to fill a want. Just as her father might come here, for sugar or slaves.

There were a cluster of other people watching the proceedings with interest. She turned to one of them, a moon-faced man with a battered cocked hat held under his chin with a scarf.

"Where are they going?" she asked.

The man smiled roundly, showing one brown tooth. "To hell, as I wish," he said.

Daisy edged away. A withered old woman in a smock pushed the man impatiently. "North," she said in a rasping voice. She held out a hand. Daisy gave her a penny from her purse. A penny a word was a dear rate, but it had to be when there was so little to sell, and to buy. Then she motioned to Cuffy, and led her to the ropewalk. She had noticed Tom in these parts on her visits to the Sugar House. Many of the refugees, renegades, deserters, scratched a living by making rope, it was well known. She winced at the word deserter. He'd run to save his boy, and now his boy was being taken away; all the family he had. She remembered that day he'd come to the Sugar House wharf and the Liberty Woman had pointed to him, and she herself had become part of the crowd for the first time. They'd taken his boat. She, Daisy, gave the word, and they took it. All he'd been left with was Ned.

There were five or six lumbering men in the ropeshed, white and black, half naked, winding hemp into thick rope. Tom was nowhere visible, nor on the walkway, nor in the dark space underneath. She asked several people, but no one would say anything. They looked at her shrewd eyes, and she was sure they knew where he'd gone, but wouldn't say. Of course not. Even in her plain brown cloak they could see she was a rich girl, a merchant's daughter. Her hair, her thin leather shoes, her pale face and hands with no work or wear in them, nor poverty. Her Negro slave. How could they trust her? She was the Sugar King's daughter.

She and Cuffy roamed the streets of New York for hours. As the day wore on to afternoon, the air grew cold. People jostled them, spat. The redcoats were on the whole polite enough, believing her to be one of their own and too wealthy and well-connected to be safe prey. But the people of New York were different, the drunken men staggering out of taverns, the gutter people on the lookout for rubbish to pick up, a piglet, or even a cat or dog to make off with or a pocket to pick. And whores, everywhere. The whores didn't thrive, they were as raggedy as the rest, but they did a brisk business even if there was not the wherewithall in New York to get wealthy on it. One of them, a red-faced, coarse-featured girl, far-gone with child, pawed at Daisy for money and wouldn't leave her alone. She said her trade had been off since her belly showed. She was from Staten Island, she said, and was a good girl until the soldiers were garrisoned there and the temptation was too much. Daisy resented giving money to a whore who slept with British soldiers, but she gave her some anyway. The afternoon wore on and the winding streets wound into each other like hemp into rope. The sharp, wary, sometimes emaciated faces from the crowd loomed at her and hands flapped open, hands everywhere—it was a city of hands, questing, questioning, beseeching hands, hands that she could put nothing into because her purse was exhausted.

At last they found themselves down by the wharves again. Dusk was falling, braziers and fires being lit, an atmosphere of celebration developing at the sight of British soldiers marching north. For no good reason there were plenty remaining. Her father had told Daisy that the British would occupy New York for the duration of the war; it was their headquarters. And in any case, if some were marching north, they were no doubt on their way to defeat some more Americans. But still, people were happy to see the back of the bloodybacks, as they called them, if only for the present. Daisy and Cuffy pushed their way through throngs that sang and danced and picked fights with each other in the torchlight. Again Daisy went up the planking of the ropewalk and peered into the shed, just to make-certain.

This time he was there. He was lying on the floor, near the wall, in the dim candlelit room, sleeping restlessly. Men still cranked huge timber beams, making rope, too busy to pay any attention to him. He was whimpering and talking in his dream. A British cockade was pinned to his chest.

Daisy approached. She stood over Tom for a moment, loath to wake him. But he sensed her in his sleep, and opened his eyes, startled. When he realized who it was, he lowered his eyes and inspected one of his wrists, on which there was an angry welt.

"Whatcha want?" he asked sullenly. "Wanta see me?"

She replied, too softly for him to hear her.

There was a long pause. Slowly, very slowly, as if coming from the bottom of the sea, his eyes rose to meet hers. "What?" he repeated.

"It's your son," Daisy whispered.

"Ned?"

"I saw him taken at the Sugar House, him and another boy. Away on the drummers' cart. They've marched north."

It was like when somebody died. She'd seen a little of death since this war began, soldiers dying of wounds and fever, people dying destitute on the streets, the fire-bucket man at the end of a rope. For a moment you didn't know you'd died, you thought life was carrying on as normal, a strange moment in which, without knowing, you took immortality for granted and so discovered a little bit of it; and then at last you realized what had happened and you changed all over, all at once, became a different thing, became a thing, as if your body could close itself as a door closes.

Something like this happened to Tom now. He waited for a moment after she had told him, as if it mattered not at all; and then his body closed in despair. "Not Ned," he whispered.

Daisy's breath stopped as she watched his pain.

Tom had gathered his things together: a knife, a strapped pouch, a canteen, a leather shirt. There was a small skiff moored to the piers of the ropewalk. He checked carefully to each side, to make sure no one could see him, and dropped his possessions into it. Then he slid in himself and began to rig the sail.

"You're going after him," said Daisy. She watched him in awe. To go north, to look for one boy on the whole continent, to intend to steal back a boy from the British army. "You've got no weapon," she said.

"I got hands," Tom replied. He cast off and the boat began to edge away from the wharf. He seemed a different man now that he was back on the river—confident, calm, in control. No longer the little man at the mercy of events, always ready to run. He moved the rudder, and the boat swung farther away from shore. "Thank you for coming to me," he said.

She couldn't speak.

"Ya go down the wharf," Tom went on. "Ya yell a man stole a boat. Ya point 'em toward the sea."

"I will, Tom," she said. She raised her hand as if to touch him across the water. The offshore breeze quickened the sail. "Oh, Tom, we should have spoke." He couldn't hear her, but he waved. "God save you," she muttered to herself, "both of you."

As she spoke, she was aware of the gurgling sound of water, but not from the river—from the side of the ropeshed. Then a sentry came around the corner, buttoning his trousers. He saw Tom and began to shout, yelling out across the water about stealing the boat, breaking the curfew.

On the ropewalk was a loose timber. Daisy had skirted it carefully before. She picked it up and walked along the planking toward the soldier, whose back was to her. Her soft leather shoes, thank God, made no noise. She raised the beam above her head. It was heavy and took all her strength. Then she brought it down on the soldier, who dropped suddenly and completely. She beat him several more times to make sure. She didn't know how hard, or how often, it was necessary to hit someone. But she was learning. She had entered the war.

Tom was only just visible, midriver. He hadn't heard or seen her. She watched him go. He was a riverman, and she'd given him back a boat. She continued to watch after he had long disappeared. Then she turned to Cuffy, who looked back, scared. The soldier lay still. Tom had the river, the task of searching for his boy, of finding his family once more. She and Cuffy had nothing. No home, nowhere to go. Nowhere except this vague unformed country that was struggling to come into existence all around them. No one except each other.

10

The small boat bucked with the eddy and flow of the river, beating against the movement of the water. But the wind was behind, so Tom made progress. Tom went past Fort George and then around the point of Manhattan Island until the dark sea, darker than the sky, was square behind him. Then he went up the Hudson itself, paler ahead than the sea was behind, with the left arm of the shore flat black, and on the right, the yellow-orange haze of New York. The little skiff wouldn't cut the water like his longboat, and the ripples of the current thudded hard and noisily on the keel. He tucked her in as closely as he dared to the New Jersey shore, fearful lest a watchful sentry should notice he was breaking curfew, or even more likely, that some of the river's freebooters and cutthroats should put out after him to see if he was carrying anything worth taking.

He didn't dare get in too close to the land, however, for fear of running up against snags, shallows, moored boats, all the clutter of obstacles that accumulated inshore. Moreover it was blacker here, as though the darkness of the land seeped over the nearby water, and Tom had a repeated dizzying sensation of steering into something solid. He would hold his course and go through, however, trusting to his experience of the river for his bearings.

At one point he heard a voice, almost in his ear, someone talking on the New Jersey shore, though it sounded so close he could have been standing on the surface of the river itself. He actually steered out a couple of rods to avoid it, then reminded himself how sound travels across the surface of river water. Even from the New York side of the river occasional faint gusts of sound would waft over, street cries, someone crying out, a woman laughing, the frantic barking of a dog. But this other voice was almost intimate and confidential, it seemed so near, a drawling aimless voice like that of a man talking in his sleep, or speaking to no one except himself. A voice from a different world, he thought, from a casual, relaxed open America; a place Tom had almost forgotten during his months in New York, scrabbling for survival amongst all the beggars, cripples, bullies, loonies, and criminals who gathered in the city as the flotsam and jetsam of the river bobs about a snag. The mellow voice laughed lazily to itself. It must be a man fishing, he decided as the skiff moved on, the voice folding back into the sounds of water, wind, and trees, where it belonged.

The orange of the city fires moved over Tom's shoulder and began to fade. He took the boat out toward the dim gray pathway midriver; it was safer now. The wind was still firm in the sail, and he was making good progress. An army couldn't march far in a day, which is all the start they had on him. He would find them; he would get Ned back. He'd looked for him last night, and this morning, on the streets of New York, but then he didn't know he was lost. Now it was different. What you had to do was say it to yourself strongly enough. It was not for them, the forests or or the soldiers, to deny you if you repeated it in your mind with authority. Your word could force its way through any obstacles, as a river would force its way through a mountain, if needs must. But if the words eddied or backed up, if they spilled from their path and dissipated their force, you would fail. It was not to be done out there, overland, in the woods, amongst the British tomorrow or the next day, by force of arms or by cunning. It was to be done here, on the river, in this boat, alone. In the mind. You had to declare it to yourself.

He had said it to Daisy McConnahay and it had heartened him. It had made him feel, yes, it can be done. He had seen how Daisy looked at him when he said that, when she saw him not as a man who ran away, but as one who chased, not as the hunted, but as the hunter. She saw him with justice at last, which was not as a man who fled from the redcoats, but as one who would desert or attack, whichever was needed to save his son. She had seen him with new eyes and held out her hands toward him. He'd been busy with the boat and had not looked back, but he could sense or glimpse her hands reaching to him from the wharf. Not taking, like that first day, when she took his boat. But reaching. He didn't reach back or even wave, because his hands were too busy with what he had to do.

He had said it to Daisy, "Got hands." That was all that was needed. But he had to say it to himself also, say it so it stayed said, no matter what. Night or day. Sun or storm. Lance or musket. Life or death. You could say words like that fisherman back along the river had, so they mixed in with the water and the trees. But you could also say them so that they were part of yourself, like your limbs or your brain.

He said them.

After the words were said, Tom's spirits rose. He felt happier and more at peace than he had since he'd sailed down this very stretch of water toward New York in the summer. And he felt more at home. This was where he belonged, out in the open, on a boat, not skulking with the other wharf rats by the ropewalk. He even wondered why he'd not lit out before, taking Ned and stealing a boat. But of course he couldn't have. That was a different story. Stealing a boat from under the noses of the redcoats was a hanging offense, for both of them. The risk made it impossible. He'd done it tonight because he had to. It was sheer luck that there were no redcoats coming out of the tavern or the whorehouse, none of the Sugar House sentries down by the wharf to notice him. But he wasn't trusting to luck anymore. He'd made his declaration, said the words.

Just before dawn, the wind failed.

He didn't think much of it at first. Something usually happened at this time. If it had been a still night, you had a dawn wind; he'd seen it so often, a gray wind rising over gray early morning water. And, like now, the opposite would happen. A wind which blew all night would go still, as if gathering strength for the day ahead. The night began to fall away.

There was no sunrise, no sense of the darkness vanishing. Simply, you became aware that you could see things, then that you could see everything. Forest on the New Jersey side, forest and farmland in New York. The trees and meadows were solid gray, like the glassy, slowly shifting water of the river; then, without anything happening to the sky, no extra light that you could make out, it was day. The gray and green of a dim, drizzly day. Fish, in response to the flat condition of the river, flipped the surface, darted cheekily after insects. It looked as if you could simply take them out of the water by hand, except that you never could and there was no net or line on the skiff. Tom felt that sick hunger of the early morning, when your body is ready to work again but has no food to work on. He looked up at the sail hanging tiredly from its rigging. The boat had so little weight, it was prone to follow the current and would soon be backing up. But by the same token, it was not too big to paddle. He took down the sail and began.

After a couple of hours he thought he'd grown tired. Then he realized it was growing harder. The touch of the damp air upon his face, the sign that he was moving at all—since the shores wound by slower than the hands of a clock—was no longer a touch but a distinct pressure. The breeze hadn't been resting, it had swung, and he had paddled through the pivot of its turn.

The British would be on the move again by now. He wondered whether to moor the boat and head across country after them. It would be safer to try to keep level with the boat and make up ground later, when the army had stopped. He needed to moor as far upriver as possible, so that he could cut square through the woods after Ned, bring him back and carry on up the Hudson to freedom ahead of the British altogether. He paddled all day. It was like paddling uphill. The wind blew harder, the waves got more choppy, the boat bounced so that it hurt his buttocks and the small of his back. His shoulders ached bitterly, and even his hands, callused and hard after weeks of ropemaking, grew sore. The weather thickened but still it did not rain. The wind made his ears ache, and his old blue jacket was soaked with scud from the waves and from catching crabs as the boat rocked. He made it as far as he could, struggling to keep up with what he guessed would be the slow marching pace of a column of soldiers. There were huge lumps of rain in the sky, and if they dropped, the going would be harder still.

The wind tailed off for an hour, midafternoon, and Tom felt sure it would storm. Shivers skittered over his shoulders and chest with fatigue, but he pushed harder on the paddle,

determined to make full use of the calmer conditions. The
sky darkened further, and then went from gray to a deep
strained blue, like a murky parody of fine weather. The
clouds rattled like army drums at first, and then deeper, like
cannon. Lightning flared along the horizon. Still the rain
didn't come. The darkening sky gradually grew dark with
evening as well as weather, and by now Tom had had enough.

The river broadened out here into a small lagoon fed by a
waterfall, where another river joined it. The army would be
setting up camp by now, and surely the rain couldn't be far
off. It was time to moor. He pulled the skiff into a narrow
rocky inlet and tied its rope to the narrow trunk of a tree
which jutted out over the water. From here the roar of the
falls supplemented the now almost continuous rumble of
thunder. The water of the falls boiled white as it descended,
a white more intense than the purple afternoon could possi-
bly justify, a thick solid hawser just below the lip of the fall
fraying into individual strands as it neared the pool. Tom,
almost too weak to move and feeling uneasy on the shore
after a day on the skiff, leaned against his mooring tree and
watched it, as he had many times before.

When you watched it, you saw two things. The first was
the terrible energy and violence of its plunge downward, so
that despite its enormous volume and mass, it fell faster and
harder than you would expect, and seemed to be not merely
falling but driving downward to the platform of water below.
The second was its stillness. If you kept your eyes still, the
water remained still also, and its movement down seemed to
be merely a repeated flickering motion across its bulk. Even
apparently random drops flying off flew off again and again
and again, so that you began to believe it was the same one
repeating its flight rather than a myriad of successive droplets
falling away before your eyes.

As he watched, half mesmerized, Tom remembered all the
violence and death he'd seen already in this war, and thought
that nothing had changed after all, no movement had taken
place—the rich were still rich, the poor still poor. Ned had
been stolen from him by the American militia and then by
the British redcoats. Nothing changed but the names. It was
true that the girl, Daisy, who had stolen his boat, had kissed
him before they fought on Manhattan, and last night had
come to him to tell about Ned. But she was still a merchant's

daughter, in love with high-sounding talk. She still had her slave with her. She had cried out to him as he headed around the point, "Tom, we should have spoke." He hadn't replied, because what had they to speak about? He was a river trader, she was the Sugar King's daughter. He belonged here, with a small boat and the noise of the water; she had a comfortable home to go back to, with music playing, and warmth, and good food. She was a creature from a different world. He ached with fatigue and hunger.

It was time to move. He was beginning to get cold, and more aware of his heavy, sodden, comfortless clothes. He reached back into the boat, picked up the British cockade that had been fastened to him yesterday, and then began to climb up among the glistening scree beside the waterfall, the spray biting him all over, getting in among his clothes, hissing on the back of his jacket, filming on his face and hands. Every few feet he rested for a moment, turning to watch the thick part of the water and the spume that rose like smoke, fell like rain, drifted in the air like snow, rainbowed suddenly in the dim light. Then he continued upward, the path as stiff and ungiving as the water of the Hudson had been. The noise was huge from this proximity, and he could no longer hear the thunder of the sky, but at intervals the stones and vegetation up which he was climbing would spring toward him from the dimness as lightning flickered.

When he got to the top of the fall, there was another ahead of him. He'd known it was there, of course, since you could make out its topmost reaches from the Hudson below, but he'd never had cause to climb up this cleft in the hills before. The upper fall was not as high as the lower. It slipped over a spur of rock on the skyline, breaking its way through the dark mass of trees on each side, and struck in a small pool a couple of hundred yards ahead of where he was standing. It then formed itself into a wide, chattering, rocky river, deepening and quickening as it reached Tom, and then becoming glassy and smooth as it headed for its second drop.

Tom trudged up the respite of the shallower incline, and then began to climb the upper cascade. It was growing darker, and he wanted to reach the top ridge in time to get his bearings before darkness fell.

When he reached the top, purple was becoming black, but as he mounted the ridge the sky was huge and still held, in its fat low clouds, enough light to show the landscape below. The river was quite narrow here, snaking away along the high ground to the right, while to the left the New York colony fell away in a great valley of dark trees, with fanglike hills beyond on the horizon. And in the middle, perhaps three or four miles away, columns of smoke angled in the north wind rose to the heavy clouds as though they were collapsing under a vast, bulging ceiling. The British camp.

It was too late to set out now, and he was too tired. He would have a few hours sleep, find a place in the undergrowth nearby, since he couldn't face climbing down to his boat again. He hoped to wake up in the early hours, when first light was beginning, so that he could reach the camp by dawn.

Night had fallen. Peasy sat outside his tent smoking a pipe. There were tents in every direction, the camp well set up. The air was cold but thick. Like summer air, but cold. There was still sudden lightning on the hills yonder, but no rain as yet. The air was loaded, though. It was like a summer storm approaching in late autumn. He thought of India, with Clive. The way the sky burned and the rain rattled down, like the thick of a battle. Clive was a scrawny runt. He'd never seen him, but he was a runt, everyone said. But a sharp general. The little shrimps were always the best officers. Not like Sir William Howe, plump and well fed, his mistress plump and well fed also, waiting for him in bed, the two of them round and plump as a pair of capons in a game shop. So they said. Clive said, "Gentlemen, you have won the lottery of life, you have been born Englishmen." It rained there as if the air was turned to water, but it was hot too. You fought the weather and the Indians, keeping in line, English-style, keeping cool, like English weather. Winning the lottery of life.

Here it was cool, but it would pelt later. But for now there was a good fire burning, his pipe bowl was warm and comfortable, and it was pleasant to sit here on his kit chest and listen to the boys. They were shuffling around the fire in a slow circle, like old men—a little bent, tired after the long day. Playing anything that came into their heads. The drummers rattling out a beat, the two new ones full of promise, as he'd thought in the Sugar House, not just clumping it out like marching feet but making the music move here and yonder, change direction like the wind, give you somewhere to march toward, something to march *for*. The fifers played wild, eerie notes, like storm wind or witch music. As they all shuffled around the flickering orange of the fire, dead slow, half lit, half dark, you could think they were all wild; not like drummer boys at all, but like those Indians over the water when he fought with Clive, or the Indians here, wild men, minds dark as their skin.

And then Lord Darling called, and they became little boys again. Peasy didn't hear him. He tapped his pipe and put it back in his mouth. Fatgut Lord Darling. There was always a Lord Darling. The little boys shuffled around the fire, tired little boys ready for bed, playing their instruments like children—all over the place, only able to take so much discipline, playing sleepy music. Lord Darling called again, this time so loudly Peasy had to hear, even over the music. The boys heard too, and the music fell away so you could almost see the last stray drumbeats skittering off over the ground, the fifes zigzagging away into the dark trees.

Lord Darling stepped out of his tent and waddled over. Peasy got slowly to attention, like a lax soldier, holding his hot pipe in his hand.

Darling surveyed him carefully. Peasy was one of those tough soldiers, hard as iron, who would obey orders to the letter, to the hilt, to the death. And yet when Lord Darling gave an order, he was always aware of a certain something in the way Peasy looked back at him, almost a comic quality, if a man like that could have a sense of humor, which patently he couldn't. Didn't have the brain, the imagination. Didn't have the warmth, the generosity of outlook. Not the sort of individual who could let anything go. Played life by the rule book. Never a peccadillo in sight. It was the odd little peccadillo that made a soldier a man. The way he treated these boys for example. Even at this time of night he was still getting them to bong their drums and play their fifes after a hard day on the march, when what they wanted was a little harmless fun, or to go to bed.

No, Peasy wasn't the sort of man to possess a sense of humor. But at the same time you sometimes gained the fleeting impression that there was a certain strange something about the way he carried out orders. The way he was standing at attention at this very moment, for example—it was absurd, the man didn't have the wit—but you could almost imagine that the man was standing at attention ironically. As though somewhere in the recesses of that huge cloak of his, he was scorning you.

Best be firm, Darling decided. Show a crisp soldierly attitude. Look the man in the eye. "Sergeant-Major Peasy."

"Sir."

"I need a boy."

There was a pause. Yes, that was it. A pause. Not long enough to be disobedient, but long enough to provide room for an irony to take root. "Yes sir," Peasy said finally.

Just the sort of attitude that should be stamped underfoot. Maintain snap and sharpness. "Did you hear me, Mr. Peasy?"

"Sir."

"I need a boy, Sergeant-Major."

"What for, sir?"

Time to ease off, the point had been made. "To polish my boots, Mr. Peasy," Darling said, and chuckled, man to man.

A gaggle of little boys by the fire, peering anxiously through the gloom as the big men talked. These were Peasy's boys, his to look after and take care of, to send to bed at night and rouse in the morning, to teach to drum and to keep on drumming no matter what, as the musket balls whipped past and the cannons crashed. Peasy's boys to comfort and sustain when they were ill or wounded, and to bury when they were dead. But he was father to these boys not in the way of nature but in the way of the army. If you soldiered all your life long, all you had in the way of nature was these dirty wretches the battalion took around with it like so much baggage. For all family warmth and comfortableness Peasy had only his drummer boys, and these were not strictly his, but his in the way of the army. Which was to say, by way of certain rules and regulations; to wit, a senior officer may give orders to a sergeant-major and the sergeant-major would obey. And there were rules also which were to be found in no book. One such said, in each battalion you would find, without fail, one officer-gentleman of the likes of Lord Darling.

He went over to the boys. "His lordship needs a boy to polish his boots," he told them, though they had heard before. They shifted nervously, like animals in a pen when one of them is going to be picked out. He gestured for them to follow him, and walked over to Lord Darling's tent, his lordship having stepped back there already.

His lordship had a manly tent, with his chest and dress uniform neatly laid out, his bed made up, and some muddy boots standing in a row. His whale-oil lamp was lit. He stood by it, patting his fat belly, which bulged out his waistcoat. The boys came in and stood in a line, right by the boots. Simple boys.

Darling approached the first one. It was Ned, one of the boys Peasy had found in the Sugar House. His lordship patted his head, felt him a little around the shoulders, then pinched his cheeks with his fat finger and thumb, as you might take a pinch of salt or flour or tobacco, or any commodity from a shopkeeper's barrel, to test whether it is to your liking.

And then Ned bit down.

Darling snatched his hand from the little savage's face. The young villain had bitten his finger. He stared at it in horror and astonishment. The dog had drawn blood. Talk of biting the hand that feeds. He wanted nothing but to show affection and interest toward these boys, and this was how they repaid him. One of his hands comforted the other while he glared at the young viper with all the ferocity his countenance could muster. If there was ever a moment when the military virtues of discipline, obedience, and deference toward authority required assertion, it was the present one.

He spoke very quietly. "Sergeant-Major Peasy."

"Sir."

"The gunner's daughter."

"Sir."

Peasy took Ned out of the tent. The other boys followed like a line of ducklings. He didn't tell them to, but they didn't think of doing anything else. One of the cannon was just beyond his tent, still on its carriage, ready for towing tomorrow morning. Ned flapped like a bird in his arms as they walked toward it, then became still when they arrived.

He looked at it blankly, as though he'd never seen a cannon before and didn't know what you did with one. The huge iron muzzle gleamed in the light from the fire. Peasy bent close to Ned. "Now you little fish, see what's come to us," he whispered. He lifted Ned up, laid him on the muzzle with feet toward the end, and flicked his fingers for some rope. One of the boys scurried off and brought some. Peasy lashed Ned's hands together around the spout and secured his body so it wouldn't slip off. Then he took off the boy's clogs, one at a time, placing them carefully beside the gun carriage. From the recesses of his cloak he pulled out a cat o' nine tails and unfolded it. He swung the whip in the air to disentangle the tails, and drew it back. He eyed the soles of the boy's feet, glowing palely in the firelight, and with one eye half shut for accuracy struck the first blow.

Neither hard nor soft. Neither malice nor mercy. By the book. Stroke after stroke, in rhythm. The training of his whole life had taught him how to beat.

Ned was a good boy. He didn't cry on the first strike, just gasped as if despite everything, it surprised him. He cried a little on the second, however, more on the third.

On the fourth Merle pushed forward, grabbed Peasy's arm, and tried to pull the whip away. Peasy slapped him off with one blow to the face. Merle spun, lost his balance on the slippery ground, and fell against the cannon himself. Peasy heard a tooth break against the cast iron, and the boy turned, buckled with pain, blood streaming over the hand that gripped his mouth. But no more than on the battlefield did Peasy shift ground or come to his aid. This was a time for duty.

He struck Ned's soles again. It was his duty to continue until Lord Darling informed him he might stop.

Lord Darling stood by the opening of his tent to watch the early blows, then retired within. He possessed a certain delicacy of nerves and temperament, despite his military avocation, and had no wish to sully his eyes with the details of brusque soldierly punishment. Moreover he was constantly aware of a tendency towards softheartedness which could so easily cloud his better judgment and prevent the administering of most curative medicine, not only to the young rascal concerned, but to the rest of that litter of puppy dogs. So he remained in his tent, which in any case happened to be conveniently situated in relation to the cannon, allowing him to hear the blows of the whip, the cries of the scallawag, the assorted yelps and whimpers from the rest of his crew. He sat on his bed, listening carefully. He felt slightly shaken himself. His finger was throbbing where the young wretch had bitten it, almost to the bone, and the anguish, anxiety, perhaps even the responsibility of arranging punishment, had triggered off his mutinous digestion, as unpleasant scenes were wont to do. His stomach had begun to stir uneasily, to mutter and gurgle in discontent.

After a while he became aware of another sensation, not far removed from his indigestion but considerably more agreeable. Strangely enough it seemed to follow each stroke of the whip. It was a drawing of the innards, and a kind of puckering, shivering sensation over the lower part of his trunk. It grew stronger as time went on, until he was aware, with each blow, of a wave of hot feeling that seemed to swoop over his body, to take him down down down to dark, intimate, exquisite places. It was extraordinary, he thought, even as he surrendered to this series of ecstasies, what strange and unexpected adventures a man of rarified sensibility could find his emotions preparing for him.

Tom awoke in rain so strong it sounded as if the trees were on fire. Branches crackled all around him and offered no protection from the ferocity of the downpour. There was no visible light, but he realised he could make out the forms of the nearest tree trunks. It was time to head toward the British camp. If he ran and didn't get lost on the way, he might be able to get there before it began stirring, find Ned somehow, arouse him from sleep, steal him away. He didn't let himself dwell on how this might be done. He'd said his word, it *would* be done.

He ran over sludgy ground, the water streaming through his clothes, weaving between the trees that marched bulkily toward him like an endless army. Occasionally he blundered into one of them, stopped, collected himself, then ran on. But after a while they became more distinct, and although he couldn't glimpse the sky, he realized it must be turning from black to gray. He didn't run fast, but he didn't slacken his pace. His stomach pained him with hunger, and his limbs ached from the hours of paddling yesterday, the cold, the wet, and the hard sleep, but he ran independently of his feelings.

He ran as straight as he could, sensing the river square behind him and the British camp ahead, resuming his original line after he'd dodged round trees.

At last he broke into the open. There was a downward sweep of land, and in a low meadow, the British camp. The sky was distinctly gray, but it was still well before dawn and only the horses, and an occasional sentinel, seemed to be stirring. He ran straight toward the camp, trusting to the cockade and to the fact that he made no attempt to conceal himself, to avoid suspicion. He could be some tradesmen, a cook or a blacksmith, who followed the troops for a living and who'd gone into the woods to relieve himself. It was like running into a whole township of tents, with each little house the same. The ground had been churned up by feet and horses and was like jelly underfoot. The rain still beat unrelentingly down. Ahead was a cannon, positioned as though to guard the flimsy tents around it.

Ned had slipped off the cannon but his hands were raised up to it, still secured. He looked like a piece of wet rag that had caught on the muzzle. Tom took out his knife and cut the ropes that bound him. Ned struggled weakly. Tom put his arms around his boy.

"It's me, Ned."

"Pa?"

"I'm here."

"Oh, Pa, I'm sorry. For—"

"It's *I* who am sorry, Ned."

An arm snaked up from somewhere below and grasped the belt of his trousers. He glanced down. The drummer boy from the Sugar House was lying there, half under the cannon. His face was bloody, his eyes pleading to be taken.

Tom looked back at Ned, then let his eyes wander around the camp. Laughter came from a tent somewhere.

Tom had said one word, to get Ned back. This he had done, though the poor boy lay here all spoiled, his feet unwalkable.

Now Tom said his second word. He looked around the British camp and said it, a short word.

War.

Tom Dobb declared his war on the British, for America, and then, with Ned slung over his shoulder and Merle holding his hand, he walked out of the British camp. Standing by the marching band's tent, inconspicuous under canvas eaves, Ben, Peasy's little drummer boy watched silently as they went. And a little farther on, near the outskirts of the camp, an Indian stared at them impassively from the cover of undergrowth, but did nothing.

11

The day began at dawn. They were packing up the camp. The tents were being pulled down, folded up, loaded onto carts. The cannon was trundled off. It was empty. Peasy towered over Ben, a soldier doll in his red coat.

"Where'd they go, Ben?"

Ben didn't reply.

"You know, Ben."

"It was a man who come and took them."

"You made no alarm."

Ben looked up at Peasy as a small boy looks at his angry father, looking through the anger for some reassurance. Then suddenly he cried and put his head on Peasy's chest. Peasy held him for a moment. He knew why Ben had made no alarm. But Ned was going to be brought back all the same. The rules could not be flouted. And the army was his family now, not some half savage father taking him off into the woods. The boy had to learn to live inside the rules. Step outside them and your foot was punished. But there was room inside the rules to live your life.

There was no room out there, in all these woods, mountains, rivers, the American wilderness. In the wild there was only room for scrabbling for grub and trying not to die, like any animal. There was no room to live right, be a God-fearing man, obey your betters, instruct your inferiors, conduct an orderly life. Ned would understand one day, when he was grown, that this was better than living like the beasts of the field, or the Indians.

But now this was Indian work. Peasy called his corporal and asked him to bring two Iroquois. The Iroquois marched with the British army, except they didn't march, they skulked in and out of trees, sniffing the ground like dogs instead of going atop of it like an honest soldier; they tomahawked and scalped their victims, painted themselves, cut their hair bald except for a great tuft down the middle, and were in general, in Peasy's eyes, a shame and a disgrace to the army. If they followed rules, they were rules in the gibberish they spoke. If they prayed to God, they prayed in that same gibberish, and no doubt the god they prayed to was some prancing painted fellow who sat not on a throne, but in a wigwam, and hollered and whooped just like they did.

But in a business like this you could make good use of them. The Dobb boy's father was all but savage himself, so they'd be of a kind. Ned told him on the march he'd been a river trader on the Hudson, as rough a bunch as white men were ever likely to be.

The corporal brought him two of these Iroquois, or Mohawks. One was as evil-looking as you could hope to see, a big fellow with an even bigger fur and hide jacket, which made him look like a bear, though his name, the corporal said, was Wolf. But that was understandable when you saw his teeth. These Indians named themselves after animals and conducted themselves as such. What did they know of families, in any case, heathens that they were? No more than a dog or a horse. They talked like animals too, raising their lips and kind of grunting, hardly using the King's English. It was said the chief of all the Mohawks had been taken to England to see the king. Of course, the king's native tongue wasn't English either, but German, so perhaps they talked German to each other and were content. The other Indian, Otter by clan title, was not so big or fearsome, but more like a regular how-de-do kind of Indian, with a tassled jerkin and matching breeches. They both had necklaces, feathers, and teeth of all sorts hanging on them. They loved collecting such trash, which they regarded as a white man regarded honest money. But Peasy had something they could use. He dug into the inner pocket of his cloak and pulled it out.

It was a knife, sharp as a razor, with a bone handle. He'd taken it off a dead soldier after the fighting on Manhattan Island, if the truth be told, but the poor wretch would have no more use for it. He knew what use an Indian would put this blade to, of course. But then, as with the knife itself, corpses had no further use for their locks, neither use nor ornament, except to savages. He held the trophy aloft.

"This is for the Iroquois who brings back my boys," he said.

Off they went. As he expected, they sniffed their way out of the camp, going on all fours on the ground one moment, reaching down the branch of a tree the next. You'd think they could see a man's shadow after he'd passed, even in this teeming rain. But then, that Dobb wouldn't be tracking through the woods like a regular man either. Indians and Dobbs, they were two of a kind as far as Peasy was concerned. And it was his duty to get Ned and Merle out of the clutches of all such and back into the ranks of the British army, where they now belonged, beating their drums like proper soldiers and Christian boys.

Ned could feel the rain, but thought it was a seething in his mind. He lay over his father's shoulder, head swinging against the small of Tom's back. He saw the trail unwind below him, all the small things, leaves, moss, grass clumps, tree roots, spiky objects which seemed to hook his eyes as he passed over, making them itch so that he wanted to scratch them. Moving over the ground this way, without touching, reminded him of something—perhaps when he was nothing but a babe in the arms of his ma or pa. No, no. That was wrong. You didn't carry a babe by the ankles. Your babylife was when you always watched the sky, day after day, and people's faces came down at you from the sky like birds. It wasn't as a baby that he'd floated over the ground like this, yet he could remember it as if it were yesterday. Before a babe, when an angel. An angel winged its way in this fashion, with no part touching.

Before he was born, when he wasn't dead but wasn't alive yet.

Or perhaps he was becoming dead now. Perhaps this was what it felt like. Drifting up just above the ground, sliding backward away from everything. Below there was the burning, but you floated away from that, you left it and you never had to use your burning feet to walk upon the ground again. You stepped off your feet and floated in the air.

* * *

As soon as Tom was out of sight of the British camp, involved in the trees, he slowed to a walk, a fast walk that had Merle trotting beside him; a walk he knew he could keep to until he got to his boat. He was ravenous and exhausted beyond all belief, but he could keep on walking because he would. He had to get away from the British because then, one day, he would be able to turn back toward them and fight. Merle had told him, gasping it out as they thumped along, who'd done Ned's feet. The drum sergeant-major with the big cloak and the lance, the bulging eyes, the unstoppableness in attack or beating.

The sergeant-major would get beat himself one day, Tom Dobb thought. He would kill him, or rear his son to do it.

The weight of Ned bore down so that his knees buckled, but he kept on, staggering a little now. Ned was a weight, a terrible weight. But not like Georgie Washington on the hunt. The doll weighed little, but it was dead stuff and clumsily straddled your every movement. Ned was weighty but he was alive, and worth the carrying.

The rain stopped, but the fragments of sky through the treetops were leaden. It was dim green light amongst the trees, and suddenly he remembered the woods of Manhattan when they'd escaped Peasy's lance and were heading back toward New York and Ned wanted to go north, to find their troops again. Tom's eyes smarted as he thought if. If. If they'd gone north, Ned would have feet to walk on. When he'd deserted the Americans, he'd deserted Ned too. And after all this time, they'd come north to find one another again.

The trees swam and swayed like river weed as Tom's eyes filled with guilt for the suffering his boy had gone through, all because he himself had been too much of a coward to fight this war before.

There was a booming ahead. Tom stopped and Merle pressed in against him. Tom thought for an instant that by thinking of it, just by thinking the word war, he'd brought it upon himself again. But his confusion disappeared at once. It wasn't the dirty, crumpling roar of cannon fire, with the powder fizzing and firing, then the drumming of the ball along the muzzle and the howling as it flew through the air. This was the clean thunder of water dropping.

Now he was running again, up the slope, out of the trees, across scrub to the scree by the bumpy river, and there, just ahead, was the smooth tip over which the water fell. He ran toward it, then stopped.

His arm shot forward and grabbed Merle, who was still running, and he pulled him back before he knew to stop running, like a hen with its head cut off.

Tom knew without knowing. He could see nothing, since they were short of the ridge over which the water cascaded. He could hear nothing save the boom of the falls. And yet he knew. Perhaps he'd learned to read invisible signs, like the Indians. Perhaps exhaustion and hunger and guilt sharpened your senses to read them. He remembered those Indians far up the Hudson, when he was with Mr. Beeley—the way they went through the woods as if they could smell, see, feel, hear, touch another world from yours, as different as their language. You could stand so near, you could touch them, yet they were in another place, where there were colors they saw and you couldn't, and sounds you couldn't hear but they heard. It was as though it was raining for you but the sun shone for them; they moved in their own weather. Tom had looked in their eyes but had seen nothing there. With a white man you could see a particle of his nature when you looked in his eyes. Tom was a quiet man and didn't exchange many words in his trading, but he exchanged looks, and he would know the kind of business he would do, whether buying or selling, by the eyes of the man he looked at. As with that drum sergeant-major when he saw him on the battlefield coming toward them, he'd seen Ned in his eyes, Ned as clear as a picture—the man had big eyes, bulging, and Ned had been in them. And also Mr. Corty, the day he took his promissory note to the commissary and Corty stood on his little platform with the Sugar King beside him, and Corty had said the war would be over in two weeks. That was many weeks ago now, months, not far off a year, and the war still went on. But even as Tom listened to Mr. Corty and watched, he'd known it wouldn't be two. He hadn't known it would last till now, but he'd known it wouldn't be two. He'd thought four. Mr. Corty's voice said two, and his eyes said four. But when Tom looked into Indian eyes, they said nothing. And he had no idea what they saw.

He didn't know what *he* had seen either. Or heard. But it

was something. Where there ought to be nothing, something. That took you into Indian places. Something, over the edge of the falls.

He left Ned on the bank, with Merle by him. Then he crept to the fringe of the woodland and edged down the sharp slope. It was impossible to see the bottom lagoon from here. The view was obscured by trees tangled together, and a large rocky outcrop just below.

He looked across at the falls. The water arced smooth and round as a fish when it leaps. The lip at the top of the fall forced it outward, away from the cliff itself, and there was a ledge just below which formed a sort of room under the fall, with the cliff as the back wall, the ledge the floor, the lip the roof, and in front the water wall, all window. All around was the spume and spray and clouds of mist. Tom crouched, then ran to the falls.

There was white which blinded his eyes, knocked the breath from his body, filled his ears with noise even when he was through. It was merely the side spill of the fall. If you ventured under the main part you would be crushed to pulp like a beetle underfoot. But he was through and on the clammy shelf, with the thick white streamers of the water before him. It was strangely warm in there, and the air was heavy and wet. Small bushes and creepers grew from the cliff face. He approached as near the outward edge as he dared and strained to see through the fall. In amongst the white streamers there were some thicker waters, not so pulped and crazed, with a glassy surface. It was blurred but you could nonetheless see through. He saw the stream under the fall go babbling along the gentler incline, then the second leap, and then into the weirdly quiet pool where the Hudson paused on its way beneath this oncoming torrent. There was his boat, tiny as a leaf. It was moving, bobbing—no, there were forms, creatures upon it, moving, bobbing. No, it was the movement of this near water. No, it was movement on the boat. A dark shadow, distant arms swinging . . . it was Indians, on his boat.

Tom watched them, chilled to the heart. If they'd come by chance, they'd be stealing his boat, not sinking it. They'd been sent by Peasy. They've have guessed he came by river and they outflanked him, overtook him. Now they were smashing his boat. Indians, two of them, and him alone with two boys, one crippled. They'd kill him, take the boys, like as not kill them too before Peasy ever clapped eyes on them again. Once, when he was up in Canada trading with Mr. Beeley, he'd heard a story of them ferrying a white person through the woods, a woman it was, the wife of an officer in a fort up there. They took her through the woods as only Indians could, and then when they were within sight of the fort, they'd started to argue about who should get the reward for bringing her safely. Unable to decide, they'd stuck a tomahawk in her head to settle the matter. Another time Tom had seen a horror for himself, in a clearing in the forest where the Indians had been. A man had been tied to a tree and set on fire. His legs had been consumed, and all that was left was his charred body still fastened to the trunk. And then, closer to home still, was what had happened to Mr. Beeley himself.

Tom wept. He'd gone through so much. In the last few months he'd experienced every form of fear, injustice, horror. First the rich bitch had taken his boat. The Continentals took his boy. They were both of them nearly killed in the fighting for New York. The sergeant-major coming at them with his lance. The hunt, with that grinning doll. His lordship, haw haw, here endeth your dream.

Tom had no dream. He'd been in a long nightmare.

And then the bitch had become Daisy, and told him about Ned going. Then he got another boat and came for him. Then he got Ned back. But Ned was injured and couldn't walk, and the fever was coming over him, so that Tom could hardly dare think about what had happened and what was going to happen. He'd thought of everything else but that, the beating, on and on, the merciless bastard Peasy beating the life out of his boy then leaving him all hurt in the cold and rain so the fever took root, so that Ned was lying up there on the grass by the top of the fall, babbling to himself and unable to speak sense.

And now the Indians were down below, wrecking his second boat, and soon they'd be coming up to kill him too. It was too much. More than a man could take. Fighting the British army was one thing, but fighting savages out here in the wilderness, that wasn't the war he'd expected.

But he'd said the word. He had no choice. He had to fight.

*   *   *

A stone fell from somewhere up above and clattered down beside the waterfall. The Iroquois looked up as though to trace the path it had made through the air. The boat was finished anyway. They left it and began to climb. Near the top of the first fall a cocked hat lay on the grass, a bit farther on, a canteen. Otter picked it up and shook it. Empty. Footprints swirled over the grass in panic. In some bushes just beyond, the branches hung wrong. They didn't move in the wind. Otter and Wolf stood side by side, observing the stillness. There was no room for a musket in there. They darted forward and pushed the foliage aside.

Two little birds were in the nest, one peering up wide-eyed, the other with his eyes shut, lips burring as he breathed. The Indians reached forward to grasp, and leapt, shrieking, from his boulder.

He filled the sky. In one hand, he held a rock; in the other, a knife. He struck the smaller Indian on his bald pate with the rock as he landed, and the skull gave. One step and the knife was in the other's chest. He pressed intimately upon the handle, working it in as far as it would go. The man's black pelt was thick, so that would take up some room on the blade. He worked the knife up and down, exploring his insides, feeling his organs, like fish underwater. The Indian ignored it. His arms came around, grasped Tom on the back of the neck, pressed down with terrible force. Only then did he notice what had happened, and die.

Both dead. Two Indians. Tom looked up at the small faces in the bush, then down again at the carcasses in front of him. He'd set the trap, dropped the things, dislodged the stone. He'd played at being a white man to get them up here. But he didn't feel like a white man at the moment, he felt like an Indian. When he'd killed, he'd swung himself in the air and thought of nothing except killing. Not thought, just killed.

It wasn't cruel, nor just. It wasn't the defending of the children. It was killing. White men, they always said, couldn't kill like an Indian because they didn't have the gift. As he leapt on the two of them, he did it clean as an animal. As an Indian.

But one thing: his son. These children. He didn't feel Indian toward *them*. He believed in family, like a Christian man, not a heathen. He stepped over the dead Indian to his boys. He'd save them, if he only could.

Merle's eyes were fixed, wide. They were not looking at him but beyond, over his shoulder. Tom turned to follow their stare.

Three more Indians stood on the ridge of the upper fall, watching them, rifles resting in the crooks of their arms. They began to approach slowly down the slope. It was too much, there was no more Tom could do. Three of them, and they'd seen him before he saw them.

Simply wait. It was almost a relief not to have to think anymore, simply wait to die. Perhaps they'd take the boys back after all. Back to Peasy.

He waited.

One Indian approached ahead of the others. He was of Tom's age, perhaps a little older, with a sharp, serious face and long hair down to his shoulders. He held Tom fixed in his gaze and drew a knife from his belt. He tested the blade with his thumb and then, still staring at Tom's face, squatted on his haunches. Only then did he look down at the big prone form of the Indian in the pelt.

He surveyed his face, then began taking the scalp. He looked up again at Tom.

"Je suis Tonti," he said. "Vous est Anglais?"

"American," Tom replied.

The Indian nodded as if he'd thought so all along. He laid his trophies carefully in a pouch suspended from a hide sash, then moved to the second corpse and started the business over again. "I hate les Anglais," he said as he worked. "I hate Iroquois. They kill French et Huron. Mon father sont Français. Maman, she was Huron."

He held out his arm toward Tom. "The man who kill my enemy est my friend," he said.

Tom clasped the bloody hand.

Tonti turned away to look at the boys. They were both still huddled in the bush, Ned in his groaning sleep, Merle shock-faced and frightened at what he'd just seen. Tonti bent over Ned, pinched and prodded him very much as he had the dead Iroquois, grasped one of the boy's legs and inspected his foot. The blood was blackening now, otherwise it looked as naked as the scalped corpses. Tonti clicked his tongue in disapproval and shook his head. Then he looked back at Tom. "Les Anglais."

"Yes."

He gestured to the other two Indians, who had been standing patiently to one side of the bodies. "My friends," he told Tom. Honehwah, Ongyata. The sons of the sister of my maman.' He pointed to Tom and then to himself. "My friends." Then he nodded his head at his cousins and they came forward. One took Ned under the shoulders, the other by the ankles, and very carefully they raised him. Merle scuttled over to Tom. "Now," Tonti said. "We go home. To my maison."

As they walked, the rain came down again. One of the Indians covered Ned with a blanket, which he'd had rolled up on his back. Merle huddled near Tom. They were walking upriver, away from the falls, toward higher ground. Tom thought: It can rain, I can climb, what does it matter? He no longer had a sense of time passing, or even of covering ground. The hills rose in huge ridges and peaks all around, too high for trees. The sky, also ridged and peaked, swept down toward them. The wind still blew from the north, stronger up here than in the valley, and the rain was icy. But it was another Tom who felt the rain and put one foot in front of another and listened to the hollowness of his belly. This Tom didn't even think. Merle held his hand as they walked, but Tom could have been holding the hand of his own pa when he was little, holding his hand and being deep in yourself, the hand taking you everywhere you needed to go, so all you needed to do was be a little boy and not do anything. Tonti led. This was the way to Tonti's house. Tom had seen Indians by the score, hundreds in the upriver settlements where he traded fur, but they were Indians who lived near to whites, drank rum by the bellyful, took Christian names like Joseph and William. They lived in lean-tos or tents, but not like Indians. They lived like whites when whites are poor. They were mean, like white men, not Indians, are mean.

He'd seen a proper Indian village also. Once, going through thick woods, with Mr. Beeley. It was strange territory to them, and they'd missed a meeting with a trapper. Got lost. They came upon huts, and a fire burning in a little clear patch. The men sat around, not saying anything, the women making things by the huts. Mr. Beeley and Tom walked through, not saying anything, not daring to move fast or to

run, but walking slowly, as if cold water were being poured
down their backs and they didn't want to move fast because
then they'd feel it, or then the Indians would feel *them*. But
the Indians saw them and took no notice. Only a dog yapped.
The squaws didn't even see them—they were busy at their
work. Mr. Beeley and Tom walked on, into the wood, not
daring to run, walking and walking.

The sky grew darker, either with darkness or rain. They
came to a long slope with the crinkle of a little valley in it, an
old streambed. Tonti led the way down the cut, around a
little ridge and to his hogan, perched in the lee of the ridge,
out of sight from everywhere except this part of the cut itself.
It was made of hide and bark stretched on frames, with piled
rocks shoving up the lower part. It was a long building
straddling the whole cut, with a bit of garden outside—a
pumpkin patch by the looks of it, because old orange rind
from last year's crop was piled nearby, everything else being
dull brown, gray, green, and the gray and purple of the sky.

Part of the roof of the hogan was left open so smoke could
come out, but now the rain beat down too heavily for it to
rise. The smoke puffed around the cut, dark and fumey, like
a great coiling snake in the rain. Tom looked at the hogan and
thought. The only thing like home here is the pumpkin peel.
Suddenly, in a high-pitched swooping voice, he laughed. It
was like someone else laughing.

Inside the hogan it was dim and warm. There was a single
long room crowded with Tonti's family—brothers, sisters,
uncles, aunts. Puppies and naked children darted about and
rolled on fur mats, some older girls were scraping fresh skins
with sharpened stones, and an old woman tended fatty meat
on the fire. The women were wearing sky-blue beads which
glowed in the shadowy room. Furs and hides were piled high
in a corner. On the walls and from the roof hung guns, bows,
spears, medicine shields, fetishes.

A young man brought some furs across for Ned and arranged them on the floor. Honehwah and Ongyata lowered
Ned onto them. Tom bolted across to his boy. Tonti once
more inspected Ned's feet, then took a spear from its place
on the wall of the hogan. He squatted, feeling the flat surface
of its blade with his fingers. Then he caught Tom's eye, and
looked at him long and knowingly. Tom understood.

Tonti gestured to the woman at the fire, and she brought

the meat she was cooking over to Tom. He tried to brush it away, but Tonti insisted, and Tom gulped it down. Ned was talking in his dream, delirious. Tom wiped his greasy fingers on his jacket and cradled him.

Tonti, still squatting, extended his spear by the handle and shoved the point into the hottest part of the hogan fire.

12

Indians sitting around the hogan spoke in their own tongue
and made signs. Over the fire one of the men mixed herbs in
a pot, and they smelled sharp against the fatty smell of the
meat. Tom's clothes were wet again as the fire warmed them,
and heavy. Merle sat in a corner among Indian children,
eating a piece of meat, nibbling it like a dog, careful of his
smashed mouth. Ned's head, in Tom's arms, glowed like a
coal. Ned was talking like the Indians, so that you knew he
was saying words but didn't know them, just a single word
sticking out here and there: *boat*, *beat daddymammy*, *please*,
and, over and over, *sausage*. When he said sausage, Tom
wanted to laugh as he had before when he came to the hogan.
And then cry. He had to hold back the noises. *Sausage* Ned
would say, then nonsense words, then *drum*, then the other
language, then *please*. Once he said *like the rain* over and
over again, and Tom listened to the rain pattering on the roof
of the hogan and remembered Ned lying by the cannon like a
bit of rag, forlorn in the rain; and then he was back further,
sailing into New York last July with the rain teeming down,
and Ned trying to shelter his bits of cooking sausage. He
looked at the hogan fire, at the boiling herbs and the spear.
Ned's fever speech frightened him, going every way, so you
didn't know what he'd say next, didn't knew what he was
saying now. He wanted to twist all the threads together one
at a time, put them in order, braid them into a rope; something for Ned to hold onto, something to tie himself to Ned.
He'd run with the dogs coming after him, dog and lordship
baying in his wake, while he was tied to Georgie Washington

so he couldn't break free, and here was Ned, his son, slipping away like a boat that had slipped its moorings.

Tom couldn't stand it. He began to talk himself, to tell Ned things. Try to catch his mind, hold it. See if he could make Ned listen. Tell him things he'd never told before. Let his own thoughts go to a new place. His past.

He remembered a cobbled street with straw packed between the cobbles. Bending down to it, trying to pick the straw out. He could remember his fingers feeling weak against the packed straw, but working away at it till it came, and the pleased feeling he had, seeing the neat earth around the cobble again.

There was an old man, a thin old man who came. Ma said, "This is your grandda." The old man's whiskery face kissed Tom. It smelled bad, like meat. Tom cried. Ma slapped him. She kept saying, "Your grandda," but Tom didn't know what *grandda* meant. He could still remember holding the word in his thoughts and looking at it all over, going from one end of it to the other and not knowing what it meant, even though he knew what it meant now. Going along the big, open sound, and then jumping off and landing on the little one at the end. He had to know what it meant because his ma would hit him, but he didn't; it was like an Indian word, only there weren't Indians then because that was in Scotland. The name came later, Scotland, after he'd gone. At the time it was just home. He got used to the old man, but not to the word. Ma said, "He's my dad," but Tom didn't understand that, since his ma was grown-up. The old man lived with them. He had been rich once. He tried to be kind. He sat in his big wooden chair with his hands behind his back, grinning. He was a very thin old man, with a hairy face, and Tom didn't like to get near him. The meat smell was around him like a cloud. He would say, "Pick an arm." At first Tom didn't know what he meant, but at last he pointed to one of the arms. Grandda brought it forth, and uncurled his hand. Clutched in it was some stuff from his supper, saved for Tom. It was turnip and some greens squashed into a ball and warm from his palm.

There were Jan and Harry, his sister and brother, smaller than him. Then some more big people came to live, but he knew them. They were uncles. They'd always been there, but now they lived with them all the time. It was one big room, like this hogan, only you could hear wheels clacking over the cobbles all the time. The uncles and the old man slept at one end of the room, and Tom and the other chiddlers and Ma slept at the other. And sometimes Dad, when he came. Usually he didn't come, but when he did he brought things. Tom could remember what his dad looked like. He was thin, round-shouldered, with dark eyes and long dark hair. Even though Tom was only a child, he knew his father was little. He was a quick-moving man, and when he was home the place was full of laughing and shouting. Tom couldn't remember his mother. He saw her every day but he couldn't remember her. Even when he looked at her, he couldn't remember her. She was his ma, she didn't have a look to her like a *person* would. He couldn't remember how she looked any more than you can remember what you look like yourself. Their home was full of people and he could remember some of their faces still.

Then they were all gone, except Ma and his brother and sister. Even the old man was gone. There were noises in the street, banging, and cobbles being thrown. He couldn't remember seeing them, couldn't remember even if they had a window or a space to see out, but he knew cobbles were being thrown, he could hear them as they fell. He must have been able to see the street because he knew there was furniture in it too, chairs and tables, and men hiding behind them. Nobody came back but Grandda. He was crying. He still smelled of meat, and changed the smell of the room when he came in. He said, "They've gone Dot." He always called Ma Dot, even though it wasn't her name. "They're tooken," he said, tears coming down his creased cheeks. "All tooken." Tom hated the old man. He watched his red lips going up and down under his whiskers. He thought that if the old man didn't say it, it wouldn't happen, and Dad and the uncles would walk in through the door again. But the old man wouldn't stop saying it. Tooken. Tooken. Tooken.

Then he recalled being in a street with Ma. There were soldiers standing about. Ma held onto him. One of the soldiers was holding him too. Ma put a hand over Tom's face so he couldn't see. He could hear though. He heard the soldier go haw-haw, laughing in a different way from anyone else Tom had ever heard laugh—through his nose, like when a pig grunts. The soldier took ma's hand away from his eyes and said, "Let him see his father." There were heads on spikes. The soldier said his father was there, but Tom only saw heads. Their tongues poked out as if they were thirsty. Some time after that his mother wasn't there anymore. She didn't say good-bye, and he always had a feeling deep inside that this meant she would come back someday, be with him again as she always had, and he would recognise her even though he couldn't remember her face.

Tom was taken in a cart to the water. He saw his sister Jan in another cart, just for a moment, her face down low because she was so small, peering between the waists of the other children. He didn't see his brother Harry, and he never saw Jan again. They could be alive somewhere, grown-up, but he knew they weren't. They had only been children. There'd been a baby too, but he only remembered the baby sometimes.

He was loaded on to a ship called the *Butterpot*, like a ship in a story. That's what the children said it was called anyway. It was really called something foreign. They were packed in like herring in a dark hold. The children said the English paid for them to go. The children always seemed to know more than him. All his life Tom noticed other people always seemed to know more about what was happening than he did, even though it was new and strange for them too. As a result he was a careful man. Even then he wondered why the English paid, if they'd killed his father. Some of the others said it was so they wouldn't fight the English like their dads had done, but Tom knew that couldn't be the reason, because they were too small to fight. Some said it was so the English could take their homes and all their things, but they had them already, and all Tom's family's things had been put in the street during the fighting. The big chair that Grandda sat in had gone. Then they said they were going to feed the cannon balls, but there were cannon balls in Scotland, there was no need to go all this way.

The hold soon stank. Not like the smell of his grandda. It was a smell hard and dense as cheese. They were fed once a day. Biscuit. Hard bread. Sometimes crumbly meat that tasted of dust. Sometimes little blocks of salted fish, chewy like strips of leather. And given watery beer to drink. The boat rocked sharply, all the sharper because you couldn't see the ocean. Some of the children began to die. Sailors would come down and weed out the dead ones and the near dead ones and take them above decks to be thrown into the sea, like in the prison ships the British had at New York. Tom didn't die. He wasn't even sick. After a while he noticed that the sound ones like himself were given a little more to eat and drink than the others. Sometimes when it rained, sailors came and told them to take off all of their clothes, and then they were herded up onto the deck to stand in the rain and be washed.

Only years later did Tom find out what had happened. There was a name for it. The Forty-five. It was a war, like the war now. You could live through something and not know what it was. Like being with his mother and not remembering what she looked like. Or the opposite. Like knowing the old man was Grandda, but not feeling that he was. Even when he knew it was the Forty-five, he still didn't know what that was. He thought forty-five people must have been killed, but he knew it was many more than that. Many many more. It seemed like everybody. For him it was. When other people had a war, your family all died. That was what he'd learned. It was more years before he learned that Forty-five was the Year of Our Lord.

He didn't tell all this to Ned. He couldn't. The memories lay underneath the words he used, but he'd never even used the words before, so he felt as if the words were doors he was opening to let the memories out to go off into the air and disappear, like dreams do. He didn't care. If his memories died, perhaps Ned would live. Perhaps his words would give Ned new thoughts, and take him away from the beating where his body had got stuck.

As Tom spoke the words he felt they carried the weight of all his life, as a boat carries its cargo: "My folk was killed in a war. In Scotland. The Forty-five. They sent the boys of the killed people over to here, to the Colonies, to be indentured. They was sellin' us like slaves."

Tom wasn't ill till they saw land. Seeing it square and blue on the horizon one day when they'd been sent up for the rain, he suddenly thought how all the sea in between was thickly, greenly moving, and he was sick. But he was not sick of fever like the other children had been, and his teeth didn't fall out, so when they arrived in harbor he was sent along up the docks with the strongest boys.

There he was indentured to Mr. Beeley, who traded along the Hudson River, buying fur and skins up in Albany and selling them back down in New York. He was a cockneyman and spoke like the English. He didn't laugh like them, though. He didn't laugh much at all, at least in the first years. He was a fierce man, red-faced with drink. He said to Tom, "This is your load. You set them traps, you little dorkle, you learn to scrape hides, and you save my scalp from Injuns if the time comes." They were the Indian years up the river. Always coming down the bank and hollering, and waving their tomahawks as you sailed past—you didn't know whether they wanted your attention to sell you something or to take your scalp off. "Your own scalp," Mr. Beeley said, "you can save after you saved mine. You're my indenture, so my scalp comes first."

Most of the trading wasn't done with the Indians, but with the upriver traders. The Indians killed the animals, sold the hides to the upriver trader, and the upriver trader sold them to Mr. Beeley and the other downriver traders, who sold them to the New York traders, who sold them to the shippers. Every hide was traded over and over. When he saw the likes of the Sugar King and Mr. Corty, Tom wasn't surprised, because for everything in this country—like a beaver or a martin or a wild dog even—there was six or ten trades, many more trades than things, so that the most of everything was the business of it. Even war. The first thing they wanted in war was your boat and your property. Your life they wanted later.

Mr. Beeley taught him the river and the traders. He taught him scraping. He taught him a bit about the Indians, but he kept clear as best he could of them. The Indians were trouble. "I don't need to buy trouble," he said. "I can make myself trouble for free. I bought trouble when I bought you." After a long long time Tom came to understand that Mr. Beeley didn't mean everything he said. It was as if he was laughing all the time without laughing. If he was fierce he was saying, Look at me, Mr. Beeley, being fierce. If he was quiet he would be saying, This life is too rough and short to be worth saying anything about. If he was sad, he was drunk. When Tom discovered that Mr. Beeley was gentle underneath his fierceness, he felt he'd lived the last years wrong, because all along he'd liked him when he thought he was hating him. All along they were friends when he thought they were enemies. One day Mr. Beeley was scalped, which he would have thought was a good joke since he was always frightened of Indians and kept clear of them; except that he was a timid man, afraid of pain and dying.

Tom was fifteen. The Indians scalped Mr. Beeley because two of them had died from drinking rum they'd got from a trader who'd been supplied it by Mr. Beeley in exchange for furs. The dead Indians must have been unlucky because Mr. Beeley had drunk plenty of rum on the way upriver and nothing had happened to him, except he'd gotten drunk. Perhaps Mr. Beeley had been lucky.

"Mr. Beeley took me on, and we traded furs. He got scalped by Indians." Tom had lowered his voice, in case the Hurons thought the information was disagreeable. "I went down the river by myself. I met your ma on the river."

Ned was soaking. Inside too, you could hear his lungs bubbling. His face was blurred as his thoughts.

"Pa?" he whispered.

"I'm here, Ned."

Like a little boy about to cry, he said, "I got a terrible dream."

"It's just a dream, Ned."

"I'm drownin', Pa."

"Hold me hands, Ned, like them's rope. Hold on ta me words, them's your net. No, I won't let you sink. Ned, you hear me?"

"Yes, Pa."

Tom's arms were tight around Ned, his cheeks next to his. If you got so near, nothing could make him go far away. He was all Tom had left. Everybody Tom knew had left him and gone off to die. Tonti took the spear from the fire. It glowed pale pink. He held it close to his face, inspecting it. He blew on it a little.

"D'ya remember your ma, Ned?"

"Yes."

"What d'ya remember?"

"She smelled warm . . . and the way she rocked me." Ned's face looked like a face underwater, not quite clear, the features drifting. His eyes were closed.

"Was fever took her, Ned," Tom said hoarsely. He wanted Ned to know. Fever was the enemy. You had to fight it. "Took everyone. Indians by the thousands. Your sister Nell. James, your brother. D'ya remember them, Ned?"

"I do, Pa."

Tonti raised one of Ned's feet by the ankle, inspecting the sole narrowly, frowning.

"I loved your ma," Tom said. "And them babes. I swore I'd keep ya safe, Ned, no matter what."

Tonti pressed the spear point to Ned's foot. For a moment Ned didn't seem to notice it, as if he'd felt all the pain he could already and there was no room for any more. And then, almost to Tom's relief, his face seemed to shrink, and twisted with pain. Tonti placed the spear against his other foot.

"Oh, Pa," Ned said, not loudly, as if to say, This is so bad I can't tell you about it. He was reared up, with his head flung back and his spine arched. He relaxed again against Tom's arm, and Tom lowered him back to the mat. He'd gone white, as if he were painted, and his breathing was shallow.

"Hold on, Ned," Tom said, pressing his face up against Ned's and kissing him on the cheek as he spoke. "Pray for your brothers and sisters."

Tonti placed the spear back in the fire.

"Talk to me, Ned. Do you remember the farm? The farm we got for ourselves?"

Ned spoke from the bottom of the sea. "Sometimes before dawn . . . I see it. I'm asleep, but I ain't. I look across, and there's Ma, holding the baby."

"Ya see her?"

"Yes, Pa."

"What's she do, Ned?"

"She smiles at me, like she knows something I don't know."

"When they burned up," Tom said, "I walked in the woods all night. If I stopped, I'd die."

Tonti took the spear out of the fire again.

Tom said, "I lost my ma when I was a little boy in Scotland. I saw the head of my pa on a stake. I never saw my ma no more. But I still got her. She's still here. Same way your ma is. In your net. Bearing ya up. She's going to carry ya across."

Ned was murmuring to himself. It sounded like a poem. "If I had land, I'd make a farm. If I had a wife, I'd love her. If I had a horse, I'd ride far as I could see." Then, as if he'd suddenly woken up, he said quite loudly and firmly: "I'd need a good dog and a rifle, Pa, and I won't let no dick-headed Tory kick me around."

Tonti took his feet; one, then the other. This time Ned said nothing, but writhed in Tom's arms, his eyes tightly shut. Tom could feel him slipping away. Tom held him with all his strength, as if you could hold someone away from dying. Tonti stepped over to the fire, took the pot, put two fingers into it and smeared the herb paste over the soles of Ned's feet.

Ned spoke faintly. "It was you saved me, Pa?"

"It was, Ned."

"Pa? I thought you was a coward."

"Did ya, Ned?"

"But you ain't, Pa."

"I was, Ned." He looked into the fire. The dim forms of the Indians sitting beyond it looked as if they were sitting in judgment on him. "Was me got you into this mess. Now what the hell did I do that for, Ned?"

"Pa?"

"Needin' ya, Ned. Needin' to hold on to ya, that's what, Ned. You're my son, what's all I got."

"Take me away, Pa. Take me away." He was still in the British camp.

"I will, Ned. I promise. I'm here for ya, Ned."

"Pa."

"I'm here, don't ya fall away."

He could feel, with his hands, Ned's body poised over a drop, pulling down, ready to go. His own fingers gripped the boy's arms till they hurt with the pressure. "Don't sink. Don't drown, Ned. Damn ya, no!" Clawing him back.

"Pa."

"Feel me, Ned. Feel me rocking ya. Like whenst ya was my baby."

Tom pulled Ned around to his chest and began rocking clumsily, jerking backward and forward. Ned opened his eyes a fraction, then shut them tight immediately, as if he couldn't bear the world. His heart was in another place.

He rocked. Water flowed. Rocking in the wind. Water wind. There was blue. He'd seen blue. Opened his eyes, he'd seen blue. Blue as eyes, below the dark eyes of the Indian girl. A mild blue water wind, blue as Indian beads. A breeze above blue water, across blue sky, so the sky gently moved, blue folding into blue. Their boat moved through purity. As if he'd died. Perhaps he and Pa had died and were floating down the sky. The British had cast them adrift. Or the Indians.

"We on the river?" Ned asked.

"Oh, Ned."

"Can feel it movin'."

"It's the wind."

Blue wind. As a bead. His father could see the wind. He

was here, on the boat. Blue beneath blue in a world that was freshly begun. Fresh wind."

"Where're we going, Pa?"

"Somewhere new."

Yes, he was here on the boat. Sailing to a new world. Once in New York one afternoon he'd seen a man hanged. The man had cut the handles of water buckets while the city burned. Burned like feet burn. The neck molded to the noose, the head lolling the way it had to go, the legs drifting in the wind. Ned could feel exactly what it was like when you were hanged. He felt the rope around his neck, rope his father had twisted. When he'd finished watching and was walking off, he suddenly felt he'd been hanged himself. How did he know it wasn't him? He knew the authority of the rope, the endless gap between feet and ground. He would have cut those handles off himself if he'd been there, him and Dick and the other Mohawks. So he was dead. So to be dead was just turning a corner in being alive. There was New York, the same as before, the buildings burned or falling apart, the harbor full of British ships, the streets full of British soldiers, mud and manure on the cobbles. He went back to the rope-walk. His father didn't know. He behaved as normal. He was warping a hawser, as usual. Ned had died all by himself.

But this time Pa was dead too. He could feel the rocking of the water, the blue wind. He understood they were sailing somewhere new. His face was beside Ned's face.

"What's it like, Pa?"

"Like nowhere else."

"Tell me."

Ned's voice was remote but at peace. And he was listening to Tom. Tell me, he said. He wasn't off by himself. He was here in the hogan, listening, even if his voice sounded far. Tom had to give him something he could listen to, something on which he could hang.

"We goin to find us a place, Ned. Some place where nobody's gonna treat us like no dogs in the dirt. Some place."

He kissed Ned, caressed his cheek, reminded him of his closeness to that place.

"Where I could shake hands with some fella and he's no better'n me." As he said it, he thought suddenly of Daisy, the merchant's daughter. Taking his boat. Kissing in that cornfield. Her telling him about Ned being taken. That's where they had to go. A place where Daisy was no better than him. "Any fella. He'd be like my brother, and me his."

Now he thought of his brother who had gone so long ago that he'd hardly been alive. He was just a name and a few dim pictures inside Tom's mind, little bare-arsed boy crawling over a dirt floor, and the hands of their mother sweeping him up. That was nearly all there was of a whole life. Long dead hands lifting a long dead baby in a long ago room. His brother was gone, and his sister, and his father, and his mother. He knew as he thought this that he would never again imagine her coming back, because she hadn't said goodbye. He would never again have that odd restless, tense feeling that she was an unfinished matter in his life and that across some ocean, in some country, she was alive. And Mr. Beeley was gone too. And his wife and his own babies. Except Ned.

His life was a country of dead people. And now it was time to make a new country, with living people to be there alongside him and Ned.

"Where we could have a wife and babies, and they could all sleep safe through the night."

"Are we there, Pa?" Ned whispered. He was sleepy, slipping away but not down, not drowning.

"Almost, Ned," Tom said. He thought of the Liberty Woman, and Mr. Corty with his two-week war. Of the recruiting sergeant. Of Long Island and the chainshot snaking over the ground. Links of blood. The only links of blood were those between him and Ned; the only rope he'd ever twisted so it held for always was the rope that tied the two of them together.

He thought of the hunt with the blank doll, and Clowski being torn by the dogs. The lord with his laugh through the nose like a grunting pig. Of Sergeant-Major Peasy, and all the British in camp.

What a word was almost.

13

The hard wind was flecked with snow. The snow flew level, stinging when it struck your face. Valley Forge was not a valley nor, any longer, a forge, but a dismal bare plateau. It was early March 1778, and the main American army had been encamped here since December, three months after the British under General Howe had marched into Philadelphia.

Despite the loss of the home of the Continental Congress, 1777 had been a year of balanced fortunes in the war. Although Sergeant-Major Peasy and his detachment had joined a British encampment at Fort Lee, close to the New Jersey Palisades, the main thrust of the British advance had not been north, but south.

The bulk of the British army had spent the winter of 1776–7 in New York, and by the following spring the city and its environs had been stripped of provisions. Foragers had been sent out to New Jersey, and a series of vicious skirmishes with Washington's troops had taken place, until the British troops withdrew again and the waiting game continued.

Finally, on July 8th 1777, Howe loaded 18,000 troops onto his fleet in New York harbor. Even now the situation was not clarified, because Howe left the packed ships moored in the harbor for another two weeks and then spent most of the rest of the summer cruising in the Atlantic. He didn't land at Elke River in Maryland until late August. Washington began to bring his troops south to meet the British, who, after resting for a while to recover from their cramped, sweltering weeks at sea, in turn started to march north. The two armies met at Brandywine Creek.

British discipline and experience won the day, but didn't bring about the disintegration of the American forces which still blocked Howe's way into Philadelphia. A couple of weeks later, however, Howe succeeded in decoying Washington's army away from its defensive position, and on September 26th 1777, he occupied the city. A large body of British troops was bivouaced five miles to the north at Germantown, on the east side of the Schuykill River. On October 4th the Americans attacked them.

It was a foggy day, the American lines of communication failed, and once again the British won the engagement.

However, far to the north a different story was emerging. General Burgoyne, in command of the British troops in Canada, had persuaded the government in London to allow him to attack the rebellious colonies from the north and march down the Hudson. He set out in June, and by early July had taken Fort Ticonderoga at the head of Lake George. As the British offensive from New York had been directed at Philadelphia, not north to support the incursion from Canada, the northern department of the American army under its new commander, General Horatio Gates, and his brilliant subordinate Benedict Arnold, was maneuvering confidently and gaining support from the local populace. In early October, after a stalemated battle at Bemis Heights, Burgoyne found he could advance no farther, and on October 17th the British surrendered at Saratoga.

But if the American triumph at Saratoga could be seen as a counterbalance to the loss of Philadelphia, there was to be no equivalent of Valley Forge, ever. It was a bare piece of land about twenty miles from Philadelphia, by the Schuykill River. The area was sparsely populated, and the autumn battles had deprived what farms there were of their stock. The soldiers lived in tents until they had felled trees and built themselves comfortless huts. They had no soap—not that it made much difference, according to George Washington, because they only had one shirt each in any case, so had to wear it dirty. All through the winter the American troops in the camp were aware of the British eating good beef and butter in Philadelphia, attending balls and parties while they ate thin soup full of leaves and dirt, and the dreaded flour-and-water firecake.

Albigence Waldo, one of the army's surgeons, kept note of the menu: "What have you for dinner, boys?"

"Nothing but firecake and water, sir."

"Gentlemen, the supper is ready."

"What is your supper, lads?"

"Firecake and water, sir."

"What have you got for breakfast, lads?"

"Firecake and water, sir."

"The Lord send that our Commissary of Purchases may live on firecake and water till their glutted guts are turned to pasteboard."

Two thousand American soldiers died during the winter at Valley Forge, and many deserted. There may not have been a valley, nor a forge, but the two words developed meanings of their own; hunger, cold, suffering.

Two carts approached the camp along a dirt track. Though the wind was bone cold and the snow hit you level, it was warm enough for mud, a greasy inch or two, with ice like iron beneath it. The carts slewed and rocked as they galloped. Daisy, her face weathered from wind and a year of war, drove the first cart, a white flag on a broom stick stuck beside her. She was wearing a blue swallowtailed coat with brass buttons, both manly and nautical, strange on her. Beside her sat Cuffy. She had also aged in a year and also wore a man's jerkin, a plain brown broadcloth. The cart was loaded, the goods protected from the weather by a canvas sheet. The cart behind was similar and also driven by two women: Carrie, blond hair springing from her cap, the reins in her hands; and Bella, in her teens, with quick, dark, wary eyes in an intent face. All four looked frozen, underfed, frantic with haste, yet merry.

Sharpened stakes bristled along the perimeter of the camp, the great shafts probing outward at whoever might be insane enough to want to get in. Daisy knew from previous experience that it would be more appropriate to point them the other way. If soldiers left the camp, it would be to desert, to get shot by the British, or to plunder the few wretched inhabitants of the area who had anything at all worth plundering or that might seem worth plundering when you were starved. As she reached the gates, she fumbled for the pass that allowed her to go in and out, but the guards recognized her and greeted her loudly and enthusiastically, waving them in. And as they trundled through the camp over churned earth, soldiers cheered. The merchant's daughter was bringing merchandise.

She waved, enjoying their pleasure and approval and above all, the sense of comradeship. But at the same time she felt a twinge of guilt. They were in such need and so easily pleased by the two small wagons. The supplies were a drop in the ocean.

Sergeant Malin grabbed the traces and brought the horses around. He was gruff, unsurprised, steady. Daisy dug a small pouch from the pocket of her jacket.

"Brought your tobacco," she said, passing it to him. "Best Virginia."

"Thought you would," Malin replied in his terse way. "What you bring this time?"

Daisy rattled it out. It didn't take long. "Five pigs. Four sheep. Three barrels of fish. As much cheese as we could lay hands on. And there's sour grass, camomile, and mistletoe for the medicine chest." She thought of some of her father's inventories, all the goods he must have supplied the British with in the last year. Her cartload would hardly have filled the larder at home.

"Get them goods unloaded," Malin called out. Soldiers, only too eager, ran to the carts, stripped back the covers, and began. Daisy noticed how their coats seemed too big for them—they'd got so thin. You'd think they were boys, except their faces were old. Perhaps they *were* boys. "Captain Cray," Malin yelled. "Here's a couple of wagons."

Just beyond the open patch of mire where the wagons had pulled up, was a large open-sided hut. Inside, even from here, you could see men on litters scattered about by the open, smoky fire like bales of cordwood. Cray stepped wearily between them and came out hunched against the cold. He nodded briefly at Daisy and the others, then inspected the carts with what would have been interest if his fatigue could have made way for it; businesslike attention anyway.

"I'll need you and your carts," he said. "I've got sick men to be taken to the hospital at Yellow Springs."

Daisy remembered how another surgeon, Dr. Sloan, had once regarded her: "This is no place for you. Go home to your mother and sisters." Suddenly she had a feeling of self-disgust. Was this why she had busied herself over the last year? In order to convince herself and others that she was grown-up? Even worse, in order to be treated as if she were a man? She glanced down at her swallowtailed jacket and thought of all the froth and foolery she and her sisters had worn at home. Was this all the war meant to her, an opportunity to drive a cart of provisions with dash and swagger, pleading, bargaining, issuing receipts and promissory notes, a girl playing at being a merchant as she had once played with her doll's house? What an unnatural and selfish way that would be to treat a great cause. Was she unnatural? Here she was, driving side by side with a black slave as if they were of the same race and class, sharing quarters with her, eating, talking, swapping thoughts with her. That had nothing to do with independence; indeed, they said that George Washington kept slaves, and Thomas Jefferson, and many others of the great southern gentlemen who had done so much to promote the cause. Perhaps she suffered from some perverse and destructive urge to abandon the good things that had been showered on her from her birth. She knew that's how her family must see her—as a mad, petulant, willful girl, a girl who bit the hand that fed her.

Suddenly she thought of that absurd evening when Martha entertained the two British gentry, or rather, when she had endeavored to offer up her two daughters to them. How she, Daisy, had behaved toward Lord Hampton! Call that biting the hand that fed you! Martha had been beside herself with rage as she saw her plans collapse with the slow collapse of Lord Hampton's person around its anguished pivot. She could laugh with glee at the thought of it even now, although it seemed like another time, another country from these gray wastes of Valley Forge. Absurd and trifling. And yet . . . and yet, perhaps one could say that the young lady who comported herself thus in relation to his lordship's so-called manly part was in character not dissimilar from the girl who stood here in slush and mud, proud to wear a battered man's jacket, pleased to be treated as a colleague by Mr. Cray, happy to be recognized as a comrade by these thousands of soldiers in Valley Forge.

And only as a comrade. There was, for her, no nobler part to play. But perhaps this reflected some deficiency in her own nature? Certainly these men were hungry with more than a hunger for food, but she had found no difficulty in ensuring that they treated her simply as one of themselves. Was that natural? Had Dr. Sloan been right after all when he told her she ought to return to her mother and sisters, take her rightful place among the other petticoats in the parlour and the drawing room?

No, surely not. She remembered the Liberty Woman in New York. It was a matter of being *for* a cause, not *of* a sex. Her mother and sisters could offer her no comfort, because they sided with the British. As did her father. Or rather, he sided with anyone who would give him good business. There was no home for her there. And in any case she was not immune to emotions and sensations natural to one of her sex. A year and a half ago she had given her heart to the cause and then to a man. There was no contradiction between the two. And when she had struck the sentinel on the wharfside while the little boat floated out into the middle of the river, she was striking a blow for Tom at the same moment as she struck one for America. The motives were bound up inextricably within her breast.

To clear her mind of this torrent of reminiscence and self-questioning, she went over to the hospital shed and peered inside. The faces of the men were sallow, exhausted. They looked back silently at her. She hurried back to the wagon and whispered confidentially to Malin, "Sergeant, those men are dying."

"Yes, ma'am," Malin replied in his abrupt way. "That's why they must go."

"Get them loaded now, Sergeant," the surgeon said. The goods Daisy had brought had already been dumped on the ground and were being sorted into heaps by the soldiers.

"Yes, sir," Malin said. He called out orders, and soldiers went into the shed to begin the loading of the men on litters.

Women helped carry their men. One of them seemed familiar. She was wearing a long soldier's jacket, had a baby in a pouch on her back, Indian style, and was pregnant with another. She looked at Daisy with exactly the expression of half recognition that Daisy must have shown her. Then her faced cleared.

"I know you," she said in a strong Irish accent. "Miss New York. So you've come to the war."

"I remember you too." It was the girl who had tried to board the transport to Long Island, had promised to meet her lad in the hay, and *had* met him in the wheat, back on Manhattan Island. "You had a fella."

"Bill was killed at Fort Washington." Her features, designed to be plump and jolly, were strained and sad as Abby remembered her loss.

"Is that his son?" Daisy asked quietly.

"Yes." She glanced back at the hospital shed, at the men on litters. "This one's Jack's," she said, patting her belly, her voice trembling. She went back in to her man.

There were some stalls nearby, narrow planks on trestles, a strange sort of market where there was hardly anything for sale and almost no money to buy. A market in mime. But there was business at the grog bench. A soldier stood, having his jug filled with rum. As with Abby, there was something familiar about him. He was quite tall, wearing a battered blue army jacket and carrying a rifle decorated in the Indian fashion, with silver studs and a feathered lanyard around the butt. An Indian was standing beside him and they were talking familiarly. No, she didn't recognize him after all. The meeting with Abby had made her feel the camp must be full of her acquaintances, just as once she had known all the wealthy set of New York.

Then the soldier glanced across, and noticed her, "Daisy?" he called.

She looked at the lean, hard, young face. It seemed an exact mixture of the familiar and strange.

"Daisy," he called again, and hurried toward her. He was limping a little. "It's me. Ned."

Her heart missed a beat. Surely not. "Ned?" she asked, hardly daring to believe it.

He caught her confusion and looked down at his rifle, at the Indian leggings beneath his jacket. "I'm a scout," he said proudly.

Suddenly, in his boyish pride, she caught sight of the child of a year ago. She ran forward and flung her arms around him. He hugged her as tightly.

"Oh, Daisy," he said.

"You're safe," she whispered. Then she held him at arm's length and laughed. "You've grown," she said. "You've got a rifle. Look at you. Ned, oh, just look at you." He looked back, pleased. A little embarrassment crept in as the first shock of the meeting subsided; and then, for Daisy, fear. She looked down at the ground, hardly daring to ask.

"Is your pa all right?" she finally said, then bravely looked him in the face.

He nodded, his eyes bright with pleasure.

She felt herself go scarlet. "Take me to him, Ned," she asked, her voice uncertain, wavering.

Ned took her arm and led her across to a nearby hut. There was a crudely painted notice tacked to the log wall: 4th Tracking Troop. Ned pushed the skin door aside and held it for Daisy. She stepped inside.

It was a dim room, no windows, lit only by a brazier in the center. There were animal skins heaped on the floor and tacked to the walls. Two Indians sat by the brazier, one of them pouring melted lead from a long-handled ladle into a musket-ball mold. No, she realized, he wasn't an Indian. He was wearing a tassled hunting jacket, leggings, and boots, like a hunter rather than a soldier, and he was a white man. He looked up straight into her eyes when he'd finished pouring.

Tom.

He jumped as he saw her, like a man who'd seen a ghost. His eyes stared fixedly at her, uncomprehendingly.

"Daisy," he said, but not by way of greeting, nor by way of a question. It was simply the only word he could think of for what he saw.

For a moment Tom thought he must be dead. Not that Daisy looked like an angel in her man's jacket and wet skirts, just that she was there at all. Being dead was the only place he could think of where they might meet. Or in a dream. Across the shimmer of the fire and the smoke, it was like seeing a figure in a cloud or a mist.

She moved toward him. "It's me, Tom," she said. It was her voice.

He stumbled to his feet. "Are ya smoke or real?" he asked.

She almost laughed, but her eyes were too intent. She came nearer, and as when the eyes come into focus, he saw her sharply. Then they were in each other's arms and she was crying and laughing against his neck. At last they let go.

"I prayed for you, Tom," she said. "So much."

"You're thin," he said.

She just stood, laughing at him, her eyes searching. Ned slipped out of the hut.

"Do ya want some soup?" Tom asked. There was a pot on the brazier. Soup and musket balls. He poured some for her into a bowl. "It's thin," he said, passing it to her. "I got salt."

"You've got salt?"

"Yeah." He sprinkled some in her bowl.

She put it to her lips. "It's good," she said. She surveyed him yet again. "You're an Indian now," she added. Tonti squatted by the fire, watching the flames and thinking his own thoughts.

"I'm a scout. In the army."

"I never thought I'd see you again."

"Tell me, Daisy, what happened to you?"

Daisy looked down at her bowl, then back at him. He could see there was so much to tell.

"Well," she said, "Cuffy and I, we left New York. We fled to Philadelphia, where there were partisans. We smuggled— food, muskets, flints. And I learned to sail."

"Did you?"

"Yes. Up the Chesapeake."

So many things had happened, underneath her words. Tom could see it from the look in her face as she spoke. Not that she was trying to hide things, keep secrets from him, but that there weren't enough words to say it all. Just as he couldn't tell her all that had happened to him, and to Ned.

"I can see ya wearing a captain's coat," he said.

"That's Captain Stanhope's," Daisy replied, glancing down at it then back at him, her eyes amused. "He gave it to me. He taught me to sail, in a skipjack on the Chesapeake. We sailed and smuggled."

"You sailed together, you and this Captain Stanhope?"

"We did, Tom."

They looked at each other in silence.

"Look at my hands," she said. She put the soup bowl down and showed him. As if this were a sign of intimacy, Tonti slowly rose to his feet and left. "See how rough they got?"

Tom inspected them carefully. "Lot a calluses on them," he said.

"That's from the ropes."

At the word he looked her straight in the eyes. She looked straight back. "From sailing," she explained. "I can sail any- where with you now, Tom."

"Could ya, Daisy?"

"Yes. I could."

Ned stood outside the hut. The wind was still cold and searching. He hugged himself and stamped his feet. The

Indians had a little fire out here and were roasting a pumpkin. He stood as near it as he could, but it only warmed his feet. After a few minutes Tonti came out and divided the pumpkin up. He gave Ned a piece, and he ate the hot, sweet watery stuff greedily. Where the pumpkin had come from he didn't even ask. The Indians seemed to be able to spirit them out of nowhere.

Across the way, outside the hospital hut, the sick men were being made as comfortable as possible on the carts. Then girls climbed up to the driving boards. They shook the traces and the carts inched slowly forward, waddling through the mud with their heavy loads. Women and other soldiers walked near them, with the surgeon, Cray, trotting on his horse alongside. Malin was by the lead wagon, while Cuffy drove. Carrie was driving the second, with a new girl sitting with her and Bella walking alongside.

Ned called in through the gap in the doorway, "Pa, wagons coming."

After a few moments Tom and Daisy came out, looking foolish. Ned felt almost as though he were the father and his father the son. And Daisy was nearer his own age than Tom's. He felt his first stirrings of jealousy. Nobody had ever possessed anything he wanted before. It wasn't that he'd never wanted anything, but that he'd never been near people who *had* anything. It wasn't a matter of Daisy herself, but of the conspiratorial intimacy she shared with Tom. For the last year he and his father had hardly been out of each other's company for a moment.

Ned remembered nothing after being tied to the cannon, except twisting his head up and seeing Peasy's face—not angry, not cruel, just blank, with the whip hissing past it. The next face he'd seen was Pa's coming through layers of pain, like the sun through clouds. Now he watched him as he smiled with the same warmth upon Daisy.

Tom helped Daisy up onto her seat beside Cuffy. Then Ned realized that the girl who had been walking beside the second cart was in front of him. She looked directly at him, her eyes deep and dark, her face narrow, pure, sharp-witted. She looked as if she were about to laugh, but didn't. She told him her name was Bella. The carts began to move off. She continued to walk beside the second one, and Ned hurried along with her. His father continued beside Daisy's.

"My father's Israel Davis," Bella said. "The gunner. I'm his daughter."

Ned glanced across at her to see if this was some kind of strange joke, but it wasn't. The laughter was still near her face, but it wasn't that kind of laughter. "I came in the wagon," she added. "I came to be by him."

"Pleased to meet you," Ned said.

"You got a limp."

"It's nothing."

"Were ya wounded?"

"I was captured. My pa saved me."

"I'm glad."

"Are ya?" Ned asked, genuinely surprised.

"Of course. If you weren't saved, I'd never have met you, Mr. Dobb."

They were at the gate. The women showed their passes, and the carts trundled out on to the muddy road. Ned and Bella watched them go. He glanced at her again and thought, How does she know my name? And then, with a thumping of his heart, he answered his own question: She musta asked.

Tom ran beside Daisy's cart as it gained speed down the muddy track. She looked down at him, laughing, and urged the horses on.

"Ya going to sneak back into Philadelphia?" he panted out.

"I don't know," she replied. "Where are you going?"

"I'm gonna scout here rest of the winter. After, I don't know. Indians wanna go back to their families. But I don't know."

The cart began to move away from him. She was going, and he had an urgent, panicky feeling that there was something important they should have said. He called out the first thing that came into his head: "This captain . . . Captain Stanhope. Is he a good sailor?"

"Yes, he is," Daisy called back.

"Is he at Philadelphia now?"

"No."

She was getting far away now. He called at the top of his voice: "Do ya love him?"

Her voice came back, faint on the wind: "No. only you, Tom Dobb. Only you."

The carts wound on over the bleak plain. Tom stood panting, watching them dwindle under the garish winter sky. It began to thunder.

No.

It was hooves, horses, breaking out from behind a low ridge perhaps half a mile off. Redcoats. Drawn sabers. British dragoons, twenty or thirty of them charging the carts. Tom began to run.

He ran, slipping in the mud, weeping as he ran, running fast, faster than he'd ever run, even on the hunt, weeping with fury at being so far off, so impossibly far. The carts slewed to the right, trying to turn back, but they were heavy and cumbersome compared with the mounted soldiers. The second one turned too sharply and toppled over. Daisy's continued across the plain, the dragoons in pursuit. There was the dull crackling of musket fire from Valley Forge behind him, impotent at this range.

Daisy felt, with an intense bitterness that came with the approach of death, no noble, uplifting sentiments, no peace and resignation, but a burning outrage that events should have turned upon her in this way. She thought, Here you are, Daisy McConnahay, where you always wanted to be—in the thick of battle, with swords and muskets all around you. A spoiled girl's dream.

She twisted around. Carrie's cart had gone over and there was a cluster of redcoats around it like flies around meat, stabbing down at the people on the ground. The remainder of the soldiers were right behind her.

In a moment Daisy would die and the adventure would come to its end.

Then beside her a narrow, cruel, silly face called her name. "Daisy McConnahay!" it shouted. At first she thought she must be thinking it herself. Then she realized she wasn't. "Daisy McConnahay! You are a traitor!"

It was Lord Hampton.

Her bitterness crystallized into a dark merriment. She knew what she had betrayed as far as his lordship was concerned. Behind her the sick cried out, slithered and struggled as they died in the mud. The thin blade of Hampton's sword swept toward her face.

*   *   *

Tom saw her struck and collapse on the driving board. The cart skidded wildly, out of control. Bodies were spilling from the rear. Cuffy was bending over Daisy, and he could make out sketchy screams and the thin haw-hawing of the British officers. Dragoons grabbed the traces and the cart and red-coats swept off toward the horizon. Tom could run no more. He stood in the distance, unable to help, unable even to imagine what had happened to Daisy.

It was only a small ambush. One of thousands. A minor skirmish. The firing from Valley Forge died away.

14

As the spring went on, easing the cold, Valley Forge underwent unexpected changes. For one, the appointment of Nathanael Greene to be in charge of the quartermaster's department transformed the system of obtaining supplies and forage, and both troops and horses saw the threat of starvation fade away. For another, morale and military discipline improved after a rumbunctious Prussian appeared at the camp in late February. He called himself Frederick William Augustus Henry Ferdinand, Baron von Steuben, although in fact he was Captain William Steuben, a soldier of fortune who had once served under Frederick the Great and who had transformed his limited experience into a distinguished career as a lieutenant general, quartermaster general, and Frederick's own aide-de-camp.

Despite his zest for telling tall tales about himself, Von Steuben knew only one word of English: goddamn. Nevertheless he could swear profusely in German and French, a feat that rapidly won the respect and affection of the soldiers at Valley Forge. Shocked at the indiscipline of the American troops, he wrote them a drill book, which was translated into English by his seventeen-year-old secretary, Pierre Duponceau. Then Washington gave him the opportunity of drilling a model company at Valley Forge as an example to the rest, and Von Steuben—one of those strange charlatans who somehow contrives to be the real thing—set about his work with gusto. Captain Ben Walker stood beside him on the parade ground, translating his French and German invective into English profanity. The men immediately developed the amused

148

affection for him that soldiers anywhere in the world will feel for an extrovert, hard-swearing drill master.

At the same time, Steuben was aware that the soldiers under his command were Americans, not Prussians, and that they had to be disciplined differently. As he wrote to a colleague in Europe, "You say to your soldier, 'Do this,' and he doeth it, but I am obliged to say, 'This is the reason why you ought to do that,' and he does it."

The Americans, however demoralized and uncertain they might be, were fighting this war for themselves; and now they set about learning the art of it. A Hessian officer fighting with the British was to complain that whenever an American knapsack fell into his hands, it proved to contain among its wretched shirts and torn breeches a copy of *The Instructions of the King of Prussia to his Generals*, and similar works. "This was a true indication that the officers of this army studied at the art of war while in camp, which was not the case with the opponents of the Americans, whose portmanteaux were rather filled with bags of hair powder, boxes of sweet-smelling pomatum, cards (instead of maps), and then often, on top of all, novels or stage plays."

But by far the most important reason for the improvement in the fortunes and morale of the Americans had nothing whatsoever to do with the turn of the seasons, the increase in supplies, or the acquisition of military discipline; indeed, it had nothing to do with Valley Forge at all. It resulted from an event that took place three thousand miles away, in Paris.

In early 1778 the French decided to enter the war on the side of the Americans.

The rumor went around Valley Forge: the French have joined our cause. Vive Lafayette! The war will be over in two weeks. The rumor reached Tom, taciturn and grim in his hut. It did not fill him with elation. It wasn't the first time he'd been told that the war would end in two weeks. And in any case, he felt differently about the war now. It was his war. He didn't want the French to fight it for him and he didn't want it to end quickly. He had battles of his own to fight.

Ned had been farther away, by the gates of the Forge when the attack took place, so he hadn't seen what had happened. It was like watching insects moving about on the blue, cold plain. But he had joined the detail that had collected the bodies of the sick men who'd spilled off the carts and of the two women who drove the second one—the one

Bella had come to Valley Forge upon. Daisy and Cuffy had been taken off by the British.

Bella was teaching him to read properly. He could struggle through bills and receipts, but she wanted him to read whole books. He would stare at the pages for hours, baffled how such little black marks could be living, breathing people and great doings in the world. That was how it had been to watch the ambush from all that distance away. He had seen it, and yet hadn't.

Ned watched his father cleaning his weapons, casting musket balls, or just sitting staring at the brazier for hour after hour, brooding. Hour after hour.

Tom was thinking of something that took the tiniest part of a moment. A sword had been uplifted and brought down. The whole ambush had only taken a few seconds, but Tom struggled to read the event as Ned struggled to read words. Tom's mind went through it over and over, walked all around it, inspected it from different positions, tried and tried to find something else in it, such as Daisy not being struck, or he, catching up with the cart, or the fusillade from Valley Forge striking home. But there was nothing there for his mind to feed on. He had to content himself with the faint hope that perhaps, perhaps, Daisy had lived, and that one day, from among all the people in all this continent of America, he would find her again.

Once Ned would have been jealous at the thought that there was room in his father's mind for only one person: Daisy McConnahay. But now Ned had a young lady of his own to think about. Tom still lived in a winter of his own as spring came to Valley Forge, but Ned found himself in an entirely new season.

Bella was quiet and droll. Her father, Israel Davis, was noisy and droll. He was a Jew, and Ned feared he wouldn't wish his daughter to consort with a Christian. But he needn't have worried. "My girl is a Jew," he told Ned, "and you seem to be some sort of redskin. A redskin with a game leg, to boot. Neither the one nor the other of you is ever going to eat off a china plate."

He told Ned stories about Bella's pluck in battle. At the Battle of Brandywine she had been reaching for a new cartridge, and as a result had placed one leg as far in advance of the other as it was possible to reach. At that moment a cannon shot from the British passed directly between her legs without doing her any harm apart from carrying away the lower part of her petticoat. She simply glanced down, said in her dry way that she was glad it hadn't gone any higher or it would have fetched away something else, and continued to load the cartridge.

"Valley Forge," Israel had told Ned, "is a strange place to make court, but it can be done here as well as anywhere else."

So Ned and Bella sat for hours in her father's hut, poring over reading books, hands intimately clasped—as Israel was quick to note—beneath the table. They walked together down the muddy pathways of the camp and Ned bought her small trinkets made by soldiers' wives and put up for sale in forlorn little heaps upon the boards of the market. They even found a small dell in a meadow to the south of the camp, where they could sit together when the warmer weather had dried out the ground, their conversation and embraces interrupted only by the occasional looming form of a horse in search of fresh grazing.

The events of early May set the seal on their happiness. On the first of the month General Washington officially communicated to his troops the news that the French had entered the war. A great *Feu de joie* was organized, a firework display in which cannon and musketry provided the explosions and flashing lights. The sounds boomed along the Schuykill River, and re-echoed from the surrounding hills.

A week later came news that Sir William Howe had resigned as commander in chief of the British Forces in the American colonies. From the beginning of the war it had been clear to both sides that he would have preferred conciliation to confrontation, and he'd been subjected to criticism from the British government for his failure to follow up his victories on the battlefield with sufficient expedition and ruthlessness. Certainly in his nine months in Philadelphia he'd not heard the sound of gunfire, unless the noise of the celebrations at Valley Forge had somehow reached his ears. His place was taken by Sir Henry Clinton, whose first order, received the day after he took command, was to evacuate Philadelphia, as Washington's spies reported back. There was no need for the Americans to fight; they simply had to wait and the city would be theirs again.

Sir Henry, furious at having to depart, held out as long as he could. Finally though, by mid-June, his time ran out. He loaded his sick onto transport ships anchored in the Delaware, along with about 3000 Loyalists who wanted to make themselves scarce before the rebels took over the city. On July 18th at three o'clock in the morning the main body of his army marched out of the city and headed north for New York. It consisted of 10,000 soldiers and 1500 baggage wagons, many of them containing various comforts of life acquired during the long winter in Philadelphia.

Sergeant-Major Peasy had not acquired many comforts during his time in the city. But he stowed his drums and drummer boys on their cart with his usual care, muttering gloomily to himself all the while. He was a man who believed in rules. That was what being in the army meant. But this was a war in which the rules of warfare did not seem to hold sway. Apart from Saratoga the Americans had won no important victories, and yet they seemed to grow stronger. The British army meanwhile, in secure command of the city of Philadelphia, was now moving out without a shot being fired.

It was a war in which defeats were victories and victories defeats. Orders, though, were still orders, and General Clinton had to obey the ones he received from London, just as Peasy in his turn had to obey, and his men and boys in their turn, and so on.

The reward for the sacrifice of obedience, for willingness to allow yourself to be part of a great military machine, was that the strongest and most efficient machine would prevail. But in this cursed land of North America the rules seemed to work backward, with the British army retreating before a parcel of half-starved ragamuffins, just as if a cat were fleeing the onslaught of a mouse.

The streets of Philadelphia were full of celebration. The atmosphere was different inside Independence Hall, however. People milled about desks in search of their lost. Always desks. Tom thought of the commissary in New York. For every boat, horse, and soldier, there was a piece of paper; for every battle, great ledgers, toting it up, just as Ned and his Bella pored over books.

America was writing itself into existence.

There were women behind the desks. Tom pushed his way toward one of them. She looked up, busy and a bit annoyed.

"I'm lookin' for someone," Tom said. "She was hurt at Valley Forge. I saw the British take her."

The woman looked the way people behind desks always look—as if she'd heard it all before. How do you say, it was Daisy? he wondered. How do you say what she was like? How do you say what happened?

The woman thought she knew already. She didn't care; she couldn't. If you worried about every one of them, you'd die of worry. If you grieved for them all, you'd die of grief. Whatever people said about being a member of an army or a citizen of a country, you were on your own. He'd got Ned back by himself. No, not by himself. Daisy had helped. Tonti and the Hurons had helped. But they weren't people behind desks, they were out of doors, in the middle of things.

"I've searched everywhere," Tom said hopelessly. "I hoped she might be listed here."

The woman pushed across her big book and pointed at a mark on the page. "That mark," she said. She didn't seem annoyed anymore. She spoke quietly, sadly, sympathetically, as she had a hundred times before. "It means dead."

Tom looked at the book. His hands felt big and clumsy. Suddenly he wanted to weep. He could put up with so much, with cruelty and loss, without weeping, but when a woman gave him a book and he couldn't read it, he wanted to cry like a child being told off by his teacher. If she'd expected him to be ignorant, it would have been all right, but she expected him to know, and that made him feel it was his own fault that Daisy was gone, that if he knew his way round these pages as he knew his way up the river or scouting overland with Tonti and the others, he'd be able to find her. But no. Straightaway he was tied up in the ink, lost amongst all these pages.

He looked around for Ned and Bella. They'd all come in together. Where'd they got to? The two of them spent enough time reading together, they should be able to help now. But they'd gone, skipped off amidst the crowds, leaving him to cope with this matter himself.

He turned back to the woman. Her expression began to change. He couldn't read the book, but he could read her face. She was thinking: A man his age and he can't read his own woman's name.

"Daisy McConnahay?" Tom asked.

With weary patience she drew the book back and began to run her finger down the list of names, her plump, pink woman's finger tracking pathways that Tom had never been able to explore.

Ned and Bella wandered curiously through the throng that milled through the vast space of Independence Hall. It was the first time Ned had been a part of a city crowd for over a year, and it felt strange to him, stranger than being with Indians or the army at Valley Forge. He looked about with careful eyes. There seemed to be an invisible wall around each person, which he had to skirt. Ned remembered a story of his father's about wandering through the forest upcountry with his master, Beeley. They had stumbled into an Indian village by mistake. The men were together by the fire, the women sitting by their huts. Beeley and Tom walked through on tiptoe, terrified lest the least wrong move on their part bring the whole tribe around their necks. In just such a way did Ned find himself regarding the good citizens of Philadelphia. It amused him even while he felt nervous. He was awkward, gangly, uncouth in city company, even amongst these sad people who were searching. Bella seemed quite at home.

A bit later, when Tom had finished his business here, she wanted to go out on the streets and try to buy something for their wedding day. Ned retreated to a pair of double doors and pushed against them. They opened, and he and Bella went in.

They entered a huge room. The doors shut behind them and all the yammering, the searching, the distress, died away. There was slanting light from the great windows, and motes of dust spiraled slowly up and down. Everywhere there were pieces of furniture, opened crates, heaped-up pictures. It was quiet, even ghostly, despite the afternoon sunshine, and in the corners the shadows were deep. Bella wandered off, deep in her own thoughts. Immediately the light and shadow broke up her form, and like some Indian, she seemed to vanish amidst her surroundings.

There was a stirring at the far end of the room, and a man approached. As he came, he pushed and pulled at things in a vain attempt to insist on order. He was red-haired, young, busy-looking, amused.

"Hello," he said, as if Ned were an old acquaintance. "The army made a terrible mess before they left."

"What are you doing in here?" Ned asked.

"Congress," the young man mouthed confidentially back at him. "They're going to meet here as soon as it's been renovated."

"Congress," Ned repeated in amazement.

"You know what they're like," the man said, as though Ned had any idea. "They fight such a lot, wave their arms and knock each other about. I have to be so careful how I arrange them. I'll put Mr. Jefferson here and Mr. Adams over there." Each time he indicated an empty space with a make-believe chair and an imaginary, irate member of Congress placed at a safe distance from possible rivals. "And Mr. Franklin by the fire." In a lowered voice he added: "He gets a chill. My name's Roger Otis." He offered Ned his hand. Ned recoiled a little, inspected it curiously, then regarded Otis in obvious puzzlement.

Otis looked back at him speculatively. Good heavens, what a young savage! He didn't know what it was to shake hands.

An emblematic encounter perhaps, and an alarming one at that. On the one hand, here *he* was, Roger Otis, privy to the deliberations of the great. When Congress sat he, Otis, arranged the seating. On the other hand, here was this young warrior, battle-hardened already, familiar with the wildest places and people on the whole continent. It was a meeting between the head and the active limbs, and there seemed no connection between them.

This gargantuan conception of America as a sprawling giant set off another literary recollection in Otis's mind, Jonathan Swift's *Gulliver's Travels*. In the fourth book, Gulliver found himself in a strange country inhabited by disgusting savages who swung from the trees and grunted at each other. They were naked, hairy, and covered in unspeakable filth. They caught sight of our hero as he approached and lumbered toward him, gibbering and crying out. When they got near, one of them swung his arm aloft, much to poor Gulliver's alarm and trepidation. It was only after some moments that the innocent reader could understand that Gulliver had simply met up with a family of human beings, one of whom had offered to shake hands with him. Our fellowmen were being seen without the forgiving eye of partisanship, in their true and disagreeable colors.

Not that there was anything disagreeable about the form of this young brave, despite his accoutrements. Nevertheless it was hard to remember that the deliberations that had taken place in this room, and would shortly resume, could have anything to do with the world he inhabited.

Perhaps it was as well to remind oneself of the opening line of the Declaration of Independence: "We hold these truths to be self-evident, that all men are created equal," and so on, and so forth. One might, of course, quibble with the words "self-evident." Anyone with eyes to see and ears to hear must surely agree that it wasn't evident at all. People were large or small, wise or foolish, vicious or virtuous, interesting or dull. Needless to say that was irrelevant to the true drift of the Declaration, which did not concern itself with individuals' qualities, but with their ultimate worth in the eyes of the Almighty and with the consequent legal and constitutional rights and privileges deriving from that absolute worth. Nevertheless Otis could not prevent himself from stumbling a little over the words "self-evident," and he suspected that better men than he would do so subsequently.

There you were again—better men. Could one, or could one not, conceive of such beings? And if so, in what sense?

It was necessary to put this logic-chopping to one side and take the main principle to heart. America, and Roger Otis, were at the service of this fellow; and no doubt he in his turn had, and would, provide splendid service of his own.

Otis continued his introduction: "I'm secretary to Mr. Laurens. What regiment are you in?"

"The Flying Scouts."

"With Indians?"

"Yes." The boy waved his rifle at Otis, who saw that it was covered with feathers and other Indian decorations, including—oh, heavens.

Otis cautiously reached forward and fingered the alarming objects. "That's human hair," he whispered, both horrified and pleased. He'd never handled a scalp before. He inspected the boy more narrowly. Perhaps he was an Indian himself, after all. His face was weatherbeaten. Of course, he spoke English like a native, but then, they said Joseph Brant, alias Thayeadanegea, chief of the Mohicans, had an excellent command of English and had translated the New Testament into his own impenetrable tongue.

"What is your name?" he asked the boy.

"Ned Dobb," he replied.

That sounded English enough. Otis wondered what strange adventures had brought Ned Dobb to this place with Indian attire and an Indian rifle, complete with scalps.

Ned had begun to walk around the Guild Hall, examining it in more detail, and Otis noticed that he walked with a limp.

"They're all gonna sit in here?" Ned asked, obviously awestruck at the thought.

"Yes."

"Where do *you* sit?"

"I don't. I'll stand against the wall and take notes."

Ned probed a crate of books. The poor boy probably couldn't read. Otis reverted to his earlier train of thought. The mind and the limbs of America. No doubt Ned, in his own way, was thinking something similar. And yet, perhaps they were both wrong. It wasn't the high idealism of the Declaration that had evicted the British from Philadelphia, nor any feat of arms from those soldiers who had suffered all winter at Valley Forge. Instead it had been the wily diplomacy of Benjamin Franklin, Silas Deane, and others, manipulating France into open war with Britain. London now would be preoccupied with trying to wrest the West Indies—a far richer prize than all of North America—from French control, and to defend the Floridas from French attack. The course of this war was being determined by certain calculations and conversations that took place in the courts of Europe in the good old-fashioned manner, not by the earnest ideas generated by Congress, nor by the bravery and suffering of men like Ned Dobb.

Otis watched Dobb inspecting the books in the crate, and wondered what the boy expected from the struggle that was now under way. He remembered how the cunning Ben Franklin had suggested, when the Declaration was being drafted, that a certain significant rephrasing should be adopted. Jefferson's original draft had listed, among the "unalienable rights" of all men, "Life, Liberty and Property." The last word had worried Ben. It looked like a promise of goods and chattels, a promise that Congress would never be able to redeem. At his suggestion the document was rephrased and the promise became more resonant, and less meaningful: "Life, Liberty and the pursuit of Happiness."

If the war came to a successful conclusion, it would be as

the result of such sharp and pragmatic intelligences as that
possessed by the rotund and genial Franklin. What could—
what was he called?—a flying scout, in heaven's name; what
could a flying scout like Ned Dobb understand of the strategic and diplomatic considerations that such a one as Benjamin
Franklin had to wrestle with? All men are created equal, Otis
thought again. And then he looked at the matter from another, more mundane angle: What property would Ned Dobb
and his ilk expect at the cessation of hostilities? Or would
they be content with the pursuit of happiness?

Presumably, flying scouts were good at pursuing things.

Ned had begun on another box, full of shiny objects in
brass and silver.

"Scientific instruments," Otis told him. "The British were
intending to steal them."

Ned pulled one out and stared at it as a child might at a
new toy. It was a beautifully crafted astrolabe, and Otis
hurried to Ned's side, partly to demonstrate its workings and
partly to prevent him from handling it roughly or dropping it
to the floor.

"Mr. Rittenhouse made it," Otis said, taking it from the
boy's hands. "It's a model of the sun and planets." He wound
up the clockwork and the cluster of heavenly bodies resumed
their orbits where, in British hands, they had last left off. "This
is the earth," he told Ned. "And that's the moon."

The boy watched the planetary dance in obvious amazement. Otis could see his intelligence, unused to abstract
considerations, wrestling with the task of relating these small
objects to the greatest phenomena of the universe. The distance that lay between calculations pertaining to the nature of
the solar system, on the one hand, and those appalling blood-
stained scalps that dangled from Ned's rifle, on the other, was
truly astronomical.

Ned pointed at the moon. "How far's that?" he asked.

"Two hundred thousand miles."

Ned stretched his hand from moon to earth. "Don't seem
that far," he said. "How do you know?"

Lord, Otis thought, the questions these innocents ask!
How *does* one know? "I went to Harvard," he replied. There
was an answer to everything, he'd learned that from Congress. "See how the planets turn," he went on. "Each makes
its own revolution around the sun. Mr. Jefferson says that's

the idea of America. A revolution. A new turn." He touched the brass ball of the earth.

Ned stared at the astrolabe in silence, but whether at its pretty effect or at the profound philosophical truths implicit therein, who could say?

Then the doors of the Guild Hall swung open.

Ned turned to see his father in the doorway. As so often, Tom's face was sad and stubborn. "She ain't here, Ned. Still missin'. But I know she's alive, and I'm gonna find her."

Washington addressed his troops. They cheered and stamped. In pens on the streets of Philadelphia slaves watched the celebrations, the comings and goings, in puzzlement. It was hard to keep up with all these changes of ownership. The usual rumors spread through the American ranks. "We're going north to chase the British into the sea. The war'll be over in two weeks."

The army began to march. Column after column of soldiers; the drums and fifes gave them "Steady, boys, steady." From a small hill on the outskirts of Philadelphia the great snake could be seen uncoiling itself and winding through woods and meadows on its way north.

On a grassy slope near the top of the hill a small group were attending the wedding of Ned and Bella. The bride, groom, Israel, Tom, Merle, and the pastor made up all the company. The sounds of marching soldiers, the clatter of baggage carts, the ebb and flow of martial music, weaved in and out of the simple service.

When they were married, Israel, solemn for once in yarmulke and well-brushed soldier's jacket, gave the young couple his blessing. Tom kissed his daughter-in-law and shook hands with his son. Merle, more resplendent than any of the other members of his party—with all the straps, braids, gold trimmings, of a drummerboy—beat a skirl. And then the wedding party winded their way down the hill again and rejoined the army.

On the back of one of myriad carts sat Abby with her little boy and her newborn baby.

"What are you going to name him?" another woman on the cart asked.

"Jackson," Abby replied. "Because this one's Jack's son."

The other woman nearly laughed. There was a plump

cheeriness and resignation in Abby that made you almost forget that her children had different fathers because her men, in turn, had died in the war. She overflowed with life, yet all her loving had turned into death.

"And," Abby went on, breaking through the silence that had developed, "because he's born in sunlight."

The army marched north in the sunlight. Indeed, the sun grew hotter and hotter. On June 28th the Americans clashed with the British at Monmouth Court House in temperatures of more than one hundred degrees. It was an odd, controversial battle, with both sides claiming victory. General Arthur Lee, commanding the American vanguard, didn't want to engage the British at all, since he felt that since they were withdrawing from the environs of Philadelphia of their own free will, it would be foolish to put obstacles in their path. Better, he claimed, to construct "a golden bridge" to help them on their way. Perhaps not surprisingly in view of this attitude, he withdrew his men at the first contact with the enemy. Washington, riding up a little later, swore at him, according to General Charles Scott of Virginia, "like an angel from Heaven," and immediately sent the troops back.

At the end of a fierce battle both sides were ready to rest by early evening. The following morning, when Washington's army stirred, they discovered that the British had already continued their march north, and no further attempt was made to stop their progress.

By now the French fleet had sailed toward the American continent in support of their allies, and the focus of the struggle moved to the sea. Monmouth Court House was, in fact, the last major engagement of the whole war in the northern American states.

15

Bella punked the touchhole.

The cannon roared, the shell made its complaining whine, the barrel was lowered to be loaded again. Israel, smoke-blackened, squat, and long-armed—as though the constant loading of shells had stretched them beyond their natural size—took another from the pile and swung it to the cannon's mouth.

All around, other cannons blasted. The pall was so strong you lost any sense that you were firing at anything, and perhaps you weren't. The artillery's task was to soften up the enemy, gunners were always being told, and Bella rarely felt that what they were doing had any effect on individual men, or particular strategic emplacements, or buildings belonging to real people. Instead she thought of the enemy as a single huge dragon in its cave. By repeated pounding from cannon, some part of the creature's bulk could be made sore enough for it to change its position, twist around a little, lick its wounds. But all this happened out of sight, at least as far as the artillery were concerned. The eyes of the army were elsewhere.

The eyes, as far as this emplacement was concerned, were farther along the cliff, in a sandbagged vantage point which overlooked a small bay. The eyes belonged to Tonti, Honehwah, Ongyata; and to Tom and Ned Dobb. They were spies and snipers.

On the far side of the bay the other arm of the cliff arced into the sea like a mirror image of their own; near the top palls of mist resembling the clouds that crown the summits of huge mountains, marked the British artillery that balanced the American guns. Scattered about over the face of the cliffs were lookouts peering back at their American opposite numbers.

They sprang into detail as Ned raised his old spyglass to his eye. Its brasswork was battered and dented; once, on the banks of the Hudson River, it had leapt from his hands like a living thing when a musket ball struck it. The view became abruptly remote and enormous, and Ned, disorientated by the change of perspective, had lost his balance and fallen to the ground. The glass was undamaged, however, despite the pockmark it had acquired, and in fact had become more valuable to Ned as a result of its battle scar. Sometimes when scouting at night in a full moon, he'd raise it to the sky, and looking at the strange, pitted, broken surface of a new world, recollect his conversation in Philadelphia with Roger Otis. Now, however, he was watching an enemy sniper. The sniper in turn was taking a bead on an American farther along the cliff.

"Two stretches to the right, Pa," Ned called out crisply.

Tom shifted his rifle to the new position. Not content, he stuck his thumb in the flashpan and blackened his front sight. Then he looked down the rifle again.

"I'll take him," he said.

He fired. A scream, small as the distant screamer, followed the discharge. Ned's cold lens resumed its roaming once more.

"There's another one," he said. "Behind the facing."

Tom was still loading. Ongyata took aim, fired. They heard another pinprick of sound in response; faraway pain. More of the enemy cliff traveled within Ned's glass. And then he stopped, transfixed. Beside him Tonti was firing at something he'd seen.

"Pa," Ned said quietly; then louder, "Pa." He handed the glass to Tom and pointed with his finger at the opposite clifftop. Tom looked.

There, captured in the small disc of Ned's lens, was the English sergeant-major.

The man was farther along the enemy cliff than their previous targets, and the sun angled on to the glass, making him glow first amber, then violet. But it was Peasy. Tom adjusted the telescope and achieved sharp focus. Even though Peasy was out of range, he seemed near. He was drinking water from a canteen, and Tom felt he could be beside him, the effect was so intimate.

Peasy was brown, as if he'd not washed for all these years. Tom felt he could put his hand over the end of the spyglass and Peasy would be his, extracted from the clifftop, plucked from his army as Ned was stolen from the Sugar House and taken up the Hudson Valley. To be beaten near unto death. Tom said it over and over in his mind, as he had many times before. To be beaten near unto death. To be beaten on the feet until he was nearly dead; just a boy. To misuse a child like that.

It was a warm October day now, along the ocean shoreline in Virginia four years later, but Tom didn't even need to close his eyes to see the rain beating grayly down in New York, with a strong northwest wind behind it, and the boy hanging from the cannon, beat down by the rain like a bit of old rag. And Merle underneath, like a dog at his master's heels, his mouth broken for trying to help; Ned so hurt, those hours in the rain, the fever coming, the boy near drowning in the pain of it. Beaten near unto death. He would like to run at Peasy now, grab hold of him, tear at him with his bare hands, kill him not by the feet but everywhere, so that there was nothing left of him. And then the gray rain and the mud like jelly and his near-dead morsel of a boy would be gone from Tom's mind and his dreams, and never torment him more.

Ned was grown now, a tall man, strong; he could use the woods like an Indian, and handle a boat like his father. Married. But still, that beating was there. Tom would watch him when they were quiet in camp and Ned was poring over Bella's books, and he would wonder what the boy was trying to find in them, what question he was trying to answer. And he would think that perhaps Ned still felt his life not ready to start yet, even married as he was and living a soldier's life in this forever war. Perhaps Ned felt he was not complete because of that beating; that something had been taken away from him which he must take back if he was ever to be whole again. He still limped. He would always limp, agile and handy as he was. Perhaps he limped in his mind too. Perhaps Ned also needed to kill Sergeant-Major Peasy.

Ned hadn't moved. He had learned patience since those days on the wharf, under the ropewalk. So had Tom. In the three years that had elapsed since the British evacuation of

Philadelphia, they'd fought a small, busy war. As spies they'd developed a deep Indian patience, a quality of silence.

The Flying Scouts had been with Washington's main Continental army, or rather, on its periphery, in New Jersey or up the Hudson River, always in the New York region where the British headquarters was still located. Of course, they knew that the main action of this war was taking place elsewhere—on the ocean, around the West Indian islands, and in the southern states, where vicious fighting had taken place over the last few years. General Gates, the hero of Saratoga, had lost his reputation in the south. Having been defeated by Cornwallis at the Battle of Camden, South Carolina, he departed from the field upon a racehorse which took him, in the space of three days, one hundred and twenty miles away from danger, and the same distance into disgrace.

Cornwallis and his troops continued to win in the south, but not to triumph, as Howe and Clinton before them had in the north. Nathanael Greene, a New Englander, was given command of the American forces in the area, and he conducted what he called a "fugitive war" with great brilliance. As his phrase implied, it was a war that devolved upon relatively small-scale skirmishing which required great mobility. As Greene himself claimed, he was an excellent runner. "There are few generals who have run oftener, or more lustily than I have done. But I have taken care not to run too far, and commonly have run as fast forward as backward, to convince our Enemy that we were like a Crab that could run either way." Perhaps more than anyone else involved in the War of Independence, Greene understood the peculiar paradoxes of victory and defeat. The British "got the splendor," as he put it, "we the advantage."

But if Washington's army in the north was primarily undertaking a holding operation, ensuring that the British remained bottled up in New York—and didn't try to regain Philadelphia, for example, or make a break up the Hudson—the Flying Scouts saw their share of action. They reconnoitered New Jersey and the Hudson for British foraging parties, and fought when they discovered them. They protected and guided supply missions for their own army, sometimes boating along the river they knew so well, more often probing the woodland on either bank. They came up against local marauders, cowboys who were willing to work for or against either side, as long as they were always working for themselves. It was two such roughnecks who captured the British spy Major John André as he made his way from West Point after his secret discussion with the traitor Benedict Arnold. The cowboys haggled with each other for some time over which side would give them the best return on their prize, finally deciding to hand him over to the Americans. Thus the dashing André was hanged, protesting only at the ignominious method of his death, and Arnold lived on to fight for the British. It was against village mercenaries such as these, as well as against the outlying units of the British army, that the Flying Scouts had to fight.

While the main American army during this period had few engagements of historical note, Tom, Ned, and the Hurons had engaged in a whole series of confrontations and conflicts whose scale was small but in which the stakes—their lives—were as high as they could have been in pitched battle. They had learned how to stalk, how to observe, how to fight, and above all, how to be patient.

The American army as a whole was showing patience during the siege of Yorktown. The British commander, Lord Cornwallis, despite the splendor of his victories, had withdrawn into Virginia and moved to the tidewater of the York River, where he could obtain supplies from British ships and build an anchorage for the Atlantic fleet. Washington, meanwhile, feinted an attack on New York from his base in New Jersey, and while Clinton waited anxiously for the maneuver to begin, brought the French and American armies down through Philadelphia into the region of Yorktown. The French fleet meanwhile controlled the entrance into the Virginian capes, so that Cornwallis's army was trapped.

The Americans consolidated their position skillfully and carefully. Sappers dug trenches nearer and nearer the British redcoats, artillery was dragged up from the York River and put into position, and while the subsequent cannonade kept the British preoccupied, further trenches were dug. By October 11th 1781 the earthworks had reached to within three hundred yards of the enemy lines. The engineering of these parallel trenches was of text-book quality, and the advance of the Americans was slow, careful, relentless. In the town itself piles of bodies, many lacking heads and limbs, were heaped up and began to rot.

Only now and then did an American soldier become foolhardy. One militia man stood on the parapet of one of the parallels, and shouting "Damn my soul if I will dodge for the buggers," brandished his spade at the oncoming musket balls and batted them away successfully for several minutes before being shot. For the most part, though, the American army, after years of experience and discipline, had become a professional body of men on a par with its French allies. No longer disorderly nor prone to panic, conscious of the possibility of a final victory after its long history of defeats, it calmly and patiently tightened its grip on Cornwallis's troops.

Like their comrades, Tom and Ned patiently waited and watched what Sergeant-Major Peasy would do.

Peasy seemed at first in no hurry to do anything. He finished with his canteen, stoppered it, and put it away. It was strange to feel so near him and yet not be noticed. Once while they were patrolling in the forests of New York, Ned spotted through his glasses a member of a British foraging party who had somehow acquired a wooden bathtub, and having filled it with stream water, was making good use of it. They didn't dare come up close enough to capture him, for fear his comrades might be concealed in the woods nearby. So Tom picked him off from their cover with his rifle. It felt like a betrayal—not killing the man, but disturbing him when he was naked and engaged upon private business. Of course, they would have felt no such compunction about Peasy, if the range had been possible.

Peasy began, in his turn, to survey the scene before him. He was looking intently at a particular point on their cliff. Tom took the glass from his eye and attempted to follow the direction of Peasy's gaze. He seemed to be eyeing an artillery spotter who was positioned farther down, in front of the guns. Tom picked up the glass again. Peasy was collecting a patrol together—another British soldier and a couple of his Iroquois.

"What's he doin'?" Ned asked.

"Qui est là?" said Tonti.

"Le sergeant anglais," Tom told him.

"Ah." Tonti knew well enough who they meant.

A little farther along the line an American sniper was jolted back and died. Musket fire threaded the air in a huge, invisible knot. Nevertheless Tom and Ned kept their heads exposed, still watching. Peasy adjusted his leggings, took up two muskets, and began to lead the patrol down a trail that led to the face of his cliff.

Tom, Ned, and the Hurons ran along their own lines

through a pall of smoke and roaring artillery, picking their way over the dead and wounded until they reached a corresponding pathway from their clifftop. Then they scrambled down a steep pathway alongside a thin stream of water that poured down the cliff, and dashed over a small bridge.

Peasy led his patrol into a deepening cleft, almost a cave. The artillery spotter was just across the bay, not quite in range, but the beach area was dangerous, offering little cover from the American fire. He peered out from behind a great pillar of rock.

It seemed quiet enough. Huge sharpened stakes leaning toward the American cliff bristled along the perimeter of the British lines. The sea lapped peacefully against the shore, unaffected by the thunder of cannon and the insect whine of musket shot above, except that the seawrack was thicker upon the tideline and Peasy's eyes, missing nothing, made out ship's timbers, bits of sail, bloated gray bodies of men tangled amidst the other debris.

His eyes roamed the beach again. Nobody there. All quiet. Yes, you could say all quiet, despite the roaring from the cliffs. In battle how often had he noticed them, these quiet places in the lee of struggle. When you entered them, you seemed to become invisible for a moment and could collect yourself. For a moment no ball would penetrate, no bayonet strike. You could hear and see the battle all about you, but that was only sight and sound and did not affect the stillness. Upon such islands Peasy had stood from time to time, feeling—as he so rarely had during his soldier's life, but so often had before, as a child—feeling alone. He would refresh himself by thinking of his drummerboys beating out the battle formation, and of the whole vast military family of which he was a part. Then, having stood aside, he would plunge back in again, renewed, and fight shoulder to shoulder with the other men. These places of silence were safe, but he had no wish to remain in them long; only so long as it took to prepare to return to the other places, where there was danger.

His childhood in Yorkshire had been a place of silence. His mother had married a soldier boy who had gone away. She told him the story bitterly, and often. She always called this father of Bill Peasy's a boy, though he must have been a man.

"My boy went away," she would say, looking resentfully at
Bill, so that he began to feel the Gypsy trick had been played
on her—his father taken and him put in place instead. He
and his mother lived together in a small dark cottage on the
edge of a Yorkshire village. As soon as he could, he took the
king's shilling and joined the army, like his father before him.
It was a place of noise, life, and activity.

The beach was quiet. And yet he had a sense of movement
among the American stakes that pointed toward their British
counterparts like an array of mute cannon. Just a flicker
somewhere amid them. The play of light on wood, perhaps.
Nothing was visible now. Yes, Indians. Surely. Indians could
move without disturbing the silence. They were creatures of
the silence already, as he had been in his childhood; they
lived alone, without loyalty or any sense of comradeship.
He'd watched his Iroquois squatting for hours at a time, side
by side, staring straight ahead, never so much as passing a
word. He, Peasy, liked to be convivial, watching his drummerboys practice, yarning with his men, smoking a pipe by
the campfire and feeling his family all around him. He'd
never discovered his father, nor anyone who knew of him by
name. The army, of course, was a big place—as big, almost,
as the world; though it would become a little smaller if the
rebels stole North America.

There was no movement now. Or perhaps just a something, over to the left.

Suddenly, as if he'd raised a glass to his eyes, they became
visible. Three of them—three Indians. Tawny, on the sand,
amongst the timbers. Peasy touched his Iroquois, but they'd
seen them already. He touched his corporal, Birdsall, and
pointed. Birdsall saw, nodded.

Peasy led them out, leveling muskets. Then, from a clear
sky, it hailed—all around, puffs of sand, the angry whine of
musket balls. They were being shot at from above, somewhere up the British cliff. The silence was gone forever.

The Iroquois dropped silently on the beach. Then Birdsall.
Then Peasy felt a burst of pain in his side and he was sitting
suddenly on the sand, leaning against one of the stakes.
Birdsall was writhing a yard or two off, still exposed. Peasy,
like some bulky creature of the seashore suited to neither
land nor water, began to work his way across the sand. He
didn't dare stand for fear of attracting another shot, and also
he didn't know whether his legs would obey, so he pushed

them uselessly before him. He'd been hit before, but never in all these years disabled. Only flesh wounds, which encouraged the men because they could see blood streaming down, their worst fear, and yet you were still on your feet, still shouting orders, still loading your musket. So they would think, It's happened to him, but he's still going.

But this was different. Of course he'd seen it happen hundreds, thousands of times. One moment a man would be whole, the next, a part of his body had become stupid. You hardly ever saw the hit, just the change. It was as though a section in your unit mutinied. Peasy had seen that too—soldiers out of nowhere saying enough is enough, first one, then others, crowding together in their rebellion, feeling secure in each other's company. Never Peasy. Never. However bad things were, you stuck it out together, as he saw it. You couldn't choose whether things were good or bad, you took them as they came. You didn't choose your army or your country. These matters were ordained. It wasn't up to you, it wasn't your concern. Any more than you could choose your mother or father. Stepping out of your army, deserting, wasn't a matter of changing sides, because once you'd abandoned your own people there was nothing left. You could never belong to the enemy. They might feed you, pay you, but they would never be your people. No good could come of it. Like Benedict Arnold. When Major André was captured by the Americans, they said they would hang him unless Benedict Arnold was sent out to them in his place. If it had been Peasy's decision, he wouldn't have hesitated. André was a loyal servant of the king, who had only done his duty. Arnold was a traitor who had sold his country for money. If you could be allowed to change your country at will, then this whole war had been a waste of time, because that was exactly what these Yankees wanted to do.

Wounding was like a mutiny. Some part of you refused to take orders, as the lower part of his body was refusing now. When soldiers mutinied, you had to kill them. Once, when it had happened, when they spread the word disobey, his colonel had ordered that three of the mutineers should be shot and the others forced to witness it. Peasy commanded the firing squad. The first one had fallen clean. The next kept crying and pleading and talking about his wife and children, but he'd died quickly too, when the shots struck him. The third one said nothing before they fired, like the first, but he wouldn't be killed, and lay on the ground struggling and crying to himself. You could mutiny in the company of other renegades, but when you died you lay on the ground and died alone. When a soldier disobeyed orders, he had to be cut down; so with a limb. But when you died, your whole body disobeyed you.

He tried to bring himself to a focus. Birdsall couldn't be left out there alone. There was blood on his chin—he'd been shot in the chest, or the guts. Peasy thought of Ben, little Ben, who was so frightened of dying, who was so frightened of everything. He had coughed blood, then died. But till the last, Peasy had told him to live. The same with Birdsall. He and Birdsall had been together a long time.

"Don't leave me, lad," Peasy whispered hoarsely, just as he had to Ben before. He clutched hold of Birdsall's shoulders and began to struggle back toward the stakes. He could hear the sea roaring, or maybe the roaring of the cannon, or perhaps it was his mind roaring. Birdsall was so heavy. When a man was whole, he was easy to carry, however big. When injured or dead, he was nothing but baggage. He pulled him back to the stakes. They made grooves in the sand.

Peasy got his back on one of the stakes, as he had before, and hoisted Birdsall up so that he was resting on his chest. Birdsall's head lolled. Perhaps he was dead already. There were Indians standing nearby. He nearly gave an order, but then realized they weren't Iroquois but Hurons. They just stood and watched, like Indians always did. Then there were some more men, a young man and an older one. The young man was tall, rugged, a proper soldier, half Indian by the look of him. His musket was leveled at Peasy, but as he watched, Peasy kept forgetting that this was the enemy, about to kill him—he just thought, This is a soldier; I've lived among soldiers all my life, he is my kin, my friend. The lad could have been one of his own boys. But the rifle was pointing, like a staring eye. The boy would have the killing of him.

He tried to look at him properly, but his eyes felt strange, and the boy became unclear, dazzling, haloed. The sea was behind him and sun sparking off the sea so that there was a sheen all round the boy. The Angel of Death. Like any life-soldier Peasy had always known that there was a musket, a trigger finger, a soldier waiting for him somewhere, and this boy was the one.

Colors shivered and swam about him. Above was the blue of the sky, like the sea, as if the boy had come from the depths of the sea to claim him and drag him down.

In the army you lived your life by order. Unto death. That was being a soldier. You didn't shirk in the line of fire. There was a proper way to do all things, including dying. Now was Peasy's time to go through the drill for dying. He knew the rules as he knew all the rules and regulations by which you conducted yourself as a sergeant-major in the British army. He knew his orders. They were: the twenty-third psalm: "The Lord is my Shepherd; I shall not want. . . ."

Even as he spoke, Peasy wondered how a fighting man like himself could obey a shepherd. But he had no authority to query any of superior rank. You didn't write your drill.

He maketh me to lie down in green pastures; he leadeth me beside the still waters.

Hot-eyed, Peasy inspected the beach once more, tawny as an Indian. Not green. There was no green here. And the sea. No still waters. The waves seemed bigger than before; they roared in his ears. But not for him to question, or disobey.

He restoreth my soul; he leadeth me in the paths of righteousness for his name's sake.
Yea, though I walk through the valley of the shadow of death, I will fear no evil: for thou art with me; thy rod and thy staff they comfort me.
Thou preparest a table before me in the presence of mine enemies: thou anointest my head with oil; my cup runneth over.

In the presence of his enemies Peasy thought how he should prepare for death. He hoped he didn't cry and call out after he was done for, like the third mutineer they'd shot. But how could you prevent it, since death itself was a sort of mutiny? They said Major André, when the Americans hanged him, had died quiet at the end of his rope, not struggling as hanged men usually do. Perhaps his neck had broken clean. Or perhaps he had the self-discipline to hold himself still and wait for the end.

It was time to die as he'd lived—like a soldier. Peasy raised his eyes to the gun once more. The sea thundered. He felt he was drowning.

Ned said, "I got him dead, Pa."

Tom watched Peasy squirming across the sand, dragging the corporal. "Don't leave me, lad," Peasy was saying in a dry, faint whisper. Don't leave me lad. They came up against the stakes. Peasy began to pray.

Tom waited for Ned to shoot. The boy had a right. It was his war.

No, not war. Peasy was finished with the war. He was out of it. Now it was a matter of revenge.

Why not? Peasy's shadow had fallen over Ned's life these last years; he would limp to the grave. Peasy had haunted them both like a figure in a dream. Sometimes Tom felt that all the fears, all the suffering, all the foul emotions that these last years had brought with them could be tracked back to this man. He was the one you saw in battle when your lines collapsed and panic set in. He was the one who marched the streets of your city when the enemy were in occupation. He was the one who, when your child was lost, was abusing him and bringing him to death's door.

Years ago Tom had said the word that Peasy should die, and now here was Ned, all ready.

Ned lowered his musket. "No. I ain't going to do it," he said.

Tom lurched with relief. Yes, it was true—their war was over. Ned was whole again. The past was over, and the future had begun.

The gun was lowered. Peasy gazed at it. Perhaps he'd been shot so quick he hadn't even heard the blast. No. There was the roaring of the cliffs, of the sea, and the weight of Birdsall on his chest. He could walk out of the valley of the shadow of death.

Sergeant-Major Peasy ordered his legs to obey. He rose to his feet. He bent down, grasped Birdsall under the armpits, hoisted him up over his shoulder.

Then, knees buckling with the strain, side screaming with agony, feeling nothing, Peasy carried his corporal from the beach, back to the British lines.

*   *   *

On October 16th 1781 Lord Cornwallis made a last desperate attempt to escape from the trap of Yorktown. He began ferrying troops across the river to Gloucester, hoping he would then be able to march his army back to the security of New York. But after about 1000 men had gotten across, the weather turned and a storm blew up, bringing the evacuation to a complete halt. By the time the wind fell, it was too late to continue and the men were ordered back into Yorktown.

The next day a drummer stood on the British ramparts and beat a parley. Merle was ordered to stand upon the American earthworks and beat a return. As he did so, Ned remembered how they had drummed together on the boat to Long Island as they went to their first battle. Beat daddymammy.

A little before noon on October 19th the document was signed. The entire British army at Yorktown had surrendered: 7000 men, 200 cannon, 6000 muskets, 500 horses, 2000 pounds in cash. At two o'clock that afternoon British troops were marched out of town between the French and American lines. Their band, drums cased in black and fifes hung with black ribbons, played one of the popular marching tunes of the time, "The World Turned Upside Down":

> If ponies rode men and if grass ate the cows
> And cats should be chased into holes by the mouse
> If summer were spring and the other way round
> Then all the world would be upside down.

As Ned listened, he remembered Roger Otis's words in Philadelphia about the revolution. A revolution was when the planets turned. The earth had turned now, and it was a new world.

In the streets and environs of Yorktown dead bodies were heaped up everywhere.

16

Tom and Ned were back at last in New York. But it was a different New York from the one they'd known before. True, the houses and streets hadn't changed since the occupation, except that more of them were ruined now. Graffiti was scrawled over the derelict house where the Sugar King, Joe McConnahay, had once resided with his family. GONE TO CANADA. TORIES OUT. The windows and doors swung open, but there was nothing left to loot. For years the city had been forced to prey on itself, its buildings consumed for fires; its goods and chattels, trades and commerce supplying the wants of an impoverished community and an always-hungry army. The Loyalist bastions that had come through these depredations almost intact were now assaulted by the rebels in acts of revenge. Their owners went to Britain, Canada, or like the rebels before them, lay low.

But if the city was wretched, there was jubilation also. People danced in the streets, got drunk. Kissed, organized cockfights, shouted and sang.

But these celebrations weren't unalloyed. Soldiers were cashing, or trying to cash, their notes. People were seeking out old friends and relatives at addresses that no longer existed in streets that were now a shambles. There was confusion, anxiety, parting.

Tom and Ned had changed even more than their city in the years that had passed since they last sailed in on their long-boat to trade pelts. They were rangy, weatherbeaten, with Indian rifles, knives, and hunting jackets, and they led a strange and motley crew. Bella, Israel, Merle, Tonti, Honeh-wah, Ongyata; Part of the American army. They had a few horses and a small cow. They were one group among many who had come back to New York in 1783, now that the peace treaty was finally signed.

Tom and Ned left the others and pushed their way through to a small trestle table guarded by soldiers. Behind it stood a sergeant with an eye patch and an empty sleeve. His bristling, aggressive manner made his injuries seem like threats, not losses. They testified to action, but you gained no picture of him lying on the battlefield or moaning in a field hospital. He was simply battered, as a rock might be after years of lashing by the sea. Beside him was a tattered notice. Ned read it, even the word in the middle: PENSIONS, REDEMPTIONS, BACK PAY.

Tom eyed the sergeant curiously. His glance was hard, cocksure. The living eye had hardly more expression than the patch. His face didn't give an inch. You could see why they put him in charge of the money. There was something familiar about him, but then all sergeants tended to look alike—cynical, foulmouthed, amused. Tom passed him the primissory note, creased and yellow now with age. The sergeant squinted his remaining eye at it.

"Boat and providents, seventy dollars. July 1776. Ya had this a long time."

He counted out notes. His one hand, expert and busy, rattled through the pile with the quick movements of a squirrel collecting nuts. It seemed unconnected with the rest of him—a small, independent, wary animal.

"Forty dollars," the sergeant said. The hand pushed the little pile across the board to Tom. The eye looked at him, bright, expressionless, challenging.

"It says seventy," Tom said.

"Ya got forty. That's what it's worth, now."

Tom remembered how he'd carried that bit of paper all these years of war. How he'd given it to Ned to keep in his boot when they were rowing over to Long Island at the very beginning, so that the boy would be left with something if he was killed in battle. When he lived on the wharf, under the ropewalk, he'd wedged it in a gap between the planks. He'd had it tucked in a pocket inside his jerkin when he raided the British camp and in all the years since, over fields, woods, on the river, right through to the Battle of Yorktown. And all the time the paper was worth less and less.

"Ya give me my money," Tom said.

"Ya got ya money."

"And my land," Tom said. "There's a hundred and fifty acres I got owing."

The sergeant grinned at him and shook his head, as if astonished that a grown man could think like a child. Tom thought of Mr. Corty and the Sugar King at the commissary— the way Corty had given the men all that oily talk of the notes in your hand being worth more than gold, and of the English being shoved into the sea in two weeks. Corty would oil the men up and then turn to the Sugar King for more lies, and the Sugar King would whisper him some and look over all the rabble of poor men who had lost their small stock of bits and pieces, and sneer, because the war was just a business matter to him, win or lose. Seven years later, at least Joe McConnahay had been driven to Canada. But now here was this sergeant giving him the same story. There were lies at the beginning, and there were lies at the end. What kind of revolution was that?

"The land," the sergeant said, but Tom knew what he was going to say: The land is gone.

"What d'ya mean?" Tom shouted. The soldiers grabbed him. But the lie was savage and insulting. People had died by the thousand. He'd seen the dead pile up at Long Island, on Manhattan, in Valley Forge, at Yorktown. But the land was still there. What could happen to the land? "I got a hundred and fifty acres coming."

"Sold off," the sergeant said. "To speculators. The country needed its money too."

"But it was mine!" Tom yelled.

The sergeant tutted and shook his head. "Tell Congress," he said. "It ain't my business."

"I'll tell you," Tom said, "because you're in front of me, here."

"I don't want to talk to you. Shut ya mouth."

"I'll open my mouth to anyone I please. We fought for something, and I want it."

"D'ya think I didn't fight?" the sergeant asked. "Look, what ya complaining of? Ya got two arms and two legs, haven't you? Ya still alive."

Tom looked again at the sergeant's mutilation. Whoever had made a profit out of this war, it wasn't him. Again he had a sense that he knew him. Suddenly the thought struck him that this could be the sergeant that recruited him seven years before. And as soon as it did, he felt his rage build up once again. That man had stolen his boy, like the British did later. But then Tom thought, Perhaps it wasn't him after all. You had to put so much back together to get back to the past, not just the arm and eye, but time as well, youth; you had to go back through battles and marching and winter camps into a world that had gone. And good riddance, for the most part. Maybe he *was* the recruiting sergeant, maybe not. What did it matter? Even if he was the same man, he was a different one now.

"Where is this Congress, then?" Tom asked.

"It's coming here soon."

There was nothing more to be had. No back pay, no gratuity, no pension. Just sign out and go. Make your own way in the new America. Be independent. Tom signed. He'd learned to sign a bit better than he had seven years ago, when he'd been recruited. Ned's Bella had taught him.

Ned signed his discharge too, and they walked back. Ned had heard, but he couldn't believe. He asked again, "Where's the land?"

Tom said, "The land's been sold."

"But it was *our* land."

"It's all our land," Tom said. "We won the war. But we don't own a morsel of it." He nearly said: How could we get anything from a war that began by taking our boat? But he didn't. Ned was deep in gloomy thoughts. Tom knew just what those thoughts were. He'd gone into the army for money and a piece of land, to make up for the loss of the boat. He'd brought his father in too. And for seven years they'd been fighting. For nothing. They hadn't even been given all the money promised in exchange for what had been requisitioned.

Forty dollars. After seven years.

As they rejoined the others, a cart trundled past. On it sat Abby, her pregnant belly thrust proudly forward on her lap. Three boys squatted behind her.

"Oh, Abby," Bella called. "My God, look at you. You're pregnant again."

Abby pealed with laughter and pointed back at Bella's own

rounding belly. Tom thought, Why not? The one thing you see plenty of in a war is men, whichever way they're running. At you or away. Forward or back. Always men. You can pile the corpses up in heaps, but there are always men. Where they go in peacetime, God knew, but in a war there were men everywhere. Of course women got pregnant. What could you expect?

Then he stopped himself. He didn't want to be bitter. The land was beginning again. You needed new people for a new country. Abby's womb strode forward proudly, like a vanguard; and Bella's small hillock, his son's child. Life had been made, as well as death; joy and love, not just misery and destruction. He knew why his thoughts had been so bleak. It was jealousy. He was remembering his own children coming. And now it was his child's child, and his wife dead so long. And Daisy dead too, as she must be, he thought. While the war continued, he thought of her as alive somewhere, somehow. There was unfinished business, nothing had been finally decided. If that was true of this great matter of the war, it could be true of one person's life as well. But when the war ended, Daisy ended too. She had only existed for him through the war. Shouting on the wharf. Telling him about Ned, and helping him on his way. In the hut at Valley Forge. She was a woman born of the war. Not that she lacked gentleness and love, but she was a fiery woman who believed in those words that were dead on the tongues of people like Corty and her father, the Sugar King. Liberty. Independence. Equality. When Tom thought of the true America and the real war, he thought of her. But not here, not now. Not in this America where the land was sold off and the promissory note wasn't honored. This was Joe McConnahay's America, even if he had fled north. Daisy was dead.

Abby said, "This time I've got me a live man." She pointed to a giant sitting beside her on the board, holding the traces. He grinned slowly, as slow as her laughter was quick. Abby had never learned to read or write, and never would. She never tried to grapple with the principles of revolution and its words, like Tom and Ned did. But her laughter was quick and intelligent, as was her loving, and her grief. Her man was obviously slow, but perhaps this one would last. "This is Jim," she went on. "He's got a farm upstate." She patted her belly. "We're gonna plant." The laughter again. The cart clattered off, to mix with all the others, as though people might pass into the gaze of the times and then rattle away into their own secret lives again.

The Indians were tying travails to the horses, long poles lashed with webbed rope. Bella lay on one of them. Tom pressed the forty dollars into Ned's hand. "Here," he said.

"Pa?" Ned said, looking at the money. "I don't want it *all*."

"Ya take it." He nodded toward Bella. "She and the baby gonna need more than one skinny cow."

"Oh, Pa." Then he realized. "You ain't coming."

Tom looked at them in turn: Bella, the Indians, Merle, Ned. His family. The war had given them something after all. Each other. A new family. They would never have met each other, or been together, if it hadn't been for this fight. But something had been lost too, and not just the boat and providents. Daisy had gone, and he couldn't go off and live his life as if she had never existed in the first place, like his family back in Scotland. Except that you never did that in any case. The people of the past lived in your dreams. And because he never knew what had happened to his mother, he went through years of his life hoping in some part of his mind she'd come back to him, that she was out there really, that she'd just gone off a few minutes ago and one day would turn a corner or open a door or go around a bend in the river to some new place and there she'd be, and she'd have been there all along.

The trouble with thinking like that was that it made you more alone than ever. If you kept forgetting someone was dead even when you knew they were, then they had to die again each time you remembered. He couldn't leave matters like that with Daisy. He had to find out what had happened to her. The war was over for all these people milling about in the streets, it was over for this family of his, which was standing here about to go off and start a new life. But Tom wasn't ready to start his yet. He needed to kiss his past farewell. Daisy wasn't just going to be one of the anonymous dead, like those corpses heaped up at Yorktown with no one able to take notice whose mother's sons they were, whose husbands or sweethearts. Daisy had experienced the worst: a young rebel girl fallen into the hands of British dragoons. He'd seen the sword slashing down, and even from so far he thought of his lordship slashing at the guy line and haw-

hawing. When you tried to understand your life, you kept seeing the same things happen and the same people doing them over and over again. Like with the redemption sergeant. When he thought of what had happened to Daisy, he saw the mean, pinched face of that lordship in the hunt, and his laughing, and what he said about killing the dream.

The man with the sword had killed Daisy, Tom told himself, and he hoped it was quick. He'd killed Daisy, but he hadn't killed the dream of Daisy. Tom had to do that for himself. He had to know what happened, how she died. He had to bury her in his heart. Then perhaps if there was a new life for him, he could begin to live it, like this family of his. That was business for later. At the moment he couldn't go off and be a citizen in this new country. A new country needed new people, like Bella and Ned were making, and Abby and all the others. Even though he'd fought so hard and so long in this war, Tom felt that he belonged in another place, where so many of those he'd been close to and loved had gone already.

"No," Tom said. "I ain't comin'. I can't."

Ned stared at him, his eyes filling with tears. Tom pulled the hat up on his head, as he had years ago, when his uniform was new and too big and they were rowing over to Long Island.

"Go to the East River," Tom went on, "and cross Hell's Gate. Take the Hudson to the Mohawk Trail, then up as far as she goes. Tonti says there's farmland nor'west, where the rivers begin. That's where ya go settle . . ." He paused. "Like ya dreamed."

"Pa," Ned whispered.

"I got things to do, Ned. They ain't right yet." He wanted to say something more, but couldn't think what. "I can learn to read."

Ned laughed, and they hugged each other. Then Tom pulled away. "Ya ready, Tonti?" he asked.

"Oui, Tom."

"Then ya better get off." He stepped over and clasped Merle. "Don't forget no good tunes," he said.

"Won't," Merle replied.

Tom kissed Bella, clasped hands with the Indians. Then Ned mounted and they moved off. Tom held his bridle and walked beside them for a stretch.

"Name your children for old friends, Ned."

"Yes, Pa."

Tom let go of the bridle and slapped the horse's flank. Ned looked back and waved. Then Tom suddenly, urgently, called out: "Tell them how we fought. Tell them how far we come."

Ned called back, "I will, Pa."

Then, like Abby before them, they merged into the crowds.

Tom stood, watching them go. A swirl of dust blew up from the road and stung his eyes. He shut them tight. When he opened them again they were still blurred with water and the crowds on the street walked past him, billowing and shrinking. For a second one of them came into sharp focus, a black woman's face, and then swam away. He blinked. His eyes cleared. He stood and looked. The black woman had gone. He stood a little longer, and then he ran.

He had the impression she'd gone to the right, toward the Bowling Green. He pushed and shoved through the crowds, down a narrow street, into the open area of the Bowling Green itself, which the plinth of the king's statue still dominated. People were dancing on it now and swarming all round, people of all shapes and sizes, mostly wearing poor clothes, tattered from war, but singing and merry; everybody here you could imagine, except that one black face. In a corner of the Green a little stage had been erected and a man was standing on it, haranguing the people. Over and over again he was shouting "Liberty and property!" There was a familiarity in the Irish brogue, in the combination of threat and flattery. Even while Tom searched the faces that swarmed around him, the voice threaded its way into his mind. "Do you want these ruffians to run New York?" it was asking. "Or men of honor and integrity?" Surely he recognized it? Surely not. He'd been recognizing too much this morning as it was. The voice droned on; the faces flowed past.

Every face you could imagine, except the one he wanted. Merry and laughing as most of the faces were, they began to seem unfriendly and forbidding. He became aware of gap teeth, bulbous noses, scars, animal features, even while the people hugged and danced and sang. No, that wasn't right, it was how you looked at them. He blinked and they settled down to men and women once more, celebrating their peace.

The common people—his people. It was just that he was
alone, and the one black face that he searched for was nowhere to be seen. There were many black faces in the crowd,
of course, but none like the one he'd glimpsed, or thought
he'd glimpsed. He'd only seen Cuffy twice before. A quick
sight of her on the wharf, when Daisy had broken the news
about Ned being taken off; a handshake at Valley Forge,
when Daisy was about to climb onto the wagon that took her
into disaster. That was all. He couldn't even say what she
looked like. It was just that the face he saw by the Battery
had some familiarity in it.

The politician's voice continued its harangue. "A vote for
Corty is a vote for integrity." Corty. The man by the Sugar
King. The man who said their promissory notes would be
redeemed in gold, and who said the war would be over in
two weeks, seven long years ago. Wherever you went, the
past came back to you. Except the one part of it that you
needed.

A movement at the far side of the Green caught his attention. A woman turning down into one of the little side roads.
A black woman.

Tom ran again—down the road, across Wall Street, into a
narrow entrance opposite.

This street was one of the winding alleyways of New York.
A knot of people surrounded a cockfight near the middle part
of it, and a bit farther down a small mob was hammering at a
door. Perhaps a stray Tory had gone to earth. Then there was
a building with a ramshackle balcony—the old whorehouse.
The stars and stripes flapped from it now, with some new
writing scrawled on an old sheet alongside. Tom couldn't
read it, but he knew what it must say. The whores had to
keep an eye open for business, like everybody else.

The street wound down toward the Sugar House wharf.
The building was even more dilapidated than it had been
during Tom's time at the ropewalk, when it was a prison. It
wasn't anything now. The boarding was sprung, and the door
sagged open on its hinges. It looked like an old discarded
eggshell or broken nut, as though whatever had been inside
had burst out and left the ruins behind. Its sign was gone.

The woman wasn't here, so if she'd come this way at all,
she must have skirted the dock and gone on along the water-
side. Tom leapt into a moored boat and then into another,

cutting across as though the little dinghies were stepping-stones. He climbed up the rope ladder of a barque moored on the far side, ran across its deck and up to the wharf. The roadway snaked around a couple of buildings, and as he passed the second corner, he saw the black woman again, quite close, and some children playing beyond. In the middle, in cocked hat and plume, and green jacket, her skirt billowing out beneath, a woman was playing with them. The black woman was heading toward her, and as she sensed her approach, the other woman turned to look.

Amongst all the people, he saw only one face. It was lean, weathered, intense. The power of his dark eyes watching her gave her a shock; eyes that had drawn her to look back in the first place, devouring eyes. And then the face became familiar and for a panicky moment she couldn't speak or breath. She was leaving Valley Forge again and galloping across the wintry plains with the huge sky above, calling back to that watchful face: "Only you, Tom Dobb, only you!" and hearing her voice swept away by the wind. Tom's arms went up. It was half a wave, half a gesture of triumph. Then his figure became smaller and darker as the wagon swayed on along the slushy track. There was the thunder of hooves and the bright flash of red in the chilly gray scene. The British dragoons were bearing down on them. The other cart overturned. Even as hers bulkily turned and bounced off across the grass, she looked back to see the dragoons pumping their swords down at the wounded on the ground and the women. The bastards! Then Hampton's sneer, the sword—and then all she could see and remember was blood.

She was writhing in a wood somewhere. Hands were mauling her. Cuffy was whimpering and groaning nearby. She tried to open her eyes, but they were stuck with blood. Hampton's voice. It was a silly voice, high-pitched, drawling, affected, but that made it worse when it was coming at you out of the dark from somewhere above and you were so completely in its power. She heard over and over again that word he'd called her during that evening with the harpsichord, the wig, the warship: Whore. She felt as she had then—that the word itself, coming from that vile man, made her one. Perhaps, at the back of her mind, she'd felt so ever since, during the years that had gone by.

Her hand instinctively rose to her scar. Tom was approaching. She had another sudden memory of Valley Forge, the killers pumping their sabers into the wounded; and beyond that, the smoke billowing from the guns at the ramparts of Valley Forge itself; and between, the distant form of Tom, running and running but getting no nearer.

He was running toward her now. And then they were in each other's arms.

**BANTAM
SHOP·AT·HOME
C·A·T·A·L·O·G**

Special Offer
Buy a Bantam Book
for only 50¢.

Now you can have an up-to-date listing of Bantam's hundreds of titles plus take advantage of our unique and exciting bonus book offer. A special offer which gives you the opportunity to purchase a Bantam book for only 50¢. Here's how!

By ordering any five books at the regular price per order, you can also choose any other single book listed (up to a $4.95 value) for just 50¢. Some restrictions do apply, but for further details why not send for Bantam's listing of titles today!

Just send us your name and address and we will send you a catalog!

DON'T MISS
THESE CURRENT
Bantam Bestsellers